A SILENT DANCE PARTNER

The glow from headlights and streetlights out front illuminated the northern end of the room and a trickle of moonlight from the back windows cast shadows along the south side. A broad stripe of light fell into the room from the hall. My eyes went to the stereo system; if someone were going to rob Graysin Motion, it was about the only thing worth stealing. Present and accounted for. About to return to my office to wait for Rafe, I sniffed. Something didn't smell right. I gazed around the room more deliberately, scanning each section in turn.

Nothing by the front windows. The curtains were too sheer for anyone to hide behind. Nothing in the center of the floor. The odor grew stronger as I stood there and my legs started to tremble. Beneath the southern windows, one of the shadows was strangely static, not shifting as clouds and tree limbs skipped through the moonlight. I groped for the switch on the wall, my eyes never leaving the immobile shadow.

Light drenched the room and I slid down the wall until I squatted on my haunches, unable to approach Rafe where he lay under the window. I felt like I'd just plummeted into a death drop, but Rafe was not there to catch me. The beach ball–sized pool of blood congealing like a macabre halo around his shattered head told me it was too late for bandages or CPR. Too late for kissing and making up . . .

D0121963

Quickstep to Murder

A BALLROOM DANCE MYSTERY

ELLA BARRICK

AN OBSIDIAN MYSTERY

OBSIDIAN
Published by New American Library, a division of
Penguin Group (USA) Inc., 375 Hudson Street,
New York, New York 10014, USA
Penguin Group (Canada), 90 Eglinton Avenue East, Suite 700, Toronto,
Ontario M4P 2Y3, Canada (a division of Pearson Penguin Canada Inc.)
Penguin Books Ltd., 80 Strand, London WC2R 0RL, England
Penguin Ireland, 25 St. Stephen's Green, Dublin 2,
Ireland (a division of Penguin Books Ltd.)
Penguin Group (Australia), 250 Camberwell Road, Camberwell, Victoria 3124,
Australia (a division of Pearson Australia Group Pty. Ltd.)
Penguin Books India Pvt. Ltd., 11 Community Centre, Panchsheel Park,
New Delhi - 110 017, India
Penguin Group (NZ), 67 Apollo Drive, Rosedale, Auckland 0632,
New Zealand (a division of Pearson New Zealand Ltd.)
Penguin Books (South Africa) (Pty.) Ltd., 24 Sturdee Avenue,
Rosebank, Johannesburg 2196, South Africa

Penguin Books Ltd., Registered Offices:
80 Strand, London WC2R 0RL, England

First published by Obsidian, an imprint of New American Library,
a division of Penguin Group (USA) Inc.

First Printing, September 2011
10 9 8 7 6 5 4 3 2 1

Copyright © Laura DiSilverio, 2011
All rights reserved

OBSIDIAN and logo are trademarks of Penguin Group (USA) Inc.

Printed in the United States of America

*To Amy, Lin, and Marie, who make
my books better and the writing more fun.*

ACKNOWLEDGMENTS

Since my knowledge of ballroom dancing was limited to a few ankle-bruising lessons with my hubby, I am most grateful to Deborah and Richard Love, ballroom instructors extraordinaire; Marie Layton, critique partner and ballroom dancer; Dan Messenger, competition organizer and *Dance Trends Newsletter* guru; and all the dancers—amateur and professional—who chatted with me at the Denver Star Ball, for sharing their knowledge of ballroom dancing, competitions, studio ownership, and related topics. They get the credit for what's right and I get the gong for any errors.

Thanks also to my dedicated and long-suffering critique partners; Danielle DiSilverio for explaining unions to me; the world's best agent, Paige Wheeler; and my sharp-eyed, insightful, and tactful editor, Sandy Harding.

Finally, hugs, kisses, and bunches of gratitude to my husband and daughters, who fill my life with laughter, joy, love, and meaning.

Chapter 1

I've always thought of myself as a quickstep sort of person, full of joie de vivre, zing, and fun. Dancing the quickstep, a mix of the foxtrot and the Charleston, usually transports me to the 1920s and Zelda Fitzgerald, champagne and flappers. But it's tough to have much joie in your vivre when you're dancing with a partner you loathe, especially when he's the ex-fiancé you caught boffing a Latin specialist. Sometimes, though, you just have to suck it up and fake the zing, like when you own a ballroom dance studio and eight members of a wedding party who want to learn to dance before the big day are watching you demonstrate the quickstep.

Rafe and I glided across the smooth floor of our jointly owned studio, Graysin Motion, with the light and complex footwork that had won us more than one quickstep title. My sapphire dress belled out as we chasséed and spun the length of the ballroom to the corner in preparation for our run. Staying energetic and light on our feet, we skipped and hopped diagonally across the floor, our bodies staying upright and solid while our toes appeared to barely skim the ground. I tried to lose myself in the strains of Louis Prima's "Sing, Sing, Sing" as it poured through the speakers, but Rafe broke into my reverie.

"You've got to listen to reason, *querida*."

He kept his voice low, which deepened his sexy Argentinean accent. At least, I used to find it sexy until I discovered he had the fidelity of a mink.

"Don't call me sweetheart," I said through my smile.

"Stacy, the studio . . . barely covering costs. Must expand . . . class offerings."

Talking and quickstepping are pretty much mutually exclusive activities since you're moving at about the rate of a sprinter attempting a four-minute mile, but Rafe and I were in superb shape and my anger drove me to gasp out a response. "If you think . . . I'll let . . . you wreck . . . reputation . . . finest ballroom studio . . . D.C. area . . . by teaching hip-hop and tap and becoming . . . recital mill like Li'l Twinkletoes . . . No."

I was a pro. Despite my anger and frustration, I smiled at him, my expression a nice blend of mischief and carefree gaiety. I tried superimposing Jay Gatsby (the Robert Redford version—yum) over Rafe. It didn't work.

"Need the money."

"Maybe *you* need money. I'm fine." We slowed for a moment for him to bend me into a deep arch in the corner. "I didn't just buy a Lexus."

"Gift."

His dark eyes locked onto mine and for a second, a nonquicksteplike passion that had more to do with anger and frustration than the volatile chemistry that had brought us together as ballroom partners and then lovers bled into the dance. We'd been engaged for two years and had bought Graysin Motion before the chemistry exploded the afternoon I found him practicing a horizontal mambo with Solange Dubonnet. I had ended our engagement on the spot—was it really four months ago?—but severing our business relationship was proving more difficult since neither of us could afford to buy out the other's share of Graysin Motion. We moved apart for some Charleston-inspired side-by-side figures and I recovered my bright smile.

As the choreography brought us into a closed hold again, Rafe said, "Listen to reason, que—Stacy. Adding . . . bigger variety . . . children's classes and . . . hosting . . . recital would bring in—just in costume sales—"

"Over. My. Dead. Body."

The music ended and the bridesmaids and their escorts clapped. I dropped into a graceful curtsy, trying to catch my breath without looking like a gasping fish, the swishy sapphire of my demonstration dress draping around me.

"That was fabu," the blond bride said. "Now you can see why I wanted us all to learn to quickstep, honey. Doesn't that look like fun?" She cast a sweet smile at her groom, a hulking young man who looked like he'd be more at ease in a rugby scrum than a ballroom dance studio.

The groom nodded, gulping, as the best man said, "If you think racing around a dance floor at the pace of a zebra trying to outrun a cheetah looks like fun. It'll be especially fun in a tux."

The bride ignored his sarcasm. "Can you teach us to dance like that?" She gestured to her bridesmaids, who looked eager, and the groomsmen, who looked like they'd prefer a root canal to dance instruction. Not unusual, in my experience.

"When's the wedding?"

"Saturday," she said sunnily.

Teach these neophytes to quickstep in four days? Four *weeks*, maybe, if they were talented, coordinated, and aerobically fit. Rafe and I exchanged a look that said, "Yeah, right." Our moments of agreement were rare these days and I suppressed a sad smile.

"Of course," Rafe said, offering his hand and a roguish smile to the slender bride. "Why don't we get started?"

The wedding party had barely limped out of the studio, the maid of honor complaining she'd be too stiff to walk down the aisle, when Taryn Hall and Sawyer Iverson, teenage dance partners preparing for the upcoming Capitol Ballroom Dance Festival, strolled in. We were taking advantage of spring break to work in some extra private coaching. I sipped from my water bottle as the teens put on their dance shoes and stretched. Sunlight streamed through the front windows of the studio, which ran the length of the town house. It showed scuffs on the oak floor that President James Madison may have trod when the house belonged to his cousin. I mentally factored the cost of refinishing the floor into the year's budget and sighed.

"Rafe! Yo, man, watch this." Sawyer dropped his lanky body to the floor and executed some tricky hip-hop moves, ending by twirling on his head.

"Where do you think you will use that?" Rafe asked with a grin. "*America's Got Losers*?"

I'd always liked the way he connected with the teens and even the kids in the beginners' class.

"Cold, man. Cold," Sawyer said, shaking his head. The stud in his ear glinted. "The chicks dig it."

"In your dreams," Taryn said, sinking into the splits and stretching forward until she lay flat against the floor.

Rafe clapped his hands. "Let us get started, *niños*." The couple took their positions as he cued the music. I moved with them as they danced, changing an arm position, giving a reminder about keeping their frames up. They took the corrections in good part, focused on becoming better dancers.

"No, no," Rafe broke in over the foxtrot music. "Taryn, come here. Let me show you. Watch, Sawyer."

Taryn hurried toward Rafe, her smile showing her pleasure at the prospect of dancing with him. With midnight-dark hair and a milky complexion, Taryn was a wisp of a girl whose slightness belied her strength. She looked even paler today, I thought, as she stretched up within the frame of Rafe's arms. They circled the room twice, Rafe narrating each piece of footwork, each gesture, as they danced. Sawyer glowered at the twirling pair until I offered him my hand and dragged him onto the floor.

It ought, of course, to have been me demonstrating with Rafe. But the awkwardness between us made it difficult. I knew next month's Blackpool Dance Festival, the prestigious invitation-only ballroom competition in England, would be our last competition together and it saddened me. He was the perfect partner for me in many ways; he was just the right height and his olive complexion and dark hair made a striking contrast with my paleness. In the heat of my fury and hurt at his betrayal, I'd initially told him I wouldn't dance with him any longer. But after I'd auditioned a couple of prospective partners who answered my ads on the Internet dance sites (Disaster 1 and Disaster 2, I called them), and Rafe had danced with a couple of women who didn't meet his standards (too whiny, no personality), we decided to keep our dance partnership intact until after Blackpool. To bolster the studio's reputation, we agreed.

Deep in thought, I didn't see how it happened, but suddenly Taryn was on the floor. "I'm okay," she said weakly as Rafe helped her to her feet. "I don't know why . . . I felt dizzy . . ."

Sawyer broke away from me and hurried to where Taryn stood supported by Rafe's strong arm. "Taryn, let me—"

"Don't fuss," she said. "I'm fine. Maybe just some water."

Sawyer jogged to her gym bag and pawed through it, searching for her bottle. Rafe said something to her in a low voice and she shook her head vehemently. When Sawyer trotted up with the water, Rafe stepped aside, but his eyes were full of concern as they dwelled on Taryn. Watching the way she trembled as she brought the bottle to her lips, I wondered if she had an eating disorder. Unfortunately, in a sport that prized thinness and a ripped physique, eating disorders were all too common. Taryn's symptoms fit the bill—dizzy, thirsty, weaker than usual, thinner than a daffodil stem. I'd find a way to take her aside later, sound her out about it. Anorexia was nothing to mess around with, especially as a teen. A friend of mine from my ballet days had had to go away for several months to a live-in facility in Arizona to recover. She was thirteen. She'd never returned to dancing.

I walked over to the girl and put my arms around shoulders that felt bony through her thin sweatshirt. "Come on, Taryn. I'll call your mom and you can wait in my office until she comes. Maybe some cheese crackers would help. I've got some in my drawer."

"Oh, no! I couldn't eat anything." She put a hand to her mouth like she might throw up, confirming my suspicions.

The music started up again as I led Taryn out of the studio. Sawyer trailed after us, but Taryn stopped him with a shake of her head.

"I've got the car," Taryn told me. "I can drive myself home."

"Are you sure you feel up to it? Maybe Sawyer—"

"Yeah. The fresh air will do me good." She managed a wan smile. "Thanks, Stacy."

I watched as she navigated the stairs that ran down the side of the house, creating a separate entrance for Graysin Motion just off my office. Her shoulders were slumped, whether from the weight of her dance bag or something else, I couldn't tell. As I returned to the studio, I wondered if I should share my suspicions with her mother. No, I decided. I'd talk to Taryn first.

Two hours later, I slouched into my office, kicked off my dance heels, and put one foot on the desk to massage it. *Ahh.* I was exhausted. Resting my head against the chair, I stared at Rafe's desk, set at a right angle to mine. We used to work in here together, with him doing billing and payroll stuff while I worked on schedules and choreography. He hadn't spent much time at his desk since our split, preferring to work from home on his laptop, and dust coated his computer and keyboard. Somehow, that film of dust made me want to cry. It wasn't the empty desk that bothered me, I told myself; it was Rafe's escalating irresponsibility.

Rafe had walked out today without a word of explanation not long after Taryn left, leaving me to teach a beginning Latin class on my own. I'd wanted to put a spear between his shoulder blades but had to act like his leaving was no big deal. *Grrr*. His behavior the past month had grown increasingly strange—disappearing at odd times, whispered phone conversations he obviously didn't want overheard, furtive meetings in a limo I'd seen parked outside the studio several times this week—and I'd had to cover more than one of his classes when he didn't show. It wasn't like him. He knew as well as I did that reliability was critical to the studio's success. Students tended not to come back if their instructors didn't show up as scheduled. No duh, as my brother, Nick, would say.

Rafe might have fewer morals than a feral cat, but up until now he'd been a conscientious businessman, scrutinizing the books, finding ways to cut costs, charming the customers into buying packages for multiple lessons. Then, three days ago, he'd shown up in the black Lexus, acting more uneasy than thrilled. And now he said it was a gift? *Hmm*. How come the gifts I received ran more to toaster ovens (Mom), eHarmony memberships (my sister, Danielle, who never liked Rafe), or tarty lingerie (assorted boyfriends) than high-performance sports cars? I must be doing something wrong.

A commotion outside caught my attention. Barefoot, I crossed to the large front window to see what was going on. Graysin Motion was on the upper level of the Federal-era town house I lived in courtesy of Great-aunt Laurinda, who'd bequeathed it to me, and had two studios: the main dance floor where we held large classes, and a slightly smaller room suitable for one-on-one practice, which most of the pros who trained here used. We referred to them as the ballroom and the studio. The ballroom looked out onto the tree-shaded streets of Old Town, Alexandria, and if you craned your neck, you could just glimpse the Potomac River. My office sat across the wide hall and had been a small music room or parlor in another life. Now that Rafe had moved out—he'd held on to his condo when we got engaged but we'd spent our nights here more often than not—I lived alone downstairs, which made for the world's easiest commute, especially in the Metro D.C. area.

Down on the sidewalk, two dogs—a shaggy mutt and a boxer—lunged and barked at each other as their owners tried to pull them away. My gaze drifted past them and I saw the limo—at least I thought it was the same limo—that had picked Rafe up the other day. It was parked across the street. If Rafe was holed up in that limo, swilling champagne with a new lover while I worked my butt off—! On impulse, I hurried down the stairs that ran along the side of the house.

My mother always said my lack of impulse control would get me into hot water someday. It already had. Like the time in high school with the Bunsen burner and the crepe paper. It was just a dinky fire; they didn't really have to evacuate the whole school. Or the fountain incident . . . I shook the memories out of my head as I reached the ground level. Lifting my long skirt, I ran down the slate-paved walk to the street, wishing I'd taken time to put on some shoes as the hot walkway burned my soles. Judging from the cars slowing and honking, I must have been quite a sight: a five-foot-six barefoot blonde in a form-fitting gown that displayed a generous amount of cleavage and leg. I probably looked like an escapee from a charity ball or a musical revue, not the usual sunburned tourist or Ann Taylor–shopping yuppie you see clogging the sidewalks of Old Town at three in the afternoon.

At the curb, I had to wait for a break in traffic. When the light down the street turned red, I wove my way through the stopped cars, getting a couple of wolf whistles and invitations. I ignored them. The asphalt was so hot I barely touched each foot to the street before jerking it up; I felt like a prancing show horse. Panting, I reached the black limo, which idled at the curb. I couldn't make out anything behind the heavily tinted windows. I knocked on the driver's side window. Nothing. I rapped more insistently, bruising my knuckles. The window buzzed down a bare inch. I craned my neck, trying to see inside, but could make out only the dull gleam of expensive leather, a dashboard with enough electronics to pilot the space shuttle, and a sliver of profile topped by a chauffeur's cap. Music played so softly I couldn't identify it, and a hint of cigar smoke so expensive it didn't make me retch drifted out.

"Yes?" The voice was heavily accented, discouraging.

"I'm looking for Rafael Acosta," I said. "Is he with you? In there?" Boy, that was lame.

Apparently, the driver thought so, too, because the window purred up again and the car moved forward slightly, forcing me back. As there was a steady stream of traffic behind me, stepping back posed life-threatening problems.

"Hey, just give me a minute," I yelled at the car, trying to inch down its length and reach the safety of the sidewalk.

As nonresponsive as a shark, it nosed its way into traffic, pushing me aside. An Escalade blasted past, almost scraping my behind. That was too close for comfort—my rear end was one of my greatest assets on a dance floor, especially for Latin numbers that required a lot of hip rotation, what nondancers thought of as "booty shaking." I teetered backward on my heels and windmilled my arms, knowing that if I fell, no one would even hit the brakes when their tires thumped over my body. D.C. drivers during rush hour wouldn't slow down for the president or a volcanic eruption or an alien spaceship (as long as it didn't land *on* the beltway). I flung myself forward and flopped over the trunk of the limo. It crept forward again and I felt my feet leave the roadway. Yikes! My hands scrabbled over the waxed surface, looking for purchase. Nothing. I got the ball of one foot down just as the car accelerated. One minute it was there, the next it was half a block away and gaining speed. I fell to my hands and knees in the spot it had vacated.

I sucked in a deep breath and my arms trembled. Pebbles dug into my palms and I didn't even want to look at my skirt. Two women emerged from the heavy glass doors of Spactacular, the day spa directly across from Graysin Motion. They had the dewy glow and gleaming nails that spoke of facials, massages, and a gossipy interchange while the manicurist toiled. They both noted me from the corners of their eyes, the look city dwellers have perfected to avoid eye contact with homeless people, and one whispered to the other, "Probably drunk."

"What *do* we pay taxes for?" the other asked, somewhat obscurely. Climbing into the Mercedes sedan parked behind me, they angled away from the curb, almost running over my toes.

Instinctively, I put a hand to the gaping neckline of my gown and struggled to my feet. A horn blared two inches behind me and I jumped. A soccer mommish woman in a green van was making shooing gestures. She wanted the parking spot. Her bumper nudged my thigh. The hell with her. I slammed my palm down hard on the van's hood and leaped to the sidewalk. Stalking to the corner, my knees throbbing, I crossed at the light. The woman was still backing and cutting in, trying to parallel park. I waved at her in apology as I started up the stairs to Graysin Motion and she gave me the finger.

Damn, my knees hurt. I struggled up the stairs and hobbled to my office. Plopping into the chair, I hiked my skirt up. *Ick.* My knees were scraped up good and oozing blood. Just what I needed. They'd better heal before the Capitol Ballroom Dance Festival, our warm-up for Blackpool in less than two weeks. And the dress was ruined. I examined the rips and oil stains on the stretchy fabric. I didn't use the dress for competition, just for teaching, and I'd bought it for only thirty-two dollars at a Goodwill store, but still. Holding my dress at thigh height and hoping I didn't run into anyone, I scuttled to the half bath down the hall. Washing my knees with soap and water, I patted them dry and stuck Band-Aids on before sticking my asphalt-blackened feet one at a time under the cool water flowing from the faucet. *Aah, much better.* Drying my tootsies, I grabbed a sparkling water from the mini-fridge we kept in the bathroom before slinking back to the office. I settled into my chair and stretched my legs out under the desk, wincing.

"I don't know where you think we're lunching, but you're waaay overdressed for the Falafel Hut."

I looked up with a smile. My sister, Danielle, slouched in the doorway. About my height, she's thin where I'm curvy and practical when I'm occasionally—witness the limo incident—a tad impulsive. She has a long, narrow face and straight brows that give her a serious look she says is a real asset in negotiations. She's a union organizer for service and clerical workers. I don't know what she does, exactly, except she disappears for a week or two now and then to participate in a strike and she gets a lot of satisfaction from helping wronged secretaries get back at harassing bosses. You'd think her head of flaming red curls—from Mom's side of the family— would mean she has a temper, but she's the calmest person I know.

"Come on down while I change," I said, pushing to my feet.

She backed into the hall as I shuffled to the door. "What? Did you add judo throws to your class today? And I've heard of people paying obscene sums for 'distressed' jeans, but I didn't know the trend had extended to ball gowns."

"Since when are you a fashion critic?" I asked. Dani had the dullest collection of beige, navy, and gray suits ever assembled in a single closet. With shoes to match. She called her wardrobe "nonthreatening" and said it helped her connect with the pink- and blue-collar workers she represented. I'd rather starve on the street than wear beige. Sometimes it's hard to believe we're related.

Just as I reached the hall, the door leading to the exterior stairs swung open. Mark Downey stepped in, his sandy hair tousled, a grin on his face. A couple years younger than me, Mark did something with computers and danced on the side. He paid me a handsome fee to dance with him at professional-amateur competitions—common practice in the competitive ballroom world; in fact, it's how most pros made the bulk of their money.

"Stacy! Just the person I was hoping to see," he said. Two strides brought him to where I stood and he bent to kiss my cheek. I introduced him to Dani and they shook hands.

"Did we have a practice scheduled?" I wrinkled my brow, sure it hadn't been on my calendar. His button-down shirt and khaki slacks didn't suggest he was here to dance.

"No. I was just in the area and thought I'd take you to lunch. You, too," he said, politely extending the invitation to Dani.

"That's sweet of you, Mark," I said, "but Dani and I have plans. Maybe another time?"

"Sure." He took the rebuff easily. "I've got a few errands to run anyway. See you at class tonight?"

"Probably." Rafe was scheduled to teach, but I usually poked my head in.

"Great. See you then. Nice meeting you, Danielle," he said. With a flip of his hand he disappeared out the door. I could hear him clomping down the stairs.

"He's got a thing for you," Dani observed slyly.

"He's a kid," I said. "And he's got a girlfriend. She's come to watch us in competitions once or twice."

"Still. You could do worse. He's cute if you like the boy-next-door type. Beaver Cleaver or Richie Cunningham all grown up."

I didn't answer since we both knew my taste ran more to an edgy, dangerous, heartbreaking Rafe Acosta type.

We headed down the hall that ran the length of the house to a door marked PRIVATE. As we descended the interior stairs to my living quarters, I told Dani about Rafe's strange behavior and about my run-in with the limo.

"What'd they say before they ran you down?" Danielle asked as we emerged into my sun-drenched kitchen.

Although I loved the natural light, it did tend to spotlight the worn areas in the lichen-colored linoleum that was probably laid down before the Iron Curtain went up, and the stained grout on the turquoise tiled counters, remnants of an unfortunate redecorating effort in the 1960s. As soon as I had any money to spare, I was redoing the kitchen. "Zilch."

"Have you considered the possibility this was just some poor chauffeur waiting for his employer to finish at the day spa? He probably thought you were a celebrity stalker or something."

I ducked into my bedroom to change, but left the door open so I could hear Dani.

"It wasn't a celebrity," I called, shucking off my ruined dress and reaching for a pair of green capris. "The car had diplomat plates." I hadn't learned much from my confrontation with the limo, but I had noticed the license plate as it sped away; the familiar blue and white bore the country code "PR." I didn't know what country that was offhand, but I could Google it later.

"Fine. So it was an ambassador getting a hot stone massage, not Tom Cruise."

Pulling on a green-and-white-striped T-shirt, I slipped my feet into white espadrilles and joined Dani. She was seated at the kitchen table, watching a cardinal splash in the birdbath in my backyard. It's not really a yard—just a ten-by-five brick patio surrounded on three sides by a three-feet-wide grass border—but I keep multiple birdfeeders and the birdbath filled and have a bunch of containers brimming with flowers and herbs, so it attracts a lot of birds and butterflies.

"Finally," she greeted my appearance. "Let's get going. I'm starved."

* * *

Over a Greek salad at the Falafel Hut two blocks east, I told her about Rafe's erratic behavior in recent weeks. The spicy scent of gyros and the sound of kitchen clinkings permeated my story.

She took her time answering when I finished, dabbing at her mouth with a napkin before saying, "Maybe you're just a teensy bit too interested in Rafe's activities for an ex-fiancée?"

"What? You're saying I'm making this up? That I'm jealous?"

"Making it up—no. Jealous . . ." Her voice trailed off. "It's only been a few months. You can't expect to be over him so soon."

"I was over him the minute I caught him in bed with Solange," I said. I gulped some iced tea and choked, earning stares from the family standing in line to order.

"Uh-huh." Dani took a bite of her pita-wrapped falafel.

"Don't *uh-huh* me like that. Just say what you're thinking." I glared at her.

She gazed back calmly. "Okay. I think the most likely explanation is that Rafe has another woman on a string and you like poking at the wound. Maybe catching him with another woman would be even more vindication for you, or something. It's not like Solange was the first time he cheated on you. It's just that she was the first one you caught him naked with so you couldn't ignore the evidence."

Damn. This honesty thing didn't have much going for it. I blinked back tears, scooping salad into my mouth so Dani wouldn't notice. An unwelcome thought crept in: Maybe she was a teensy, weensy bit right. Maybe I was still a bit emotionally connected to Rafe. Not in a lovey-dovey way, but in a woman scorned way, which was al-most as bad. I aspired to total indifference.

"You okay?" She lowered her head almost to table level so she could look up into my face, which I kept bent over my bowl. One red curl dipped in the tzatziki sauce.

"Sure," I mumbled around a mouthful of lettuce. "Peachy. For a neurotic, jealous, spying ex-girlfriend." I pushed my salad away and flashed her a crooked smile. "You have yogurt sauce in your hair."

She straightened up, a relieved smile on her face. Us-ing a napkin, she wiped the sauce off her hair. The curl sproinged back into place when she released it. "Good. It's time to move on, sister-mine. Forget the dirtball. Coop's brother is in town this weekend—maybe we could double date."

I curled my lip. Cooper Tate, her boyfriend of four years, was not my cup of tea. He was lanky and serious and did something in security for a local university. For a wild night out, he went to a chess club. I didn't imagine any man who sprang from the same gene pool would light my fire.

She read my expression and scowled, tossing her utensils onto the tray. "Coop's a good man. At least he's never cheated on me."

That was low. "And he's never proposed either, has he?" Sisters can push one another's buttons like no one else in the world.

We glared at each other, then bussed the table and hit the sidewalk. The heat and humidity draped over us like a wet mohair blanket. Feeling bad about my verbal jab, I offered a half apology. "I don't think I'm ready to go out with anyone yet, Dani."

After a moment, she muttered, "It's okay. But you've gotta get over him sooner or later. I vote for sooner."

As we hugged good-bye, I said, "You know, just because I'm neurotic doesn't mean there's not something fishy going on with Rafe. And if it's something that can hurt Graysin Motion, I'm going to figure it out."

Chapter 2

I tackled Rafe about his disappearing acts when he arrived half an hour late for our practice session Wednesday morning. This close to the Capitol Festival and to Blackpool, we were rehearsing two to three hours a day on top of our teaching schedule. Usually we practiced in the morning and taught in the afternoons and evenings. It made for a long day. Yesterday had been particularly long since Rafe hadn't shown up to help with the evening class and I'd had to recruit Mark Downey to help teach. I was tired and achy and in no mood to put up with Rafe's *mierda del toro*.

We were in the ballroom and sun flooded through the front windows. Rafe squinted against the glare and pulled the cord to close the vanilla-colored sheers. All in black—a sweatshirt with the sleeves cut off to display his muscled arms, and slim pants—he looked fit and elegant as he jumped in place to warm up.

And now his flaky behavior was threatening to wreck all our hard work.

"You missed the Latin class last night," I said. "And it's not the first time. What the hell's going on?" I pulled up one pink legwarmer, hoping the Band-Aids on my knees held. This practice was a shorts and T-shirt affair and I had my long hair in a ponytail draped over my shoulder.

Rafe arched a dark brow. "You sound like a jealous fiancée, *querida*. Are you regretting—?"

I was tired of all the jealousy insinuations. First Dani, now Rafe. I straightened. "I sound like a pissed-off business partner. I can't teach all the classes myself. Last night was the third time you've blown off a class in two weeks. I can't count on you; the students have commented on your absences. What's going on? Does it have anything to do with that limo that's been loitering out front?"

"What are you talking about?" Rafe's face was carefully expressionless, but his nostrils flared and I thought he paled.

"Come off it! I saw you get into the limo last week and I went down to check it out when I saw it lurking at the curb again."

"You what?" Concern, maybe even fear, flickered in his dark eyes.

"I knocked on the window and asked for you."

He forced a laugh, turning away from me to sort through a stack of CDs by the stereo. The jewel cases clacked. "This is sounding more and more like a jealous girlfriend trying to keep tabs on her lover. Did you expect to find me making love to an exotic woman on the backseat? What did she say?" His voice was casual, but I could tell by the way his eyes cut to me that he was interested in my answer.

"It wasn't a she," I said. "Not unless she likes cigars. And they didn't tell me anything—just pulled away, almost knocking me into traffic." I hesitated, trying to find a way to put my concern into words. "I'm not remotely jealous and if this is just a woman who's hot for your bod, then great. But if it's more than that, if you're in trouble, or mixed up in something—"

He turned to face me and indecision played across his handsome face. For a moment I thought he was going to confide in me, but then he fixed a smile in place and said, "You are letting your imagination run away with you. You are under too much stress with the studio. If I promise not to cut class again, can we let this go and talk about how Graysin Motion can generate more income?" He made a big, mocking X over his heart with one finger.

I snorted with disgust. "If you say 'recital,' I swear I'm going to scream. If you want more money, sell the damn Lexus."

"It's leased." His mouth tightened.

That took me aback. I might only get toaster ovens as gifts, but at least they were mine to keep. "Oh." He strode toward me and stopped inches away. I caught the familiar scent of him, a hint of sweat and a whiff of musky cologne. "Are we going to argue or practice?"

"Sounds like trouble in paradise," a sultry voice said from the threshold.

Solange Dubonnet lounged against the doorjamb, all voluptuous curves and tumbling auburn curls. Her green eyes tipped up at the corners, making her look like a cat. Of course, that might just have been her personality oozing through.

"This is a private practice, Solange," I said. Since catching her in bed with Rafe, I'd found it hard to be civil to her. She'd injured her ankle not long after I caught her with Rafe and had left the studio where she'd been teaching. I didn't know if she'd been fired or had chosen to leave. Her partner had found someone else to dance with while Solange healed and did rehab, and had told her earlier this week that he was sticking with his new partner permanently. It was almost—not quite— enough to make me feel sorry for her. I'd feel a whole lot sorrier except I figured she and Rafe would team up after Blackpool, assuming her ankle was sufficiently recovered.

"I wouldn't dream of interrupting." She strolled toward us, leaning up against Rafe to plant a kiss on his lips.

He turned his head so her lips glanced off his cheek. "I'm busy, Solange."

Oo-ho. Was he bored with her already? The juvenile part of me wanted to taunt, "Nyah-nyah. You lasted only four months." The mature part of me—I was about to turn thirty, after all—asked, "What did you need?"

Her cheeks had flushed at his rebuff, but she shrugged and headed for the stereo. "I just need to pick up my CD." She flipped through the jewel cases, held one up in a manicured hand, and walked to the door, hips rolling provocatively under a silky green sarong. She looked over her shoulder when she reached the door. "Later?"

"Maybe." Rafe didn't meet her eyes. "Stacy and I need to talk business after practice."

Solange narrowed her eyes and looked from me to Rafe and back again. "Sure. Call first, if you're going to come over. I might be going out." She flung her head, swishing her hair over her shoulders, and stalked away.

Before Rafe could resume his arguments about the business, I cued up our quickstep music and turned the volume high enough to make conversation difficult. A sweaty two hours later, we'd made solid progress on our new quickstep routine and added a nifty turn series to our foxtrot. Rafe had been checking his watch the last twenty minutes of our practice time and when we finally quit he said, "I've got an appointment I can't miss. Let's talk this evening, Stacy. Please? It's important."

"Sure," I said, using much the same tone as Solange had earlier. I grabbed a small towel and blotted my forehead.

He caught my arm and I looked at him in surprise. His face was unusually serious. "I mean it. I'll come over."

"Call me and I'll meet you in the office," I agreed, not wanting him in my house, evoking memories of our good times, leaving a trace of his scent on the couch cushions. This would be a business meeting, not a cozy reunion. The thought crossed my mind that maybe he was looking for a reconciliation. If his relationship with Solange was over already, he might be having some regrets. I hardened my heart, letting my mind replay the moment I opened our bedroom door and found him with Solange. Skin, gasps, rumpled bedclothes. I threw those sheets away, even though they were almost new. I headed downstairs for a shower. It was too late for kissing and making up.

Refreshed from my shower and with new Band-Aids on my knees, I sat at my desk with a spreadsheet open on the computer, a Peggy Lee song lilting from my computer speakers. I'd only recently learned how to play radio stations from my computer and I was enjoying the novelty. I scowled at the spreadsheet. Rafe was the one with the business brain; now that he was playing least-in-sight, I had to spend a lot more time with the book-keeping and it made my head hurt. The oldies station went to news—"Crucial House Armed Services Committee vote on acquisition of next-generation helicopters for . . . Lady Gaga appearing at . . . Cherry blossoms blooming at Tidal Basin . . ."—and I closed its window. The sounds of an altercation from the ballroom gave me an excuse to leave my desk and see what was going on.

A shaky soprano voice cried, "But it's my turn! Maurice waltzed with you last week, Edwina. You can't expect to have him to yourself—even if you do need the most instruction."

"Ladies, please."

I peeked into the room to see Maurice Goldberg, our other male instructor, holding up his hands to calm the two octogenarians glaring at each other. Two couples of similar vintage practiced a stiff waltz pattern around the combatants. A handsome Great Dane splotched with black and white snoozed under the window, heavy muzzle resting on his front legs, one ear twitching. Ballroom dancing apparently wasn't as interesting as reminding cats who was boss or terrorizing the squirrels in the park. We didn't really have a pet policy and sometimes women brought their Yorkies or Malteses tucked into tote bags, so I felt it was only fair to allow the Great Dane to observe classes. I didn't want to be guilty of size discrimination. As long as the pets were well behaved, I didn't mind having them around; in fact, I liked it.

Maurice, who admitted to being sixty but who I guessed was at least a decade older, had been a dance host on a cruise ship for many years before coming to work for Graysin Motion not long after we opened. His smoothed-back white hair, furrowed where the comb plowed through it, and perpetual tan reminded me a bit of George Hamilton. With his suave air, practiced charm, and natty double-breasted blazers, he brought in a ton of business from moneyed women of a certain age who were looking for a little tingle with their tango.

As I watched, the taller woman with thinning hair who probably remembered voting for FDR shoved a shorter, well-padded dowager who clung to Maurice's arm. "You take back that snide remark about my needing more instruction, Mildred Kensington."

"At your age, you should be grateful you can still walk. There's nothing to be ashamed of in not being able to waltz any better than Hoover." The pseudosweet words came with an equally false smile.

The Great Dane raised his head and cocked it at the sound of the quarreling voices.

"Hoover? The president? What are you going on about, Mildred?" Edwina flapped her hand dismissively, a multicarat diamond on her gnarled finger catching the sunlight. "You're gaga. Your grandchildren should have insisted you stay in that home they found for you last year. Of course, being incontinent *does* get you kicked out of some—"

"Hoover, my Great Dane," Mildred said, nodding toward the massive dog.

There was a gasp from the other couples who had abandoned all pretense of dancing and were watching the Edwina and Mildred show as avidly as if they were sitting in Ford's Theater.

"Ladies, please," Maurice said again, stepping between them as Edwina wound up to throw a punch at the smug Mildred. No genteel slaps for her, apparently.

The dog lowered his head to his legs again, apparently deciding his intervention wasn't necessary, that Maurice had things under control.

"Did you need me to help demonstrate?" I asked, deciding it was time to break it up. Visions of our insurance skyrocketing if one of the old dears broke a hip moved me forward.

"Thank you, my dear Anastasia," Maurice said.

No matter how many times I asked him to call me Stacy, he insisted on using my full name and treated me like I was deposed Russian royalty.

"We were just about to embark on a waltz."

He used the remote to cue up the music and took my hand. We circled the floor several times—I enjoyed waltzing with Maurice because of his gliding step and strong lead—and finished with a flourish.

"Thank you," Maurice said, kissing my hand with old-fashioned gallantry.

"Let's talk when you're done here," I said with a meaningful look.

I struggled with the accounts for another half hour before I heard Maurice call, "Au revoir, ladies. Until next time." Moments later he stood in the doorway.

I had hired Maurice almost two years ago, and we'd developed a relationship that seemed more like great-uncle with favorite niece than employee-employer, despite the fact we never socialized outside the studio. I didn't know much about his personal life other than that his wife had died of an aneurysm in her early fifties. He'd never remarried, although I was certain he'd had plenty of opportunities, if the women in his classes were anything to go by. Speaking of which . . .

I gestured for him to sit. "Maurice, what is it with

those women? We need to find a way to keep interactions more ... more amicable. We can't have students mistaking your class for a boxing match and breaking their osteoporotic bones. Plus, we can't let a couple of scrappy senior citizens make the atmosphere so bitter that we lose clients. Lord knows, we can't afford that."

"I couldn't agree more, Anastasia." He cocked his head a bit to one side, clearly asking me how to fix the problem. One ankle rested on the opposite knee and his hands lay on his thighs.

"What did you do when these sorts of problems arose on your cruise ships?"

"Threw them overboard," he said, straight-faced.

His deadpan humor never failed to catch me off guard and I gaped at him for a moment. Then I started laughing. His mouth twitched at the corner, and he leaned across the desk to hand me a pristine handkerchief as tears leaked from my eyes.

"Wouldn't work here," I finally said. "No ocean. Although the Potomac's not that far ..." I mused.

His blue eyes twinkled.

Damn, if I were fifty years older—make that thirty—I'd probably be fighting Edwina and Mildred for him.

"If it concerns you, Anastasia, I will fix the problem." He opened his hands like a magician performing a trick. "I shall recruit two gentlemen of my acquaintance to attend the classes—perhaps I may tell them the classes are complimentary?"

"Absolutely," I said, relieved to have such an elegant solution to the dilemma. "Thank you, Maurice. The real problem, you know, is that you're much too charming. Do you think you could dial back the sex appeal a notch?" I smiled at him as he rose.

"Impossible, my dear Anastasia." A look of mischief lit his face. "It's a curse."

Moments after Maurice left the office, I heard the outside door open and the click of high heels stop at my doorway. I looked over to see a woman posed in the opening. In that nebulous range between fifty and sixty, she had a flawlessly made-up face that had probably been lifted at least once. Her hair was an ashy blond cut to jaw length and expensively styled. A pink raw-silk suit clung to her lean curves and she wore matching stilettos that undoubtedly said Blahnik or Choo on the label. If her long neck was a bit scraggy and the skin on her hands a tad mottled, she was still a very attractive woman. Sherry Indrebo, the Republican congresswoman from Minnesota. And a talented amateur ballroom dancer who paid Rafe to dance with her at competitions, like Mark Downey did with me. I'd heard rumors that maybe she got more than dancing for her money, but I'd never believed them.

"Stacy," she said with a tight smile. "Tell Rafe I'll just be a minute, would you? I need to change. Thanks."

Uh-oh. "Rafe's not here, Sherry."

Her perfectly arched and penciled brows snapped together. "He's not? Well, I'm sure he'll get here any minute. He wouldn't forget. Not with the Capitol Festival so close."

I didn't tell her Rafe had been forgetting a lot of things recently.

"He'd better not forget." The corners of her mouth tightened. "I had to completely rearrange my schedule and miss a floor vote to get here on time."

"If he said he'll be here, he'll be here," I lied. "He probably got caught in traffic somewhere."

With a dubious look, she sailed into the bathroom to change. I was back at my computer when she poked her head in ten minutes later, dressed in a few strips of orange fluff that passed for a salsa dress and showed off her excellent legs.

"Is he here?"

"I haven't seen him."

"I'll give him precisely five more minutes and then I'm out of here."

I'd hoped she'd do her waiting in the studio, maybe stretch to warm up, but no such luck. She sat in the wing chair by the window—the better to watch for Rafe, I guessed—and crossed her legs. "I'd kill for a cigarette," she said, swinging one foot.

I didn't respond to the hint. This was a strictly no-smoking building. Smoking killed your wind. And it stank. "I didn't know you smoked," I finally blurted.

The corner of her mouth crooked up in a wry smile. "Never where my constituents can see me." She popped a piece of gum into her mouth.

I wondered what else she indulged in out of the voters' sight. I tried to think of something to say to Sherry as the seconds ticked past and the tension grew thicker. Nothing came to me. Truth to tell, Sherry intimidated me. With money (from a rich defense contractor husband who spent at least half his time in St. Paul), looks, and power, she was a formidable woman. Even Rafe had mentioned once, half joking, that she scared him. At five minutes to the second, she rose to her feet and fluffed her orange feathers.

"I can't wait any longer," she said, her voice dripping ice. "My husband and I are attending a thousand-dollar-a-plate fund-raiser tonight and I can't be late. Please tell

Rafe that I was here for our practice." Her anger was way out of proportion to being stood up for dance practice, and I wondered uneasily about their relationship. "I'll expect him to call me with an explanation. And it had better be good."

"I'll let him know," I said and breathed a sigh of relief when she swept out of the office.

Without bothering to change, she charged out the side door. I went to the window and watched as a driver held the door of a black Lincoln Town Car for her. It wasn't quite a limo, but it was certainly a more luxurious mode of transportation than my yellow Beetle. An orange feather dangled out of the door, but the car moved off anyway.

I hoped Rafe knew what he was doing. But I doubted it.

At eight thirty I sat at the dinette table in my breakfast nook, eating a late dinner of spinach and water-packed tuna, wishing I could have a cheeseburger and fries. But Blackpool was only six weeks away and I didn't need an extra pound or two straining the seams of my fitted costumes. Rafe had complained during a lift last week that I was gaining weight and although I denied it, I was counting every calorie. Winning trophies at the big competitions was excellent advertising for the studio and the prize money was nothing to sneer at, either.

And now the studio's very existence was at issue. Clearly, Rafe was going to push for some decisions if he showed up tonight, which was beginning to look doubtful. Trouble was, I didn't see a solution that we could agree on. I wanted to build Graysin Motion into one of the country's most respected ballroom-dance training centers and that took time. I was willing to live on the bare minimum while we grew the business. Rafe, for whatever reason—expensive new girlfriend? Bad investments?—wasn't.

I sipped my mineral water and downed a handful of vitamins. How had things disintegrated so quickly? A few short months ago we'd had similar goals for our relationship and our business; now . . . well, I'd rather shave off my hair than turn Graysin Motion into a kiddie recital mill. If Rafe insisted on taking more money out of the business, I'd have to do something drastic. I cleared my place and tried to decide what "drastic" would be. There was really only one answer and I shied away from it: borrow money from Uncle Nico to buy Rafe's share of the business.

The banks weren't lending to small businesses—I'd already approached eight of them—and my parents, divorced, weren't in a position to invest in a ballroom dance studio. My brother and sister had less money than I did, and my lottery picks never seemed to win. Uncle Nico, my mom's brother and an entrepreneur with his fingers in many pies (not all of them strictly legal, I suspected) would happily lend me the money. The problem was, what would he expect in return? He'd loaned me a hundred bucks in high school to buy the bicycle I needed to get to dance lessons, and told me I could just do him a favor someday in return. The favor turned out to be going to the prom with the son of one of his business associates. I was a senior and the kid was a pimply sophomore who laughed in little snorts, tipped a bottle of Southern Comfort into the punch bowl, and tried to feel me up during the slow dances. Gag me.

I was trying to decide whether to call Uncle Nico now, so I could have a solid offer for Rafe, or wait until after I'd heard what Rafe had to say, when a thump overhead brought my gaze to the ceiling. Someone was in the studio. My watch read 8:45. The last class had let out at eight—Maurice taught it—and those students were long gone. A car backfired out front and then another noise, like something heavy landing on the floor, thudded through the centuries-old boards. What the—?

I ran to the stairs and pounded up them in my bare feet, impulse taking over once again. Pushing open the door that led into the upstairs hall, I expected lights, but it was almost totally dark. Slivers of moonlight, stippled by passing clouds, provided faint illumination. The studio that was like an extension of my home, a cocoon that gave me comfort, suddenly seemed eerie and alien. I hesitated before stepping into the hall. I held my breath and listened. Nothing. I took a deep breath. This was silly. I didn't need to slink around my own studio. I slid my hand along the wall to the light switch and flicked it. The sconces in the hall lit up, casting a warm glow on the wooden floors. The hall was empty.

"Hello?" I called. "Anybody here?" I was pleased my voice didn't tremble. "Hello?" I said again, louder. Nothing.

The rooms opening off the hall still lay in semidarkness, with the small studio, the powder room, and my office to my left and the ballroom running the length of the house on my right. Standing in the hall, I reached my right hand around the jamb of the small studio door and felt for the light switch. The overhead fixture sprang to life, illuminating the emptiness of the wood-floored room with its windows that looked on to my courtyard. Gaining confidence, I marched down the hall to the powder room and turned on the light. Small mosaic tiles in white and blue, white ceramic sink and toilet—that needed cleaning, I noted—framed dancing prints on the wall, humming fridge. Nothing out of place.

As I approached my office, a thin whistling raised gooseflesh on my arms. I slowed my pace and peered around the corner of the short hall that led to the stairs. The door to the outside stairs gapped slightly and a breath of wind soughed through. With shaking hands, I pushed it closed and turned the dead bolt. Could Maurice have forgotten to lock up? I leaned back against the door for a moment, then pushed away to continue my search. I was confident by now that there was no one here . . . no intruder waiting to jump out at me. It just didn't *feel* like there was anyone here.

I scanned the office: desks, chairs, computers, Oriental rug I'd bought in Turkey—all untouched. The brightness of the lights I'd left on as I progressed toward the front of the house infused me with courage and I entered the ballroom without a qualm. What is it in our DNA that seeks light, feels safer in the glare of sunlight than hidden in dark crannies? Maybe because we relied on our vision and had lost our senses of smell and hearing, relatively speaking. Our ancestors could see the saber-toothed cat stalking them but couldn't smell or hear it. Although if the tiger house at the National Zoo was anything to go by, any Neanderthal downwind should have smelled the big kitty coming. I shook my head at the goofy direction in which my thoughts had drifted.

The glow from headlights and streetlights out front illuminated the northern end of the room and a trickle of moonlight from the back windows cast shadows along the south side. A broad stripe of light fell into the room from the hall. My eyes went to the stereo system; if someone were going to rob Graysin Motion, it was about the only thing worth stealing. Present and accounted for. About to return to my office to wait for Rafe, I sniffed. Something didn't smell right. I gazed around the room more deliberately, scanning each section in turn.

Nothing by the front windows. The curtains were too sheer for anyone to hide behind. Nothing in the center of the floor. The odor grew stronger as I stood there and my legs started to tremble. Beneath the southern windows, one of the shadows was strangely static, not shifting as clouds and tree limbs skipped through the moonlight. I groped for the switch on the wall, my eyes never leaving the immobile shadow.

Light drenched the room and I slid down the wall until I squatted on my haunches, unable to approach Rafe where he lay under the window. I felt like I'd just plummeted into a death drop, but Rafe was not there to catch me. The beach ball–sized pool of blood congealing like a macabre halo around his shattered head told me it was too late for bandages or CPR. Too late for kissing and making up. Too late for . . . Forcing myself to move, I crabbed sideways on my hands and feet until I reached the door. Pulling myself up by the doorknob, I staggered into the bathroom and threw up.

Chapter 3

The police arrived within minutes of my 911 call, in a swirl of strobing lights, staticky radio transmissions, and general confusion. A quick inspection of Rafe's body and the first two officers on the scene called for detectives and crime scene investigators. One of the patrol officers escorted me downstairs and waited with me in my living room while the other looped yellow crime scene tape around the house and kept gawkers away. I watched the goings-on from the front window, my hands laced around a mug of hot tea liberally dosed with honey and a shot of bourbon from a bottle Rafe had left behind. An unmarked car parked illegally out front, and two men I assumed were the detectives strode toward the stairs. My ears tracked their progress as they clomped up the stairs and walked heavily into the studio where Rafe's body lay, just above my head. When I realized the cop—Officer Suarez, I read from his name tag—and I were staring at the ceiling, I wrenched my gaze away.

At least an hour passed before the thumpings and noises overhead slowed. I'd drunk two more mugs of tea, skipping the bourbon but going heavy on the honey.

I'd read somewhere that sugar was good for shock. Officer Suarez resisted my attempts at conversation and I moved from feeling sick and shaky to feeling sad and worried. Sad about Rafe's fate, worried about my own. It hadn't taken much thought to realize I would be suspect numero uno. Maybe numero only. I might not have any legal training, but I'd watched enough *Law & Order* episodes to know the spouse or significant other was always a suspect. Especially if he or she had recently caught the deceased cheating, had broken their engagement, and had fought—sometimes loudly—about business disagreements. Double especially if he or she had something to gain from the death: Unless Rafe had changed his will after we broke up (I hadn't yet changed mine), I'd inherit his share of Graysin Motion.

A knock on the door broke into my thoughts. Officer Suarez answered it and returned a second later to usher in two men before rejoining his partner outside. The one in the lead looked like a fifty-year-old geek with an attitude. His head seemed too heavy for his scrawny neck and was capped by thinning, dishwater-colored hair. He had stretchy, too-red lips and gray eyes behind black-rimmed glasses Clark Kent might have worn in the 1950s. An incongruous cluster of freckles spattered the bridge of his nose, his cheeks, and even his earlobes. He wore a navy suit with a spotless white shirt and precisely knotted navy-and-green-striped tie.

"I'm Detective Lissy," he said, shaking my hand briefly. "This is Detective Troy." He nodded at the other man, a stocky bodybuilder type in his midthirties.

Detective Troy also shook my hand, his palm callused, his brown eyes taking in the details of my appearance. I didn't want to think what I looked like, clad in a vomit-flecked blue T-shirt and stretchy exercise pants—Officer Suarez had refused to let me change—with my hair straggling out of its ponytail and my feet bare. I gestured for them to be seated on the lavender velvet-covered settee my great-aunt Laurinda had placed by the marble fireplace. When she'd left me the house and its contents in her will three years ago, I'd planned to replace most of the fusty furniture, but I hadn't had the time or money to do it yet, so sitting in the living room felt like emigrating to the 1930s. I returned to the wing chair by the window and sat, curling my feet up under me. Cold, I rubbed my hands together, but then thought it might make me look nervous and forced them to be still in my lap.

Detective Troy plopped onto the settee, releasing a puff of dust from the fabric, and pulled out a notebook. Detective Lissy remained standing, his back to the fireplace.

"Tell us about your relationship with Mr. Acosta," he said, his voice neutral, his gaze roaming the room, lingering on the faded drapes, the tarnished silver-plated bowl on the end table, the portrait of Great-aunt Laurinda done when she was a seventeen-year-old debutante in 1923. He crossed to the painting and tapped it with his forefinger to straighten it.

When he returned to his post by the fireplace, I said, "We were partners."

"In the business sense or the romantic sense?"

"Business," I said firmly. Maybe too firmly.

The line between his brows deepened slightly.

"We used to be engaged," I admitted in reluctant response to that semifrown, "but we broke it off a while ago."

"When?" he asked, his gaze returning to the tarnished bowl.

I half expected him to whip out some silver polish and have a go at it. "Four months ago." My eyes slid to Detective Troy, but he didn't look up from his note-taking.

"Tell us what happened tonight," Lissy said. His gaze fixed with unnerving intensity on my face and I realized his eyes weren't gray as I'd originally thought, but the palest blue.

I told him about Rafe and me planning to meet, about hearing the noises upstairs, about running up to investigate.

"You thought there was an intruder upstairs and you went up on your own?" No skepticism sounded in his voice, but those speaking brows rose a fraction.

"I wasn't sure it was an intruder—I thought it might be Maurice"—I explained who Maurice was—"or Rafe showing up without calling." Really, I didn't think about it. As usual. I just charged up the stairs.

Lissy pulled a handkerchief from his pocket and swiped it across the face of the clock ticking behind him on the mantel. "Go on."

I teared up when I came to the part about finding Rafe's body and didn't mention throwing up.

"Did you touch the body?" Lissy asked, apparently unmoved by my emotion.

"No." I sniffed and groped for a tissue.

"Do you own a gun?" Lissy asked.

I stopped, tissue halfway to my nose. He didn't seem to be watching me; he was staring into the fireplace as if wishing he had a dustpan and broom to sweep up ash traces. His question posed a problem. I owned a gun—a graduation gift from Uncle Nico—but it wasn't registered. Uncle Nico had advised against it, warning that when the Democrats came to power, which he predicted they would, they'd confiscate registered guns. "You don't want the crooks to be the only ones with firepower, Stasia," he'd said. "Keep this loaded and keep it where you can get to it. If you ever need to use it, you call me afterward and I'll help with the cleanup."

I'd consciously avoided thinking about what the cleanup might entail, reluctantly accepted the gun, shot it at a range a couple of times under Uncle Nico's supervision, and tucked it into the bottom drawer of my bedside table. What were the penalties for having an unregistered gun? Did Virginia law require registration? I didn't know, but I bet that getting caught lying to the police had worse consequences.

"Yes, I own a gun." I knew I'd taken too long to answer by the way both detectives stared at me. I bit my lower lip. "It's just a little one. A .22. My uncle gave it to me. Years ago. For self-protection. He thought the Democrats—" Shut up, I told myself as the line between Lissy's brows deepened again.

"When did you last fire it?" Detective Troy asked.

"I don't know . . . Seven, eight years ago?"

"You wouldn't mind letting us have a look at it?" Lissy said in a tone that said it didn't matter if I minded or not.

"Sure." I unfolded my legs and pushed out of the wing chair, relieved to be able to move, to escape the room and the inscrutable detectives. The rug felt good under my bare feet. "It'll just take a—"

"We'll come with you." Lissy gestured me toward the door as Troy rose to his feet.

"It's in my bedroom." I hadn't made my bed this morning and I was pretty sure yesterday's clothes, including bra and panties, were still in a heap on the floor.

How come Mother never told me to keep the house spotless in case homicide detectives might go prowling through it one day?

"Best place for it," Detective Troy agreed, either not getting the hint that I didn't want strange men in my bedroom or deliberately ignoring my embarrassment. "That's where my sister keeps hers."

I padded down the hall to my room, both detectives trailing behind. Troy whispered something to Lissy, but I didn't catch it. Pushing the door wide, I marched straight to my bedside table, a three-foot-high walnut chest of drawers that used to hold Great-aunt Laurinda's embroidered hankies and purses carefully wrapped in tissue paper. My knees sank into the carpet's deep pile as I knelt and yanked open the bottom drawer. I used it for the lingerie items I needed once in a blue moon: the slip that went with a skirt I wore only to funerals, the cami I used under a blouse that never made it back from the cleaners after the last time I wore it, the mint-green hose I'd had to wear as a bridesmaid once. I patted the slippery fabrics, feeling for the hard, alien shape of the gun. When I didn't feel it, I started tossing the filmy underthings onto the floor, uncaring now about the detectives' scrutiny. Without looking, I could sense them standing just inside the door, watching, breathing.

My hand panned fruitlessly against the wooden bottom of the drawer. I flushed with heat; then the blood receded and I shivered. Reaching for my slippers beside the bed, I drew them on. Maybe I'd put the gun in the other drawer. I knew I hadn't. But I opened it, digging through notebooks, condom packets—probably expired—hand lotions, a sewing kit, and other miscellany. No gun. I tried to remember when I'd last seen it, but couldn't. I rocked back on my heels and looked over my shoulder. Was it my imagination, or had the detectives inched farther into the room? Their faces were impassive as they stared at me in my nest of lingerie.

My mouth felt dry, like I'd been eating baby powder, and I used my tongue to moisten my lips. "It's not here."

"I know the police think I killed Rafe," I told Mark Downey Thursday morning at seven o'clock. We'd had a dance practice set up and I'd been too distracted by the night's events to cancel, although I'd called the instructors and put a sign on the door saying classes were canceled for the day. Mark had arrived for our practice session, had seen the crime scene tape strung across the doors to the ballroom, and had sought me out in my office.

"My God, Stacy," he'd said, rushing in without even knocking and jolting to a stop at the sight of me behind my desk. "I thought— I saw the tape and thought that you—" His light brown eyes glowed with concern and relief.

"Not me. Rafe," I said, thrusting my fingers through the unwashed hair I had scraped back into a utilitarian ponytail. I knew my eyes were red and puffy from lack of sleep, and I frankly was surprised Mark didn't run screaming from the room at the sight of me. I could've had a walk-on part in the latest zombie movie without needing special effects makeup. Instead, he pulled me up into a comforting hug. I clung to him for a second—he smelled like deodorant soap—but broke away as I started to sniffle again.

"Sorry," I said, reaching for a tissue. I felt like I'd been crying nonstop since detectives Lissy and Troy finally left me alone at around two this morning. They'd pokered up and exchanged a meaningful glance when I discovered my gun was missing, and the questions had gotten a lot more pointed. They'd swabbed my hands with little towelette thingies, had taken my fingerprints—for elimination purposes, they said—and had asked if I knew if Rafe had a will. I gave them a copy. I could only be grateful they hadn't hauled me off to jail.

"Rafe! What in the name of God happened?" Mark straddled the straight-backed chair facing my desk and rested his chin on its back.

Normally, I wouldn't have considered Mark a confidante—he was a client more than a friend—but nothing about this morning qualified as "normal." I slumped into my chair and told him what I knew about Rafe's death—murder—which wasn't much, and finished with my conviction that the cops considered me the prime suspect.

"Of course they don't," Mark said. "No one could possibly think you had it in you to kill someone."

"That's sweet of you," I said. Deluded on at least two counts—the cops clearly thought I was more than capable of shooting my ex-fiancé, and pretty much everyone is able to kill under the right circumstances—but sweet. "I'm sorry, but I'm not up to—"

"Of course you're not," he said, rising immediately. "Just give me a call when you're ready to practice. If there's anything I can do . . . I know you and Rafe were close, that is, that you used to be— Oh, hell."

He looked young and confused and earnest and I gave him a small smile. "Thanks, Mark. I appreciate it. I'll call you later in the week." If I wasn't being fitted for a lurid orange prison jumpsuit.

He left and I rose to make sure the door had closed after him. I felt less secure than usual in the studio—big surprise—and gave into nerves by turning the dead bolt. Returning to my office, my gaze fell on the crisscrossed crime scene tape that barred the way into the ballroom where I'd found Rafe's body. As if compelled, I walked to the open door and stood on the threshold, wondering how I'd ever dance in there again. Except for a stain—smaller than it had seemed last night—where Rafe had lain under the window, the room looked like it always did: sunny and serene. I frequently imagined ghostly Colonial-era dancers bowing and curtsying as they minced their way through a gavotte or quadrille; now there'd be another ghost dancing in the ballroom. At least, I hoped he'd be dancing.

I turned away, fighting back tears again. Maybe Danielle was right and I hadn't been completely over Rafe. Wanting to distract myself from my incessant tears, I hurried into the studio, which the police had not put off limits, and turned on the stereo, not caring what music was cued up. A song from *Wicked* came on. I warmed up with some pliés and relevés and then flung myself around the room in a whirling dance with no precision and little grace, intent on wringing the pent-up tension out of my muscles.

"You bitch."

The venomous words caught me midleap and I half turned in the air, stumbling as I landed. Solange stood in the doorway, fury in every stiff line of her body. Even her red hair seemed to bristle with electric anger. She aimed the remote at the stereo, cutting Kristin Chenoweth off midsyllable.

"How did you get in here?"

She flung a key at me and it bounced off my cheek. "You killed him!"

"I did not!"

She stalked toward me, clearly intent on beating a confession out of me. I squared up to her but held up my hands placatingly. Heaven knows there'd been a time when nothing would have given me more pleasure than scratching Solange's smug face or pulling her hair out of her scalp, but I didn't think a catfight was a dignified way of grieving for Rafe. "How did you find out?" I asked.

"The police were on my doorstep first thing this morning," she said, slitting her eyes. "They told me Rafe was dead, that he'd been shot! How do you think it felt to hear my fiancé had been killed?" She managed a little sob.

Fiancé! I saw her lying face through a red haze. "About like it felt to find him in bed with a morals-free trollop." Whoops. That comment wasn't going to do much to head off a catfight. But, damn, it felt good to say it.

Solange stopped dead for a moment, then resumed pacing toward me, looking for an opening. I figured I could take her: She was fit, with killer abs bared by a crop top and skintight jeans that just cleared her pubic bone, but I was taller, with a longer reach, and I wasn't wearing gladiator sandals with four-inch heels. I wasn't recovering from an ankle injury, either.

"Let's not do this, Solange," I said. "I'm sorry for what I said."

"I'll make you sorrier."

Without warning, she kicked at my knee. Her stiletto heel grazed the side of my leg. "Ow!" Before she could pull her leg back, I grabbed her ankle with both my hands. Her eyes widened as she hopped on one foot.

The temptation to upend her was almost overwhelming. Instead, I backed up a step and watched her teeter precariously as she was forced to hop toward me. "I didn't shoot Rafe."

"Liar. Lying bi—"

I jerked her foot an inch higher, almost to my shoulder, and she didn't even wince. Ballroom dancers have to be darn flexible. "Stop saying that. I didn't kill Rafe. And I don't know who did. Although—" The key she'd thrown glinted as a sunbeam stroked it. "How long have you had that key?"

"Rafe gave it to me a few months back so I could use the studio to practice when I needed to."

Great. How many other people had Rafe given keys to? I was having the locks changed today.

"*Would* you let me go? You're going to hurt my ankle." Exasperation beat out anger in her voice and I could see she'd calmed down. I dropped her foot. She bent to fuss with her sandal strap.

"I don't see a ring," I said, my gaze on her left hand.

She knew immediately what I was saying. She straightened and her face was rosy, either from bending over or from my question. "We were more, like, engaged to be engaged. We were going ring shopping this weekend."

Sure they were. Talk about being a liar. I felt better knowing Rafe hadn't proposed to her. I don't know why it made a difference to me, but it did. "Look, the studio's closed today. I'll keep this"—I stooped to retrieve the key—"and I'll call you later this week to let you know what the studio schedule is going to be. What with Rafe—" I stopped, suddenly realizing that we would be short a teacher. And the Capitol Festival! I'd just lost my partner for the upcoming competition and for Blackpool, too. How could I dig up a new partner on such short notice? All the good dancers were already committed and—

"I said I could teach Rafe's classes for a couple of weeks."

I tuned back to Solange to see her looking at me strangely. "You could?" A helpful Solange was new to me . . . and suspect. "Why would you?"

"To . . . to honor Rafe's memory," she said with a pious, self-sacrificing air.

She didn't fool me for one second. She had an ulterior motive. Which didn't mean I wouldn't take her up on her offer because she had teaching experience and I was in a bind. Not wanting to make a decision on the spot, I said, "I'll let you know, okay? Right now—"

Heavy footsteps thudded in the hall. "Acosta!" a man bellowed from just outside the studio door. Solange and I turned as one to see a man burst into the room with such force that the door banged against the wall. Emotion twisted his face and inflamed a bulbous nose. "Where is he?" the man asked loudly. "Where's that cowardly spic who got my daughter pregnant?"

Chapter 4

I gaped at the stranger as a dozen questions flitted through my head. Who are you? Who's your daughter? How do you know she's pregnant? The only one I verbalized was, "You mean Rafe?"

"Señor Rafael Acosta." The man oozed sarcasm and butchered the first word by pronouncing it "senior." A shade under six feet tall, he had shoulders that almost filled the doorway and hands clenched into fists the size of grapefruits. He rocked back and forth on the balls of his booted feet, a bull about to charge.

"Who are you?" Solange thrust herself into the conversation. She had her hands balled on her hips, with her chin jutting out.

"Leon Hall."

My face must have shown my shock and dismay because Hall nodded with grim satisfaction. "That's right. Taryn's dad. She's pregnant. By that wetback."

Solange gasped. "Rafe wouldn't do that! He and I were seeing each other, almost engaged. He wouldn't ch—" She broke off, eyes darting to me and then to the floor.

I took little satisfaction in her stricken expression as I asked Hall, "How do you know? That it was Rafe, I mean?" Rafe liked his women on the sophisticated side; I had trouble seeing him romantically involved with an inexperienced teenager.

"My daughter told me so this morning. So tell the miserable child molester to come out from wherever he's hiding"—his voice rose to shouting level, as if he were trying to scare Rafe out of a closet or hidey-hole—"so I can kill the sorry bas—"

"Someone beat you to it," I said quietly.

It took several moments for my words to penetrate his shell of anger.

"Wha—?" He looked confused, glancing from me to Solange. "You're telling me he's dead? Acosta's dead?"

I nodded. "Maybe we should discuss this in my office."

Solange pulled a cell phone out of her purse and started punching in a number. "I'm calling the police," she announced, her green gaze fixed on Hall. "Obviously, you killed Rafe."

Unease flickered across Hall's face. "You're crazy. I didn't even know he was dead."

"So you say."

A voice squawking into her ear distracted Solange. As she talked, I led Hall away. The door to the outside stairs was ajar, leading me to believe Solange had left it open when she came in and Hall had taken advantage of that. I'd had enough surprise visitors for one morning, so I locked it again before ushering Hall into my office and gesturing him toward the love seat under the window.

He shook his head, remaining by the door. "I've got to get to work."

"So you just stopped by to beat Rafe up on your way to the office?"

He looked at me wearily, drawing a meaty hand over his face. "What will Taryn do now? I was gonna make him do right by her—"

"You mean marry her? I thought you wanted to kill him." I eyed him skeptically. The way he tossed around terms like "wetback" didn't lead me to believe Rafe would have been a welcome addition to the Hall family.

"That was just an expression," he said, thoughts of the police obviously troubling him. "I wanted him to do the right thing, marry my Taryn and give her baby a name. Now . . ." He looked around the office as if confused about where he was, his gaze lighting on the Blackpool trophy on the corner of my desk, the framed caricature of me and Danielle we'd paid fifteen bucks for at a carnival, the sunny yellow afghan my grandma had knitted draped over the love seat's back. "I've gotta go. The foreman'll dock me."

"But the police—" I called to his retreating figure.

He didn't bother to answer. I heard the door slam shut and his footsteps clomping down the stairs. Sighing, I left the office to lock the door *again*, and went looking for Solange. She was nowhere to be found. Huh. She must have slipped out while Hall and I were talking.

Returning to my office, still sweaty from my earlier dance workout and exhausted from a sleepless night, I tried to concentrate on business tasks I needed to accomplish in the wake of Rafe's death. The police would notify his family in Argentina, Detective Lissy had said, but I needed to tell his dance partners, our staff and students, our lawyer and accountant, the bank, the Capitol

Festival and the Blackpool organizers . . . I drew up a list and stared at it, weary before I started. Did I need to write an obituary? What about funeral arrangements? I supposed his family would take his body back to Buenos Aires. Well, then, a memorial service?

My mind slid away from the dreary list and latched on to the subject that had been uppermost since the detectives left me last night: Who killed Rafe? Who hated him enough to shoot him to death? Leon Hall, obviously. My list ended there. I couldn't think of any dance student or partner who would want Rafe dead. Okay, maybe Sawyer if Rafe really did get Taryn pregnant. I flipped through a mental Rolodex of the people Rafe saw regularly. Maurice and Rafe got along fine. There were professional rivalries, of course, and dancers who resented Rafe's success. A British dancer came to mind. The flamboyant newcomer had lost the American Smooth Champion title to Rafe last year and had tried to get him disqualified. But as far as I knew, he was in England, running a studio in Manchester.

Sherry Indrebo? She'd been livid when Rafe stood her up yesterday. But shooting him wasn't going to help her win a dance championship. Like me, she was now up the creek without a partner. I realized that I didn't know much about Rafe's private life. Even before we split up, our time together had revolved around the studio and dance competitions; I'd only met one friend of his, a schoolmate from Rafe's high school days who was in D.C. on business. I'd never met his father—his mom was dead—or other family members. We had broken up two weeks before a planned trip to Argentina to introduce me to his family.

A knock on the outside door made me jump. I got up to answer it, figuring it was a cop in response to Solange's phone call. I was right. Not Detective Lissy, thank goodness. I told the officer about Leon Hall's visit and threats. "I got the impression he didn't know Rafe was dead," I finished, wanting to be fair, even though it would be nice if the police had a suspect besides yours truly.

"We'll look into it, ma'am," was all the officer said before tucking his notebook away and departing.

My phone rang as I was about to go downstairs and shower so I detoured into the office to answer with a less sprightly "Graysin Motion" than I usually managed.

"Thank God you're not dead," Danielle's voice greeted me. "Don't ever scare me like that again!"

"What are you talking about?" Just hearing my sister's voice cheered me up.

"The article in today's paper." The rustle of newspaper pages crackled over the phone. "'Alexandria police report the discovery of a body at an Old Town dance studio last evening. Name is being withheld pending notification of next of kin. Police are treating the case as a homicide.' I know it was silly to jump to the conclusion that the article was referring to Graysin Motion—there are several dance schools in Alexandria. Maybe they're referring to that Li'l Twinkletoes place?"

"It's us," I said. "I mean, they're talking about Graysin Motion. Someone shot Rafe last night."

"Get out! Rafe? Who—? When—? I'm on my way over there." The line went dead.

I had showered and dressed in an ankle-length patio dress of fuchsia and blush pink and cream—I don't own anything somber-looking—by the time Danielle *ding-dong*ed. She greeted me with a compulsive hug and an order: "Tell me everything."

When I had finished, she gave me another hug. "Are you all right?"

"Sure," I said with a grimace, "for a woman who's about to be locked up for life. Or for so long that my quickstep will be more of a quickshuffle and I'll need a walker when I try to rumba."

"That's not going to happen," Danielle said decisively. "Look, I've got to get to work. I called to tell my boss I had car trouble, but I've got a meeting I can't miss at ten. Will you be okay? I'll come back this evening. I'll even bring dinner."

"Thanks," I said, grateful for her caring.

After she left, I made a list of people who needed to know about Rafe's death and picked up the phone. I called Maurice and listened to his exclamations of shock, sorrow, and concern. I told him classes would resume tomorrow and he sounded relieved. Maurice must need the money, I thought as I hung up. I e-mailed several others, including ballroom dance organizations like Dance Visions and American Dancesport, and our students. Staring at the final name on my list, Sherry Indrebo, I reluctantly decided that she deserved a call rather than an e-mail. I found a number for her congressional office and dialed. The officious-sounding man who answered refused to put me through, saying that the congress-woman was headed to the floor for a vote. Even when I explained that I was calling about a death, he refused to give me her cell phone number or patch me through to her. His tone of voice made it clear he considered me a nuisance caller, no better than the pests who call during dinner to get you to renew your magazine subscriptions. Fine.

"Tell her that Rafe Acosta won't be her pro-am dance partner any longer," I told him, finally losing my temper. I banged the phone down on the table.

It rang almost before my hand left it.

"You can't do this to me, Rafe," Sherry Indrebo said in a voice like liquid nitrogen. "I told you I'm working on it. It's not as easy—"

"It's Stacy Graysin," I broke in. "I don't know how to tell you this, Ms. Indrebo, but Rafe's dead."

The hiss of an indrawn breath was the only proof she'd heard me. Thirty seconds went by before she said, "How? What happened?"

"Someone killed him at the studio last night," I said.

More silence. "I have to talk to you in person," she finally said. "Can you meet me at, oh, the Grant Memorial in an hour? It's right outside the Capitol."

"I don't know—" Her request surprised me and I wasn't really in the mood to trek downtown.

"Please?"

The urgency in the word got to me. I'm not sure I'd ever heard her use it before. And I had to admit I was curious. "Okay. I'll see you in an hour."

General Ulysses S. Grant presided over the memorial from atop a placid-looking bronze horse. Larger-than-life maned lions lay at the four corners of Grant's stone dais, facing out. Perhaps they were watching for danger: pigeons or taggers. I wasn't quite sure the lions worked with the Civil War–era general and the cannon behind him with soldiers draped over it, but they probably had some mythological significance. A few tourists loitered around the statues and a boy of eight or nine climbed onto the lion nearest me to have his photo taken, but I didn't see Sherry Indrebo. I was just lowering myself to sit on the marble stairs when I spotted her coming toward me from the Capitol. Her brisk walk and the way she focused straight forward set her apart from the herd of tourists.

"This is an absolute nightmare," she said as she drew even with me. A frown pinched her refined features and, despite the *oomph* of her red suit, she looked washed out and somehow older than the last time I'd seen her. Maybe it was the harsh sunlight.

Noting that she hadn't bothered with "Hello, Stacy," or a "Thanks for coming, Stacy," I waited for her to tell me why she'd dragged me all the way downtown.

"I can't believe someone shot Rafe. It's unbelievable." Her fingers twiddled the strand of marble-sized pearls gracing her neck.

I reared back slightly at her words. "I didn't tell you Rafe was shot," I said carefully.

She gave me a scornful look, completely unfazed by the implication that her knowledge was suspicious. "I made some calls after we talked," she said. "To the police. They say an arrest is imminent."

"Really?" I said, trying to swallow around the lump that swelled in my throat. "Did they say who?"

Surprisingly, she didn't seem too concerned about the identity of Rafe's killer. She waved my question away as her eyes scanned the disinterested tourists as if she suspected one of them might be taping our conversation. Paranoia: the hallmark of the true Washington insider. "What I have to discuss with you is . . . sensitive. Can I trust you not to tell anyone?"

"Maybe," I said. Why in the world would the congresswoman from Minnesota want to tell me something sensitive?

Her mouth twisted with dissatisfaction. "This is awkward." She paced toward the edge of the pool that reflected Grant's image and motioned for me to join her. My patio dress swished around my ankles as I stepped closer to the pool and stared into its inky depths. A hopeful duck swam over and looked up at us. "I left something at Rafe's condo the last time I was there," she said in a low voice. "I need you to get it for me."

"What?" I was so startled by her request that the word came out louder than I intended.

"*Shh.*" She looked over her shoulder. "I'm sure you can understand why I can't go myself to fetch it. In my position, the media would be all over me if someone saw me and they might . . . misinterpret my presence, put a negative spin on what was a completely aboveboard dance partnership."

Uh-huh. Just like I was currently misinterpreting the fact that she'd obviously been to Rafe's place.

"I can't afford to be connected in any way to a murder investigation, not when I'm up for reelection this fall."

I'd bet she didn't need her husband and chief campaign contributor getting wind of her visits to a single man's condo. "Why me?"

"Well, I figured since you and Rafe were . . . Since he and you . . . I thought you might have a key."

I did have a key, as a matter of fact. It was in a box with one of Rafe's sweaters I'd found a few days after our breakup, the bottle of contact lens solution and toothbrush he'd left in my bathroom, the half-finished thriller abandoned on my bedside table, and some other odds and ends. I'd tried to give him the box a couple of times, but he always had some excuse for not taking it, like "It's too hot now for me to need that sweater." Danielle thought it meant he still had hopes that we'd get back together. I wasn't sure what I thought it meant, if anything.

"What did you leave at Rafe's place?" I asked, my mind on sweaters and books.

She hesitated, then, obviously deciding there was no way I could retrieve the object if I didn't know what I was looking for, said, "My thumb drive. We were going over video of our cha-cha when my chief of staff called and needed a document. I got on Rafe's computer and e-mailed it to him, but then I forgot to take my thumb drive out of his computer."

Sounded innocent enough. "So why not ask the police to find it and return it to you?"

She looked at me as if I'd suggested she rent a horse and trot naked around Dupont Circle. "There are extremely sensitive political documents on it. I can't afford to have some nosy cop flipping through them and maybe passing my campaign strategy to my Democratic opponent or details of my fund-raising to the media."

It all sounded logical as she laid it out, but I couldn't help thinking she was hiding something. Of course, "hiding something" is synonymous with "politician," so maybe it was just her natural furtiveness sounding warning pings in my head. I slipped one foot out of my strappy lizard sandal and trailed a toe in the cool water. The duck glided over with little quacking murmurs to see if it was edible.

"I'll owe you," Sherry said in a voice barely louder than the duck's quack.

I suddenly remembered that I'd written Rafe some

fairly hot love letters early in our relationship. Surely he'd burned or shredded them when we broke up. I'd torn his letters into confetti and ground them in the sink's garbage disposal. I bit my lower lip. If he hadn't, I didn't want his father or—worse—Detective Lissy and company reading my letters. Maybe I could kill two birds with one stone.

"I'll try to take a look today," I told Sherry Indrebo.

The door to Rafe's condo swung open easily, revealing the familiar taupe-painted walls, the glass and steel ceiling light fixture, and the closed closet door of the entryway. I'd come here straight from meeting with Sherry, stopping by my house only briefly to pick up the key and my car. No police officer had been waiting to arrest me and I took that as a good sign, although I didn't stick around to press my luck. If Sherry was right about the police being on the verge of an arrest, I figured it might be smart to play least in sight for a while.

The living room–dining room space opened directly off the entryway and I moved forward, looking to see if anything had changed in the four months since I'd been here. Didn't look like it. Rafe's condo was decorated in what I thought of as traditional male: more money spent on electronics than furniture. A navy sofa and matching armchair faced a large-screen television and DVD player like postulants before an altar. Wires snaked from the set to a Wii, speakers, and a laptop computer resting on a glass-topped coffee table. A ballroom dance magazine and a Spanish-language periodical had slid onto the rug.

Crossing to the laptop, I saw Sherry's thumb drive sticking out from a port. When I tugged on the drive to remove it, the monitor blinked to life, bringing up a photo of me and Rafe doing the Argentine tango. Tears sprang to my eyes. He hadn't changed his computer wallpaper since we broke up. I wondered what my sister would make of that. He probably just didn't get around to it, I told myself briskly, wiping away the tears with the back of my hand. I slid the drive into my pocket. My gaze fell on the mug next to the computer, and lipstick stains on the rim jumped out at me. I suddenly felt a lot less weepy.

Ignoring the kitchen, I hurried to the bedroom, conscious that the police might be arriving at any moment to search the place. Did they search the homes of murder victims when the crime had taken place elsewhere? I was fuzzy on police procedure, but I didn't want to risk getting caught, even though I had a perfect right to retrieve my own property, didn't I? Averting my eyes from the unmade bed (king-sized, of course), I pulled open the drawer on his nightstand. On top of an address book, a notepad, and a clutter of coins and old receipts I remembered from when I used to stay here, there lay a strip of photos. They were black and white and looked like they'd come from one of those photo booths at the mall, where you ducked behind the curtain and took goofy photos with your friends. Except these weren't goofy. They featured a dark-haired woman I didn't recognize staring directly at the camera. *Huh*.

I was about to shift the photos to check for my letters underneath them, when a soft *whoosh* came to my ears, followed by a dull clunk. The front door! Someone had opened it. Someone with a key, since I hadn't heard a battering ram knocking it down. The police! I looked around frantically for someplace to hide. The closet was too obvious and the space under the bed too cramped, as I knew from having to wriggle under there once to retrieve a shoe kicked beneath it in the heat of passion. On instinct, I raced on tiptoe for the bathroom and stepped into the tub, careful not to rattle the shower curtain rings. Someone—a pre-me girlfriend, I suspected, or maybe the condo's original owners—had decorated Rafe's bathroom with a heavy fabric shower curtain in taupe and cream stripes complete with swags and tassels. I dropped to my haunches at the far end of the tub, as if that would hide me from anyone who looked in the tub, and tried to still my breathing. My heart thumped against my chest wall and I felt dizzy. Taking in a deep breath, I held it, listening intently.

Nothing. No scrape of shoes against the floor, no click of cabinet doors opening, no conversation. Not the police, then. I didn't know if that made me more or less nervous. If not the cops, then who? Had Sherry Indrebo changed her mind and decided to retrieve the thumb drive herself? A couple minutes ticked past and still I heard nothing. I found myself leaning forward, trying to get a bead on the intruder. He—or she—was so quiet, I wondered if he suspected I was here. Had he snuck into the bathroom? If I pulled the shower curtain back, would he be there, ready to pounce?

The thought tickled the flesh on my arms and I rubbed them, stopping when the friction made a slight sound. Waiting another ten minutes by my watch, I realized I desperately had to pee. This was getting ridiculous. I hadn't heard a thing since the door opened and closed. Very cautiously, I straightened and stepped out of the tub, wincing as I brushed the shower curtain, and the metal rings clinked against the rod. I froze, listening again—still nothing. I crept into the bedroom. No one lurked there, ready to jump me. I headed down the hall, moving a bit more freely as I became convinced that whoever had come in had already gone. I ducked into the kitchen, a tiny, galleylike affair with no place for an intruder to hide, unless they were blender-sized and could fit into a cabinet.

Stepping into the living room, I let out the breath I hadn't realized I was holding. No one. Whoever had come in hadn't needed to search for what they wanted. What had I missed? What was here in plain sight that someone needed? My gaze drifted slowly around the room, lighting on a remote with enough buttons to operate the *Enterprise*, a camera lens on the wide windowsill— Rafe was an avid photographer and liked photographing birds—a paper bag full of old clothes he might've been taking to Goodwill, and the laptop. Could there be something on the laptop that an intruder would want? If so, why not steal the whole computer? I approached it, and stared down at the monitor, which had gone black again. It told me nothing.

I reached toward it, unsure if I wanted to invade Rafe's privacy by cruising through his e-mail and files, and my hand brushed the mug, jolting drops of old coffee onto my wrist. I jerked back as if it had come alive and licked me. The liquid was still warm. My gaze darted to the entryway. The coat closet door was an inch ajar, not closed as when I'd come in. Understanding crashed down on me like an avalanche, leaving me cold and gasping for a breath. No one had come in while I'd been in the bedroom. Someone had *left*.

Chapter 5

Carmelo whickered at me and snuffled at the pockets of my patio dress for the carrots he was sure I carried. Mom pushed his head away, saying, "Get away, greedy."

I took a deep breath of the barn air, taking in the scents of hay and clean water and horse dung, and felt my shoulders relax. I hadn't known where to go after leaving Rafe's condo. The realization that someone had been there when I arrived, hidden in the closet, gave me the creeps. I couldn't leave fast enough. On the quiet street in front of the building, I looked both ways, nervously searching for signs that anyone was paying attention to me. A guy in a Dodge Charger pulling out of the condo garage gave me an appreciative once-over, but that didn't count—it happens all the time if you're tall, blond, and stacked. I didn't see anyone who looked like a cop, or anyone lurking behind a tree. A black woman sat at a bus stop, reading a romance novel. A pair of young mothers walked past briskly, pushing strollers. A man ran a leaf blower, spraying trash and dust off the sidewalk into the street.

I hurried to my yellow Volkswagen Beetle and got in,

locked the doors and sat there a moment, unsure where to go. If I went home, the cops might show up and arrest me. I had to go home eventually, but I wanted to delay it as long as possible. Danielle was working, so I couldn't meet her someplace. I could go to Dad's or to Mom's. After some thought, Mom won out, primarily because her last name was different than mine since she and Dad divorced, and I didn't think it would be as easy for the police to track me to her place.

"I can't believe Rafe was murdered," Mom said for the third time since I'd arrived fifteen minutes ago. "I never thought he was the man for you, dear, but murdered!" She bent to lift Carmelo's hoof and work out some pebbles with a hoof pick.

Mom does horses. Horses and basketball. That's why the three current inmates of her six-stall barn outside Albie, Virginia, were Carmelo, Kobe (a mare), and Bird, the twenty-two-year-old bay gelding I'd learned to ride on. I patted his neck, watching Mom work. She moved with economy of motion, and her slim, angular body still looked great in form-fitting riding breeches. From behind, with her graying red hair covered by a riding helmet, you'd think she was thirty instead of fifty-four. Riding might be good for her figure, but it had sabotaged my folks' marriage. My father got tired of the vast sums of money spent on horsey well-being and dressage training, and Mom's frequent absences that left him working full time and taking care of three kids as well.

When he'd said "It's me or the nags," she went with the horses and didn't even try for custody of me and Danielle and Nick. I'd been upset with that as a teenager, but I'd gotten over it. Mostly. Danielle still had issues-with Mom, but I sort of understood about passion trumping all else. When I fell in love with ballroom dancing, Mom was the one who persuaded Dad to let me keep at it—he wanted me to take up a scholarship sport like volleyball—despite the steep competition bills. She said it was important to follow one's passion. She even fronted the money for coaching and dresses with her dressage winnings, and came to watch me dance when she could. At prom time, I might have wished she'd been hovering in the foyer like other moms, snapping photos of me and my date, instead of in Brussels or Germany at an international equestrian event, or that she'd been around to take me to the ER when I broke my arm falling out of a lift, but she was around when she could be.

Picking up a curry comb, I began brushing Bird, who enjoyed being groomed. If he'd been a cat, he'd have been purring. "I'm afraid the police are going to arrest me, Mom."

"You didn't shoot him, did you?" she asked, with no more angst in the question than if she'd asked, "Do you want syrup for your pancakes?"

"Of course not!" I said so loudly that Bird sidled away.

"Then we should call my brother, Nico," she said decisively, "although I think he's in Barcelona. He's good at this sort of thing."

I didn't ask "What sort of thing?" Some questions you just don't want answered.

"Are you okay?" She straightened and brushed dust and horse hair from her jeans, her blue eyes fixed on mine.

I saw real concern in her expression and smiled to reassure her. "About being arrested or about Rafe?"

"Rafe," she said.

"Not really," I admitted, trying to still my lower lip, which wanted to tremble. "I thought I hated him, but— And he was killed in my house! Well, in the studio, but it's part of my house. And—" And now I'd have to run Graysin Motion by myself and I hated the money end of the studio, and I didn't have a dance partner, and I might get arrested and spend the rest of my life in prison, teaching the cha-cha to a gaggle of hard women doing time for stabbing their pimps or dismembering abusive spouses.

Mom seemed to understand all that without my having to spell it out. She patted my hand—a rare gesture of physical affection for her—and gave me her general-purpose prescription for all ills, physical or mental: "Let's go for a ride."

I picked up a fold of my patio dress and waved it at her. "In this?"

"You can borrow my old jodhpurs, and a pair of boots. Luckily, our feet are the same size."

Yes, but I was four inches taller than she was. However, I obediently followed her into the house to change.

It was late afternoon before I finally drove home, weary from the ride and knowing my legs and ass would punish me the next day, but feeling more relaxed than I had since finding Rafe. Horses are simple creatures—big, beautiful, and brave, but blissfully simple—and I'd enjoyed rebonding with Bird. And Mom. She, too, was easy to be with because the only things she was interested in were horses and international dressage competition and related topics. She had no interest in politics—she probably couldn't name the governor and would be interested in foreign relations only if it impacted her ability to compete overseas—and even less in popular culture.

I didn't see any police loitering on my doorstep, so I pulled into the narrow alley that ran behind the row houses and maneuvered my Beetle under the carport's sagging roof. I'd barely made it through the rear door into the kitchen when the doorbell summoned me to the front of the house. "Coming," I called, figuring it was Danielle with dinner. Good thing, too, because I was starving.

I flung the door open to see detectives Lissy and Troy and two uniformed officers. I felt myself flush red and then pale as little shivers vibrated through my body. Sherry Indrebo had been right—the police were here to arrest me. My mouth opened but no sounds came out. Detective Lissy held up some folded sheets of paper. His red lips glistened moistly and I stared at them, unable to refocus.

"We have a search warrant," he said, slapping the pages into the hand I automatically extended. "For your personal quarters, your car, and the dance studio." When I didn't move, too shocked to make my feet work, he added, "You have to let us in."

I stepped aside, and the four of them entered. Detective Lissy provided some low-voiced instructions and they split up. I finally found my voice as Lissy pulled on a pair of thin latex gloves, either because he was afraid of germs or because it was police procedure. "What are you looking for?"

"The gun," he said. "The murder weapon. It's all in there, Miss Graysin." He nodded at the papers I clutched.

"Can I call a lawyer?" I asked with absolutely no idea who I would call. There were a couple of lawyers in my classes, but I thought one of them mostly did estate stuff and the other was legal counsel of some sort for the Department of Defense.

"You may call whomever you choose, but we still get to search your house." His nose wrinkled and he sneezed, pulling a handkerchief out of a pocket just in time. Four more sneezes followed. When he quit sneezing, he sniffed the air suspiciously. "What is that smell?"

"Horse."

"I'm allergic to horses." He glared at me from watery eyes like I'd deliberately socialized with horses to trigger his allergies.

"There's some Benadryl in the bathroom," I said. "Feel free to help yourself while you're rooting through the medicine cabinet." I carried the papers into the kitchen, where I sat at my table and read them. The female cop went through all my drawers and cabinets methodically as I scanned the pages, which boiled down to what Lissy had already told me: The cops could search my premises and my car for a .22-caliber gun.

"How do you know what kind of gun you're looking for?" I asked as the cop pawed through the cleaning supplies under my sink. All I could see was her broad rear end in unflattering uniform slacks.

"Autopsy results," she said. She withdrew from the under-sink cabinet and turned to look at me, brushing a strand of brown hair out of her eyes.

An image of a saw cutting through Rafe's skull flashed into my mind and I shook my head to clear it. "Oh," I said in a small voice.

"You could call someone to be here with you," the woman suggested. "It's got to be hard having us invade your home like this."

Her compassion surprised me and I smiled at her. "Thanks. I think I'll do that." I dialed Danielle's number and learned she was only a couple of miles from the house, picking up deli salads at a grocery store. I explained about the search. "Get some ice cream, too," I suggested, after she promised she'd hurry over.

"Ice cream?" Danielle's astonishment came through loud and clear. "You never eat ice cream."

"I do. Every time the police tear my house apart trying to prove I killed my fiancé," I said.

"Ex-fiancé."

"Triple Caramel Chunk." I covered the phone's mouthpiece. "Do you want some ice cream?" I asked the cop who was now shifting cans in my pantry to see if I'd squirreled a gun behind the bag of petrified marshmallows or in the rice canister.

"Can't," she said, "but thanks." She shot me a half smile over her shoulder and then turned back to hefting my cereal boxes.

Danielle and I had finished dinner, half a bottle of Riesling, and most of our pints of Ben and Jerry's when the police finished up. Lissy's disgruntled expression told me they hadn't found anything and I let out a huge sigh of relief. "Buh-bye," I said cheerily as the four of them filed out the front door. Lissy sneezed as he passed me and grudgingly told me I could resume classes the next day.

I closed and locked the door behind them and turned to see Danielle surveying the mussed-up living room, hands on her hips. "You'd think they'd at least pick up after themselves," she said.

"I'm just glad they're gone and I'm not spending the night in jail," I said, bending to shove the sofa cushions back into place. Danielle straightened books on the shelves near the fireplace.

We worked for some minutes in silence before Danielle said, "He asked me out again." Her voice was muffled as she bent over to pick up a book.

I knew "he" was Danielle's boss, a portly man in his early forties who was separated from his wife. He'd been after a date with Danielle since his wife moved out. I was actually grateful to be able to talk about something besides Rafe's death and my status as chief suspect.

"Did you tell him about Coop like we talked about?"

"Yes, and I put a photo of Coop and me on my desk and everything, but Jonah doesn't care." She slotted a dictionary onto the shelf with more force than necessary.

"You need to talk to HR." I'd suggested this at least six times since Jonah started coming on to her.

"I can't."

"What would you tell an administrative assistant who came to you with the same situation?"

"Talk to HR," she admitted reluctantly, "and document everything."

"Sooo . . . ?"

"I need this job." She'd recently bought a new Prius and the payments were killing her.

"How about a nanny cam, then?" The idea came to me in a flash of inspiration. "Set it up in your office and videotape Jonah the next time he suggests a romantic dinner for two."

"Be serious," Danielle said huffily. "You've never had a real job, so you don't understand."

"Ballroom dancing is a real job," I said heatedly, turning to face her with my hands on my hips. "And running a small business of any kind takes more work than the average union employee puts in in a year. *And* there's no one looking out for my interests, making sure I get health benefits and regular coffee breaks and safe working conditions." She started to interrupt, but I talked over her. "*And* I have to get students to toe the line while we're rumba-ing romantically or while I'm shaking my assets in a costume that's more fringe than fabric. So don't tell me I don't know about real jobs or workplace harassment."

"Fine," Danielle said, her lips a thin line.

"Fine."

I thought she might walk out, leaving me to cope with the rest of the mess on my own, but she continued to help, moving with me into my bedroom once we'd finished straightening the living room.

"You could kick Jonah in the cojones," I suggested after another ten minutes of "you pissed me off" silence.

She made a *mrmph* sound that might've been a stifled laugh.

"Or cut a photo out of *Playgirl* and leave it on his desk with a pair of scissors stabbed through the model's Mr. Happy."

She laughed aloud at that and flung a pillow at me. "You are warped."

Grinning with satisfaction at having gotten her to laugh, I told her about Sherry Indrebo's call and my visit to Rafe's condo.

"Did you tell the police?" she asked.

"Are you kidding? I was grateful to get out of Rafe's without running into them. I was hardly going to call them up and say that while I was sneaking around his place I found out someone else was sneaking around his place."

"I can see how that would be awkward," Danielle admitted. "But you had a key, so it's not like you broke in."

"I didn't see any signs that the other person broke in, either," I said, "so maybe she had a key, too."

"Who do you think it was?"

I stopped closing dresser drawers to give it some thought. "A woman," I said, "since there was lipstick on the mug. I don't see how it could've been Sherry Indrebo 'cause I practically went straight to Rafe's after talking to her. She couldn't have beaten me there. Solange, maybe? They were dating, after all."

"Or some other girlfriend," Danielle said.

"Taryn, maybe, or—" My thoughts flew to the limo that had lurked out front.

"Taryn?"

I realized I hadn't told Danielle about Leon Hall's visit and his accusation.

"A sixteen-year-old?" Danielle asked doubtfully when I finished filling her in. "That doesn't sound like Rafe."

I was relieved that she agreed with me. It was bad enough that my character judgment was so poor I'd gotten engaged to a man whose concept of "fidelity" began and ended with investments, but I hated to think I'd been in love with a guy slimy enough—criminal, really—to seduce a sixteen-year-old. I ducked into the roomy closet Great-aunt Laurinda had created by knocking down a wall into the adjoining room, originally a tiny nursery, and began pairing my shoes up and returning them to the shoe rack. Really, how did the police think anyone could hide a gun in a size-eight satin sandal?

"It had to be Solange," I said.

When Danielle didn't answer, I left the closet to find her stacking towels in my bathroom, a space not much bigger than the pantry, with a wooden-seated toilet, a clawfoot bathtub surmounted by a shower head that drizzled rather than sprayed, and the glass shelves I'd installed myself and thus they slanted just a tad so the towels slid off after a couple of days.

"Why do you suppose Solange was there?" Danielle asked when I told her the conclusion I'd reached. She answered her own question. "I suppose for the same reason you were, to remove incrim— personal things before the police arrived." She cast me a guilty look from under her bangs.

I let the word "incriminating" slide past. "I'm going to have it out with her tomorrow," I announced, "and find out just what she was up to."

Friday morning found me mopping the floor in the main studio where Rafe had lain, dressed in a paint-stained green T-shirt, short shorts, and with my hair up in a messy ponytail. The police had given me the name of a company that specialized in crime scene cleanup, but their rates were more than I could stomach and I decided to tackle the distasteful task myself. Even with wood floors, not carpet or tile with easy-to-stain grout, it took me several buckets of water, lots of lemony cleanser, and some elbow grease to get a result I was happy with. Stepping back to see if I'd gotten it all, I noticed a streak by the wall and aimed the mop toward it.

"Excuse me," an accented male voice said from the doorway.

I whirled around, mop held level like a lance, and saw

a tall, dark man step into the room. The light slanting through the front windows made it hard to see his features, but then he moved closer and I gasped, the mop dropping from my nerveless fingers. Rafe.

Chapter 6

I scrambled backward, knocking into the bucket and sluicing water across the floor. I tried to run, but my bare feet slipped and I would have fallen if Rafe hadn't lunged forward to grab my arm. His hand, hard and warm and alive, encircled my upper arm like an iron band.

"Rafe—"

Even before my eyes registered that he was a couple of inches taller than Rafe with a leaner face and wider mouth, my nose told me it wasn't Rafe. This man smelled like fresh air and cedar, not the musky Perry Ellis scent Rafe used. And the hand on my bare skin was rougher, the nails clipped straight across without the sheen of clear polish. Wearing black slacks and a black silk-blend T-shirt that hinted at strong pecs and defined abs, he looked lethal, and I wondered if he danced like Rafe. He embodied the passion of the paso doble.

"Are you okay?" The timbre of his voice was a bit deeper than Rafe's, but his accent was eerily the same. The man released his grip, but stood uncomfortably close, ready to catch me if I slipped again. "I did not intend to startle you."

"Well, you did," I said, anger seeping in as my fear receded. "Why did you sneak up on me? Who are you?"

The man regarded me out of brown eyes uncannily like Rafe's. "Octavio Acosta. I came as soon as I got word he was dead. Murdered, the police said."

His eyes narrowed and I wondered if the police had mentioned me as a possible suspect. "From Argentina?" I asked.

He nodded.

"Is Mr. Acosta—Rafe's father—is he with you?" I dreaded meeting him under these circumstances, dreaded the questions he might ask about Rafe's death.

He shook his head. "No. He is occupied with business matters. He asked me to come in his place, to make the arrangements for Rafael's body to be returned home."

What kind of father was too busy to travel with his son's body? Maybe the shock was too much for him, I thought, trying to be charitable. "Poor man."

"Indeed."

My breathing had returned to normal. Sticking out my hand, I said, "I'm Stacy Graysin. I'm so sorry for your loss. Were you and Rafe related?" I couldn't recall Rafe ever mentioning him.

He shook my hand and looked down at me gravely. "Once upon a time, we were like brothers."

He stopped there and it didn't seem polite to query him about why they'd stopped being like brothers, so I retrieved the mop and swiped at the spilled water. "I just have to get this so it doesn't ruin the floor," I apologized. "Then I can get you the number of the detective on Rafe's case so you can ask about . . . about taking him back to Argentina."

QUICKSTEP TO MURDER 75

"I have already spoken to Detective Lissy," Acosta said.

I looked up from my mopping, startled. "Oh. Well, then, I don't understand why you're here. Unless—did you just want to see where Rafe worked?" Or where he died? The second question lingered unsaid in my mind and I wondered if Acosta was the kind of guy who reveled in the ghoulish. Thank goodness the water in the bucket was clear now with no tinge of pink, like earlier.

His thick black brows arched in faint surprise. "Why, no. I came to see what's to be done about the studio." His gesture encompassed the long room.

"What's to be done? I don't understand. We're reopening today, now that the police are finished doing police stuff in here. I'll need to hire another male instructor, unless—" Maybe that was it. Maybe he was a dancer and he wanted Rafe's job. That would be too weird.

"I have come to assess the viability of the studio and whether it would pay for me to hang on to it as an investment, or whether I should sell my half."

The blood burned through my body like someone had injected me with bee venom. "What are you saying? Rafe's will—"

"Left his half share of Graysin Motion to me." The dark brows arched again. "You did not know?"

The room spun around me and I leaned heavily against the mop. Rafe had changed his will. I had never seriously considered the possibility. I'd been taking it for granted ever since I found him dead that I would inherit his half of the studio. Now a total stranger walked in to say that he was taking over. "We made our wills together when we got engaged and bought the studio," I managed to say, "leaving our shares of the studio to each other."

"But you got unengaged, no? *You* broke it off, if I recall, because of—what was it Tía Paloma said, that American phrase?—ah, yes, 'irreconcilable differences.'"

The man's reasonable tone, the look of polite disinterest on his face, fanned my surprise and disappointment to anger. "Our 'irreconcilable difference' was that I believed in monogamy and faithfulness and Rafe believed in screwing any attractive female within hailing distance. I found him in bed with—" I stopped myself with difficulty. I didn't need to rehash the old hurt with a stranger, a man related to Rafe, to boot.

"Rafael always had a way with the ladies," Acosta said. "The girls were flocking around him and telephoning from the time he was eleven. Their forwardness shocked Tía Paloma, my father's sister. He was a little spoiled, perhaps, a little selfish. I am sorry he hurt you."

The simple words took away my anger and left me feeling off balance. "You look a lot like him," I said. "Almost like twins."

He went with the non sequitur, a half smile slanting across his tanned face. "I have heard that before," Acosta said. "But I am three years older."

That made him thirty-eight. He looked older. Maybe it was the gravity of his expression or the one or two silver strands in his collar-grazing black hair. I plopped the mop in the bucket and began lugging it toward the door. "Look, Mr. Acosta—"

"Tav, please." In a single smooth motion he was beside me, relieving me of the heavy bucket.

"Thanks." I led him to the outer stairway landing and

watched as he tipped the bucket over the side to splash the water on the grass patch below. "I guess we need to talk. Let me shower and change and we can get breakfast somewhere."

"That is very reasonable of you," he said approvingly.

I didn't feel reasonable. I felt tired and anxious, emotionally depleted by my sadness about Rafe and my worry about the future of Graysin Motion, my ballroom dancing career, and the distinct possibility of being arrested. The appearance of Tav Acosta was the rotten cherry on top of the crappy sundae life had dished up this week.

Our breakfast never happened. Tav got a call from the police as we were headed downstairs and went off to meet them, promising we'd get together later. I was relieved to be able to put off our discussion.

"Does he dance?" Maurice asked me later that morning after his session with one of the elderly students he'd be dancing with at the Capitol Festival starting next Friday. Despite an hour of dancing, he looked fresh and alert, his white hair combed straight back from his tanned forehead, one ankle resting atop the opposite knee. I'd dragged him into my office to tell him about Tav Acosta and his claim to own half of Graysin Motion.

"I didn't think to ask," I admitted, fiddling with a paper clip.

"What does he do?"

"I don't know." I tossed the paper clip onto the desk and it bounced to the floor. "I didn't ask that either. He took me by surprise."

"There's no sense fretting about it, Anastasia, until we know more about the man and his intentions," Maurice said practically. "The more immediate question is what are you going to do about Rafe's classes and students?"

"I know you've got enough on your plate, getting ready for the Capitol Festival," I said. "Solange offered to fill in and I think I'll ask her to teach the group classes. I don't trust her as far as I can throw her, but we need the help. Too bad she's not a man."

Maurice winced his understanding. Three-quarters or more of our students who competed were women, most of them north of forty, widowed or divorced, with the money for twenty-five-hundred-dollar dresses, upwards of three thousand dollars in competition fees per event, and ninety dollars or thereabouts twice a week for private sessions with their pro. As a result, male pros were in much higher demand than women. Not fair, but there you have it. I mangled another paper clip and continued with my line of thought.

"The students he was dancing with in pro-am competitions are more problematic. We've already sent in the entry fees for the Capitol Festival and it's too late to cancel. We can't afford to lose his students to another studio. You know as well as I do that they'll never come back to Graysin Motion if they hook up with a pro from another studio for the Capitol Festival. I don't suppose you could—?"

He smiled but shook his head. "I can practice with some of them, but not compete. I'm fully committed with my own ladies."

Competitions were divided into heats by age, dance, and ability level (bronze, silver, or gold). Each heat lasted one to two minutes and each of a pro's students might be entered into thirty-five, fifty, or even more heats during a weekend. It was a scheduling nightmare and I wasn't surprised that Maurice couldn't juggle another student at the D.C. event.

"I heard Vitaly Voloshin has moved to Baltimore," he said.

"What! I thought he was in St. Petersburg."

"He was, but his new partner—life partner, not dance partner—is an architect in Baltimore and Vitaly moved here after their commitment ceremony. Anya refused to come to the States to train with him," Maurice added significantly.

Anya Karinska was Vitaly's professional partner. He was a world-class dancer and if he was between partners . . . I didn't have a moment to lose. I was racking my brain to find a way to get Vitaly's phone number when Maurice passed a piece of paper across the table. "I thought you might be interested, so I got his number from a friend of a friend." He winked.

"What would I do without you?" I beamed at him and picked up the phone.

"Fret yourself into a decline, run the business into the ground, and end up working as an Avon lady," he said, rising to his feet and leaning across the desk to pat my cheek before he left.

Vitaly Voloshin arrived from Baltimore barely two hours later, eager to discuss taking on Rafe's students and the possibility of partnering with me. Off the dance floor, he looked like someone you'd find behind the counter of a convenience store: thin face with a beaky nose, stick-straight blond hair with all the luster of dried hay, and a gangly body that seemed to be mostly arms and legs. Last time I'd seen him, he'd had crooked, tannish teeth. Now he flashed a smile that told me some dentist was vacationing on the Riviera with his profits from bleaching, capping, straightening, and/or crowning Vitaly's teeth. They gleamed whitely and his smile broadened when he saw me staring at them. He tapped a front tooth with his fingernail. "My partner is taking me to the dentist as a wedding present. Very sexy, *da*?"

"*Da*," I agreed.

We warmed up in silence, stretching at the barre and marching in place as the sun warmed the quiet studio. I thought how strange it was to be here preparing to dance with someone other than Rafe. It sort of felt like I was cheating on him.

"We shall dancing now," Vitaly announced. As I started the music and moved toward him, he was transformed. It was like he flipped a switch. Power and grace and charisma flowed from him and even if he'd never be conventionally handsome, he was striking in a way I knew the judges would notice. He led exceptionally well and we worked our way through all the standard dances—waltz, tango, Viennese waltz, foxtrot, and quickstep—before stopping.

"Now you will winning at Blackpool, Stacy Graysin," he said confidently, "now that you are partnered by Vitaly. The Argentinean—he was not good enough for you. He was a—" The last word was unintelligible Russian, but I got the gist. His tone was cold and his gray eyes stony and I wondered exactly what had happened between him and Rafe.

"Let's not count our chickens," I cautioned, although the session had gone better than I dared hope. "We need lots of practice time if we're going to compete together."

His blond hair flopped into his eyes and he flung it

back. "I am not concerning with the poultry. Only with the winning together."

We set up a tentative practice schedule and discussed Rafe's students. Vitaly agreed to take most of them on. "Except not the fat ones," he said emphatically. "*Nyet*. Vitaly is not dancing with the—" He tossed in another Russian word.

"What's that?" I asked.

"You is saying 'hippies.' "

"Hippos," I corrected him.

"*Da*."

I deplored his attitude, but agreed to his demands. Only one of Rafe's serious students was a larger woman and I knew Maurice would suit her well. Vitaly also agreed to compete at the Capitol Festival with the three students who had entered the pro-am events with Rafe.

"We will also competing," he said definitively, pointing at me and then himself.

I knew we needed to compete as partners, make an impression on the judges, before Blackpool, but I didn't know how we'd get costumes done, choreograph our dances, and practice sufficiently in one week.

"Vitaly is taking care of," he said when I mentioned these obstacles. He made a brushing motion, as if sweeping aside the pesky details.

Unless Vitaly had a magic wand, I didn't know how he was "taking care of," but I went with it. I reached out to shake hands good-bye, but he caught my hand in his and brought it to his lips in a courtly gesture. "Vitaly is—"

"Not wasting much time replacing your dead fiancé, are you, Miss Graysin?" an abrasive voice said from the doorway.

I jerked my hand away and spun to see Detective

Lissy looking deceptively nondescript but precise with each mousy hair Brylcreemed into place and his tie meticulously knotted. Two uniformed police officers hovered behind him.

"Vitaly is having work visa," the suddenly agitated dancer said, apparently mistaking Lissy and his posse for immigration officers. He darted toward his dance bag and fished through its pockets.

Cold stole through my body, making my fingers and toes tingle. Detective Lissy's gaze stayed glued to my face, even when Vitaly danced forward, waving a form he'd extracted from his wallet.

"Miss Graysin, you need to come with us to discuss the murder of Rafael Acosta," Lissy said. The uniformed cops moved toward me, one of them dangling handcuffs from his hand.

This couldn't be happening. I started shivering and Vitaly looked at me with an expression of mingled surprise and approval. "But—"

"You have the right to remain silent . . ."

Chapter 7

Humiliation is not my cup of tea, but humiliation is what I felt as the cops marched me to their squad car and slid me into the back, where the molded plastic seat still smelled faintly of vomit from the last person who bummed a ride with them. I ducked my head, hoping none of my neighbors were watching. I felt more embarrassed than the time, as a neophyte dancer, I'd danced the samba walk backward. Terror blanked my mind as detectives Lissy and Troy marched me into the large all-brick building on Mill Road. I took in only the foggiest details: uniformed cops, laughter, scents of coffee and pizza, harsh fluorescent lighting. Snippets of conversations bounced off my eardrums without sinking in. "... since the Redskins traded for McNabb ... court appearance tomorrow ... can't believe she slept with ... vacation days this year." None of it made sense. My being here didn't make sense. I hadn't killed Rafe.

I clung to that thought as the very polite policeman who had cuffed me led me to a small room with a square white table, three plastic chairs, and bare tan walls. He removed the handcuffs and left, ignoring me when I said, "Don't I get one phone call?" As the sound of his footsteps faded, I rushed to the door and tried it. Locked.

My brain refused to focus, dwelling on depressing images of life as an inmate and speculating about how the world would be changed when I got out of prison as an octogenarian. I stewed for half an hour before the door opened. Scrambling nervously out of the uncomfortable chair I sat in, ready to leave, I sank back down as detectives Lissy and Troy came in.

"Thank you for making time to talk to us, Miss Graysin," Detective Lissy said. He pulled out the chair across from me and sat the way my great-aunt Laurinda did, feet flat on the floor, knees together, spine erect. Troy stayed near the door, shoulders propped against the wall.

"It didn't seem like I had much choice," I said. "Am I under arrest?"

"We found this yesterday, in the sewer near your house," Lissy said, thunking a plastic bag with a gun in it onto the table. He aligned it so the bag's edges paralleled the table's sides and slid it over to me. "Look familiar?"

I studied the gun through the gallon-sized baggie. "It looks kind of like mine," I said cautiously. "Mine was silver on top like that, and black on the bottom." I pulled the bag closer to me with one wary finger. "And mine had that P22 stamped on it, too."

Troy choked on what sounded like a laugh, then hammered his chest with a fist. "Getting a cold," he explained.

Lissy didn't even glance at his partner. "It's a Walther P22," he told me. "They all have that stamped on them. Nice little semiautomatic pistol. Ballistics tells us it's the gun that killed Rafael Acosta. Guess whose fingerprints are on it."

"Um, the murderer's?" I asked hopefully.

He smiled, an unpleasant, tight-lipped smile. "Exactly, Miss Graysin. Yours."

I gasped.

"So why don't we go over that evening again, *hmm*? We've learned a lot about your fiancé in a couple of days, Miss Graysin, and frankly, I'm sure you had good reason to shoot him. What happened? Did you argue about the business or about his girlfriends? Did he want to get back together? Attack you? If you tell us the truth now, you'll likely get a lighter sentence. Maybe it was even self-defense?"

"No!"

"No, it wasn't self-defense? Now we're getting somewhere."

"No is just no. It wasn't self-defense because it wasn't anything. I didn't kill Rafe."

Someone knocked on the door and Troy opened it a crack. A brief, whispered conversation followed before Troy swung the door wider with a rueful look at his partner. "Her lawyer," he said.

"My lawyer?" It was news to me that I had a lawyer. I turned to the door and saw a huge grizzly of a man with a full beard, vest stretched taut by a heavy paunch, and graying hair brushed back and wavy to his shoulders like in pictures I'd seen of General Custer. He looked to be in his late sixties and carried a slim leather case.

"Phineas Drake," he announced in a rumbling voice, not offering to shake anyone's hand. He didn't even glance at me as he told Lissy, "Ms. Graysin has nothing further to say at this time."

Lissy rose, at a distinct physical disadvantage before the ursine Drake. "Perhaps you're unaware that the murder weapon has her fingerprints on it. We have enough to arrest her."

I wasn't under arrest? That was news, too—good news.

Phineas Drake laughed, a sound like rolling timpani. "She owns the gun. Of course it has her fingerprints on it. Are hers the only prints on the gun?"

"Acosta's were on there, too, but since this clearly wasn't a suicide, that's not germane."

"Any others?"

Lissy squirmed. The lawyer seemed to enjoy the detective's discomfort.

"I am not obligated to share details of an ongoing investigation with you."

"I'll take that as a 'yes,'" Drake said good-humoredly. "Clearly, the gun was stolen and someone else used it to murder the unfortunate Mr. Acosta. Even a first-year law student could trump that argument, Detective. She had no GSR on her hands that night and no motive for killing Mr. Acosta."

"No motive?" Lissy laughed a slight *heh-heh*. "I'd call becoming sole owner of the business a fine motive."

"But I didn't," I said, glad for the first time that Rafe had changed his will. All three men looked at me. "His . . . A relative gets Rafe's half of Graysin Motion."

Lissy flushed an ugly puce shade. "You gave us a copy of his will, Miss Graysin, that named you as the beneficiary."

"It was an old one," I said airily.

"There you have it," Phineas Drake said with an approving nod at me. "Let's go, Ms. Graysin."

"Jenkins was checking to make sure the will was the

most current one," Troy told Lissy. From the look on Lissy's face, I felt sorry for Jenkins for not coming up with the more recent will.

"His name is Octavio Acosta," I supplied helpfully. "He said he talked to you."

"He didn't mention inheriting the dance studio," Troy put in as Lissy's color deepened.

"Perhaps you forgot to ask," I said sweetly, rising with as much self-possession as was possible in the tangerine leggings and sweaty tank top I'd worn to dance with Vitaly.

Phineas Drake held out a peremptory hand and escorted me from the room before I could antagonize the detectives further. He said nothing as he ushered me through the police department and out the doors into a day that had clouded over and was sticky with humidity. A white limo idled at the curb and he gestured me to it, climbing in after me.

"Thank you very much, Mr. Drake," I said as he settled his bulk on the rear seat and reached for a bottle of champagne chilling in a silver bucket. The limo was so big I was surprised it didn't come with a steward. Drake popped the cork silently, releasing a faint aroma of pear to mix with the scent of expensive leather perfuming the limo's interior. I accepted the glass he handed me, watching the bubbles ascend through the cut crystal.

"Thank your uncle."

"Uncle Nico?" I stared at him in astonishment. "How did he know I was here?"

"As I understand it, a Mr. Maurice Goldberg called your mother and she called Mr. Papadakis at his vacation home in Spain. He asked me to wander over and liberate you."

"Do you work for Uncle Nico?" I asked.

The big man smiled. "From time to time."

"You look expensive," I said frankly, taking a gulp of champagne. The beverage might be meant for sipping, but I'd had a morning that required swigging. "I probably can't afford you."

"Don't worry about it. Your uncle is taking care of my fees. As a favor." He smiled, crinkling his cheeks below his eyes.

I knew what that meant. Uncle Nico was all about tit for tat. I'd owe him one. A big one. The thought gave me a moment of unease, but I was so glad Phineas Drake had gotten me out of the police station that I let it drift away. Time enough to worry when Uncle Nico showed up to claim his favor.

Phineas Drake's face turned serious. "This morning was all about frightening a confession out of you, Ms. Graysin."

"Stacy," I said, finishing my champagne. "And they certainly succeeded with the 'frightening' part of their agenda. I was good and scared. Still am. What's a GSR and how did you know about it?"

"A gunshot residue test. Did they swab your hands the night of the murder?" At my nod, he said, "Standard procedure. I knew the results were negative or I'd've been rescuing you from the city lockup, not a cozy interview room."

His definition of "cozy" was a long ways away from mine, but I didn't argue the point. "What do we do now?"

Drake set his champagne flute on the burled wood table beside him. "We give the police another suspect, someone besides you."

I crinkled my brow. "You mean we find the real murderer?"

"In the best of all possible worlds. Failing that, we make sure they see the value in focusing on someone else. Who would you like to see go down for it?"

His tone was casual, but the look in his eyes gave me pause. Was it possible he was talking about framing someone else for the murder? Surely not. Some of the rumors and family whispers I'd heard about Uncle Nico popped into my head and I decided to play it cautiously. Even though part of me longed to give him Solange's name, I said, "The only person I want to have arrested is the real murderer."

Chuckling, Drake poured the last of the champagne into his glass and downed it. "Mr. Papadakis told me you were a sweet girl—'not a vicious bone in her body,' he said. Don't worry, Stacy. When Mr. Papadakis wants something fixed, it gets fixed." He settled back against the seat, arms spread across the top of it, an inscrutable smile on his face. If Mona Lisa had been a bear, this is what she'd have looked like.

Calls to Maurice and Mom thanked them for their part in springing me from Lissy's clutches and let them know I was home again. A shower washed the imaginary stink of the police department off me, and two aspirin put a dent in the champagne headache. In my steamy little bathroom, I flipped my head over to blow-dry my long, blond hair and thought about Rafe's murder, Tav's appearance, and Phineas Drake's jovial assurances. Even though all I wanted to do was concentrate on my dancing, the students, and the upcoming Capitol Festival, I reluctantly accepted the fact that I was going to have to see if I could figure out who killed Rafe. If I didn't, either I was going to end up in prison (not an acceptable outcome), or some random bystander set up by Uncle Nico and his legal eagle was going to take the fall (also unacceptable, especially if it was someone I liked, such as Maurice or one of my students).

I stood, flinging my hair back, and watched in the foggy mirror as it settled in a golden cloud on my shoulders. I decided to leave it loose and quickly donned a pair of striped capris and a slim-fitting teal shirt that made the most of my assets. I'd never been much of one for mystery novels or TV cop shows, but it seemed to me like I should start my investigation by talking to a few people: Taryn Hall and/or her dad, Tav Acosta, and Solange for starters. As I was mentally flipping a coin to decide who to start with, the phone rang.

"Have you got it?" Sherry Indrebo asked when I said hello.

I started guiltily. So much had happened, I'd completely forgotten about returning the thumb drive to Sherry.

"Sorry I didn't get back to you," I said. "Yes, I've got it."

Her sigh of relief wafted through the phone. "Thank goodness. Look, I'm tied up today, but I'll stop by this evening to get it from you." Her tone grew sharper. "We also need to talk about my partner situation. I already gave Rafe a check for the Capitol Festival and I expect you to find me an equally accomplished partner to compete with. And no excuses about it being too last minute."

"I already lined someone up," I said, thinking that her gratitude hadn't lasted long.

When she hung up, I started to dial Taryn Hall's number, hoping to catch the girl while her parents were still at work, but put the phone down before it connected. I'd probably learn more from her in person. I dug her address out of our computer files, Mapquested it, and was on the road within ten minutes.

The Halls' house wasn't far—a few miles south on Route 1 on the other side of I-495. Probably built in the 1950s or '60s, the house had pale blue aluminum siding, small windows, and a beautifully landscaped yard brimming with salmon-, white- and fuchsia-colored azaleas and spring bulbs by the dozen. Leaving my car at the curb, I strode up the pebbled walkway and knocked on the front door.

Taryn answered so quickly she must have been standing in the front hall. "I've been waiting— Oh! Miss Stacy." She peered over my shoulder. "What—? I mean, I— What are you doing here?"

"I thought we should talk," I said, noting the purse slung over her shoulder and her flustered manner. Clearly, she was on her way out and I was an inconvenience. "Were you expecting someone?"

"No. No! Well, I mean, yes. Just Sawyer."

"May I come in?"

"No. That is— My dad doesn't let me have anyone over when he's not home," she said, running her hand through her black hair. It fell silkily to the pale shoulders bared by layered cotton camis in lime and lavender. "This isn't really a good—"

"Why don't you come out, then?" I interrupted her. With my nascent detecting skill I had figured out this wasn't a good time, but it struck me that talking to her while she was a bit off-balance might be a good thing.

"Oh. Okay." She joined me on the concrete stoop and closed the door.

"You heard about Rafe?"

Tears sprang to her eyes. "Oh, yes. It's just horrible. And now my dad says I can't come back to the studio."

"Because Rafe was murdered there or because of the pregnancy?"

Her brown eyes widened until she looked like a startled fawn. "I'm not— How did you know?"

"Your father came by the studio," I said. "Didn't he tell you?"

She shook her head.

"He seemed to think Rafe was the father." I eyed her sternly. "I find that hard to believe, Taryn."

"I didn't mean for it to happen," the girl said in a trembling voice. "He was so nice to me. I didn't mean to tell— It just came out and my dad was so mad. And—" Sobs overpowered her words. Not that it made much difference—I couldn't piece together her half sentences into a sensible narrative.

Questions sparked by her incoherence tumbled in my head. She didn't mean to have sex? To get pregnant? To tell her parents she was expecting? Rafe was nice to her and so they had sex? She told Rafe something—that she was having a baby?—and he was nice to her? The only part that made sense was her dad's anger, and I already knew about that. Before I could probe further, a car door slammed, jerking both our heads toward the street.

Sawyer Iverson strode toward us, baggy jeans riding low on his pelvic bones, cheap black T-shirt outlining his thin frame, hair gelled and spiky. Not exactly the look he sported on the dance floor. "Whassup?" he asked as he drew nearer. His gaze was on Taryn, who had jumped to her feet at his approach. "How're you doing?"

"Okay," Taryn whispered. Their gazes met and something passed between them.

"Hi, Sawyer," I said, wondering what was going on.

"Uh, hi, Miss Stacy." He shuffled his feet, glanced at me for a second, then turned his gaze back to Taryn's flushed face.

"She knows," Taryn said, "about—"

"What! You told her?"

"About the *pregnancy*."

Taryn's emphasis on the last word shut Sawyer up and I again wondered what I was missing. Somehow, they were carrying on a whole conversation I wasn't in on, despite standing practically between them.

"My dad told her."

"When he came to beat up Rafe," I added helpfully.

Sawyer paled. "Oh, God. I'm so sorry, Taryn." He reached for her hand and held it tightly. "It's all because— Does he have a good lawyer?"

Taryn wrinkled her brow; then understanding hit her and she pulled her hand away. "My dad didn't kill Rafe!"

Sawyer looked from her to me. "I thought you said—"

"Mr. Hall came yesterday morning, after Rafe was already dead. He was looking for Rafe, having somehow gotten the idea that Rafe was the father of Taryn's baby." I looked pointedly from Sawyer to Taryn and back again, having my own thoughts about who had fathered the baby.

Neither teen met my eyes. Taryn inched closer to Sawyer, who threw a comforting arm around her shoulders. "We've gotta go," he told me. "C'mon, Taryn, or we'll be late."

With an apologetic look at me, Taryn let Sawyer steer her toward his Honda Accord. I watched as he opened the door for her—not too many of the grown men I knew bothered with that courtesy—and clunked it shut once she had pulled her legs in. I had a vague feeling that I should stop them, but I had no right. And no real reason, either. Maybe they were meeting friends at Starbucks or going to a movie. Just because the tension between them was tighter than a piano wire didn't mean anything ominous. I hoped.

Chapter 8

Tav Acosta was sitting in my office when I returned from Taryn's house. I stopped on the threshold and stared at him where he sat on the love seat, tapping away on a laptop. "What are you doing here?"

He looked up, an expression of mild surprise on his face. "Waiting for you." He closed the laptop and rose. "Mr. Goldberg told me I could wait here."

Music sounded from the ballroom and I heard the faint shufflings that indicated a dance class was taking place. "Oh. Well—"

"Perhaps I could buy you lunch to make up for running out on our breakfast earlier?" he said with a smile.

I suddenly realized I was famished. What with meeting Vitaly, getting hauled off to the police station, and tracking down Taryn, I hadn't eaten anything today since the yogurt and English muffin I'd had for breakfast. "Lunch would be good," I said. "Give me just a moment." I crossed the hall to tell Maurice I'd be out for a while, but that we needed to talk about the Capitol Festival when I got back. He nodded his understanding in time with the music, never taking his eyes off the couples circling the floor. "Absolutely, Anastasia," he said. "I trust you sorted things out with the police?"

"For the moment," I said, hoping it was true. Ducking into the powder room, I washed my hands, ran a brush through my hair, and rubbed some sunblock on my arms. Rejoining Tav, I led him down the stairs and east toward the Potomac River. "Have you seen much of this area?" I asked him.

"I have only traveled in the United States a couple of times," he said. "Most of my business is in South America and Europe, although, as I told Rafael, I am thinking about expanding to the United States. He invited me for a visit, but I was involved in delicate negotiations and couldn't get away." Regret sounded in his voice and when I shot a sideways glance at him his face was shuttered.

"So you talked recently?"

He looked down at me assessingly. "Ten days ago. Prior to that we had not spoken in over a year. He called to tell me he was making me the beneficiary in his will and invited me to come to D.C. on vacation."

"So you knew about the will." I said it neutrally, but my heartbeat had quickened.

"Yes." His eyes told me he knew exactly what I was thinking. "But you did not know he had changed it, correct? You were still under the impression you would inherit his share of the business."

"I didn't kill Rafe," I said hotly, responding to the unspoken accusation and causing a suited woman walking a Westie to cross the street abruptly, nearly upending the dog, who was busy marking a tree.

"The police questioned you this morning."

We had reached the Torpedo Factory by this time, a

three-story building that housed artist studios and shops. I pulled the door open without answering his question and cut through the ground level to the back door, which opened onto a plaza fronting the Potomac River. The glare from the sun-silvered water sliced into my vision and I blinked rapidly. The familiar scent of the river, a mix of fresh water, diesel fuel, and warm mud with a whiff of decay, anchored me as my eyes adjusted to the brightness. Tav's warmth crowded me from behind and I stepped forward, dodging a seagull intent on carrying off a large french fry.

"It is beautiful," Tav said, quiet appreciation in his voice.

A handful of boats glided past, sails bellied by the wind. Tourists milled about with cameras and melting ice-cream treats, reddened shoulders and noses testifying to a morning spent at Mount Vernon or wandering the streets of Old Town. Two mallards swam near the pier, hoping for handouts. Being near the river always lifted my spirits and I smiled as I headed for a food cart, letting the past days' sadness and anxiety drop away for a moment. Sandwiches and bottled waters in hand, Tav and I wandered a hundred yards up the river and settled on a river-facing bench to eat.

"Look," Tav said, crumpling the sandwich wrapping and shoving it into his pocket. "I don't think you killed Rafe."

"Gee, thanks," I said around a mouthful of turkey sandwich. Despite my sarcastic response, I was a teensy bit pleased by his words.

"The police said your gun was the murder weapon, though, so how do you explain that?"

"I don't. I can't. Someone stole it."

"Who knew you had a gun?"

I'd already been thinking about that. "Dozens of people," I said gloomily.

He looked startled. "Really? How is that?"

"Six or eight weeks ago, at one of our social dances—that's where we invite students from all the classes, and people from the community, too, to come on a Friday night and dance for fun—one of the women mentioned how unsafe she feels going out at night. She was nervous just walking the two blocks from the parking garage to Graysin Motion. Someone said she should get a gun and carry it in her purse. Rafe went downstairs and got my gun to show her, even demonstrating how easily it would fit in her purse. So," I said gloomily, "lots of people knew I had a gun."

"But they wouldn't know where you kept it," Tav objected.

I gave him a look. "If you had to search a woman's place for her gun, where would you look first?"

"Bedside table."

"Bingo."

"Point taken." His brows drew together as he thought. "So if someone went to the trouble of stealing your gun, then Rafael's death was premeditated, not a crime of passion. Although . . . something was bothering Rafael."

"I got that feeling, too," I said, staring at him. "He didn't used to worry about money, but recently he was obsessed by it, trying to cut costs at Graysin Motion, trying to talk me into having kids' hip-hop and tap classes and an annual recital. What did he say when he called you?"

"Nothing specific."

I eyed him, wondering if he was telling the truth. He had stretched his long legs out and let his head rest against the bench's back so I couldn't read his expression in profile. "So he just called up, told you he was making out his will in your favor, and hung up? And you said—what? 'Have a nice day'?"

"Pretty much," Tav said, turning his head slightly to face me, a slight smile quirking his lips as he took in my frustration.

"Liar."

"I am wounded." He put a hand to his heart, but his expression told me he was only making fun of me. "Actually," he said as I jumped to my feet with an impatient exclamation, "I tried to get him to talk, but he said he had to go and hung up."

"And you left it at that."

"I did." His expression grew somber, his sensuous lips folded into a thin line. "Now I wish I had pushed him harder, called him back."

I could understand that. I didn't feel I knew him well enough to offer any words of comfort or absolution, though, so I stayed silent. After a moment, he rose and said, "We should be getting back. I've got a meeting later to prepare for."

"What do you do?" I asked, stuffing my lunch debris into a trash can. We headed back toward my house and I caught him examining the ornate doorways and cornices and wrought-iron fences on the row houses we passed.

"I'm in the import-export business."

"Oh." Part of me had hoped he'd say "I'm an internationally acclaimed ballroom dancer." I knew that wasn't even a possibility, though, because if he were that good I'd've heard of him.

"Do you dance?" I asked.

He looked down at me, a rueful smile curving his lips. "Not a step. Football is my game—what you call soccer."

"Oh."

"I am a huge disappointment to you, right?" He didn't sound like it bothered him.

"No," I said. "It's not that. But if you're not a dancer, inheriting Rafe's share of Graysin Motion has got to be more of an inconvenience than anything, doesn't it?" Which pretty much put him out of the running as the murderer, as far as I was concerned. Not that I really thought he'd traveled from Argentina to D.C. to put a bullet in Rafe in my ballroom.

He put a hand to my elbow to guide me away from a skateboarder careening down the sidewalk. "Not necessarily. Are you interested in owning the business outright?"

I didn't know if he was asking me to make an offer or just sounding me out, but I said honestly, "I can't afford it. We aren't turning a profit yet—probably won't be for another couple of years at the earliest—and even though it's worth less now than before Rafe got killed—"

"Really?" Tav sounded interested.

"Definitely. A lot of a studio's worth is in its reputation, its name, the success of its pros and students. Rafe was a big draw—a huge draw—for us. We'll lose some students to other studios and pros now that he's dead. Also, I need a new dance partner. I've got one tentatively lined up—on approval, you might say—but it's unrealistic to expect that we'll do as well at Blackpool after only a few weeks together as Rafe and I would have done." I pushed a hand through my hair and sighed. "Frankly, the studio'd be in better shape if *I'd* gotten shot; a male pro brings in a lot more business than a female because the biggest student demographic is women."

"I am sure you bring in more than your share of business," Tav said, his tone more assessing than admiring.

We turned the corner on to my block as he spoke, and the sight of the black limousine hovering across the street from my house shocked an exclamation from me. The conviction that whoever was in the limo knew something about Rafe's death grabbed hold of me and I broke into a run. The car idled at the curb like before, windows rolled up, wholly anonymous. My momentum almost carried me into the passenger side door, but I stopped in time. Knocking on the window, I called, "I need to talk to you about Rafe. Just tell me what you know about him. Please."

A British-accented voice from behind me said, "I don't know anyone named Rafe, but I'd like to get to know you, luv."

I whirled to find myself facing a cadaverous-looking man in his late sixties being escorted out of the spa, someone I vaguely recognized as a seventies rock star having a successful comeback tour. Resurrection tour was more like it, I thought, scanning his gaunt face. Wearing leather pants and with highlighted hair sticking out at all angles, he gave me a rakish grin as the chauffeur came around to open the door for him. "Whaddaya say?" The rocker gestured toward the interior of the limo.

I stepped back, appalled by my mistake. "I'm so sorry. I thought you were—"

Suddenly, Tav was at my side, his hand on my shoulder. "Stacy?"

The rocker gave us a knowing smile, raised a hand, and said "Ta, then," as he slid into the limo. It glided away from the curb and I saw the license plate: Virginia. Not diplomatic plates.

My face blazed with heat, and I scuttled across the street to my house, weaving my way between cars stopped at the light. Reaching the other side, I realized Tav had followed me. I felt like an utter fool and was doubly embarrassed to think that he had witnessed what must have looked like my frenzied pursuit of a musician old enough to be my grandfather.

"I'm not really a rock groupie," I said.

"I did not think you were." He studied my face. "What was that all about?"

"You wouldn't believe me if I told you," I said wearily.

"Try me."

What did I have to lose? He probably already thought I was mentally unstable and, really, was it any more humiliating to confess to spying on Rafe's trysts or meetings or whatever they were in the suspicious limo than to have Tav think I lusted after Sir Whoever, the has-been rock star? I unlocked my door. "Come on in."

As I pushed my door open, a voice called my name from half a block away. "Stacy!"

I looked around to see Mark Downey hustling toward us, dance bag in hand. His sandy hair flopped across his forehead and he slowed as he came up to us, his brow wrinkling as he studied Tav.

Glancing guiltily at my watch, I told Tav, "We'll have to talk later. I've got a practice session scheduled with Mark. Mark Downey, Tav Acosta."

"I thought you might be related to Rafe," Mark said, offering his hand. "Your brother? What an awful thing. My condolences."

"My half brother," Tav said. "Thank you." He looked at me. "We will continue our conversation later, then?"

"Rafe was your brother?" I asked, confused that he hadn't clarified the relationship earlier.

"Half." Tav's face closed off.

Mark glanced from me to Tav. "I didn't mean to interrupt . . ."

I detected a slightly huffy note, which was justified since I'd already canceled on him once and almost missed this practice. "You didn't, Mark," I said. "Let's get started." I smiled apologetically at Tav and started up the stairs to the studio, Mark behind me.

An hour into our ninety-minute session, we paused for a water break. "So," Mark said, "that guy is Rafe's brother? I suppose he's here to make arrangements about the body and stuff?"

"That, and to check out the studio," I said, draping a towel across the back of my neck. I used the end to blot sweat off my face.

"The studio?" Mark asked.

"He inherited Rafe's share."

"What!" Seeming to realize he'd practically shouted the word, he asked more quietly, "I thought the studio must be all yours now?"

"Nope." I shrugged like it didn't matter to me.

"So what will happen?"

"That's what we need to discuss."

"Do you think he'll sell? I've got some money saved and I've been thinking it might be a good time to go pro." He screwed and unscrewed the cap on his water bottle as he talked, his words rushed. "I'd have to keep my day job for a while, to make ends meet, but if I bought into the studio—"

"Oh, no," I said involuntarily. Mark was a good amateur, but he was never going to be a top-flight pro. He didn't have the pizzazz, the sizzle, the certain sort of something, as my mom would say. And although I liked him okay, I couldn't see being business partners with him.

"No?" His water bottle crinkled in protest where he gripped it.

"I mean, no, I don't think Tav is planning to sell," I improvised. "He said something about wanting to expand his business interests to the States." I wasn't exactly lying, just being disingenuous. I crossed my fingers behind my back for good measure.

Mark's shoulders lost some of their tenseness. "Oh, well, maybe he'll change his mind if he gets the right offer."

"Maybe." I made a mental note to find out from my lawyer or from Tav if there was some way I could have approval over a buyer if Tav decided to sell his share of Graysin Motion. I hadn't thought about it previously, but I realized now that the wrong partner would make me want to give up the studio entirely. One more thing to worry about. I sighed and strode to the middle of the floor. "Let's try the waltz again from the reverse corte."

After Mark left, I spent the afternoon trying to sort out the studio's finances. I'd already had calls from three students—all well-off women—who said they wouldn't be returning now that Rafe was dead. "You know, it wasn't ballroom dance I liked so much as Rafe," one of them admitted. "I hope they catch the witch who shot him," she added.

"You think it was a woman?" I asked, curious.

"Bound to be," the caller said with a short laugh. "A woman or a jealous husband. Husbands always know more than we think they do, don't they? Oh, I'm sorry—you used to be engaged, didn't you?"

She knew full well we'd been planning to marry. I managed a civil good-bye and hung up, thinking about her comment. Unfortunately, I didn't get very far. Literally dozens of women filed through the studio on a weekly basis and who knew how many other women he met on his own time. Danielle had always contended that Rafe was cheating on me long before I caught him with Solange, and I began to realize she was right. Monogamy was not a concept Rafe had ever gotten his head around.

Shutting down my computer, I wandered into the ballroom to turn off the lights and sound system. We didn't have a class tonight and I was looking forward to a quiet evening at home—take-out sushi for dinner, followed by a DVD. *Four Weddings and a Funeral*, maybe, or *My Best Friend's Wedding*. Something to make me laugh. I was headed toward the outer door to lock it, when it opened and Sherry Indrebo stepped in, svelte in a royal blue suit with satin lapels and turned-back rhinestone-crusted cuffs. A ruffled blouse mostly disguised the crepey skin on her neck. Swanky. I had to admit the woman dressed well.

"There you are," she said as if I were an hour late for an appointment. "Where's the thumb drive? And I want to hear all about the new pro. He'd better be in Rafe's league, and not some second-stringer who's available because no one else wants him." She shot me a "you can't put one over on me" look and walked into my office uninvited.

Reminding myself that I couldn't afford to lose any more students, then counting to twenty, I followed her. She sat in the chair in front of my desk, legs crossed at the ankles, as comfortable and in charge as if it were her House office. I told her about Vitaly and she was finally impressed.

"Vitaly Voloshin? That's excellent. I thought he lived in Ukraine or in Russia."

"He recently moved here," I said. "Your practice times will be the same as they were with Rafe. I know your schedule is tight."

"It certainly is," she said with a thin smile. "Being a public servant is a twenty-four–seven occupation. Some might say prison term. Speaking of which . . ." She glanced meaningfully at the platinum watch on her bony wrist. "If you could just give me the thumb drive, I've got a function to attend tonight. Ruben—my husband—is waiting in the car."

That explained the suit. "I don't think I've ever met your husband, Sherry. Does he dance?"

She looked pensive. "You know, he did when we were younger. I first got interested in ballroom dance because of him. He was so smooth. But he broke his ankle skiing eight years ago and it didn't heal right. So now he just works. This dinner tonight is an opportunity to network with some movers and shakers who can help his company land an important military avionics contract. I really can't complain," she said with a forced laugh, "because I'm a workaholic, too."

Anxious to be rid of her and get on with my sushi and movie plans, I reached into my desk drawer and extracted the thumb drive. "Here." I slid it across the desk to her.

I knew better than to expect profuse thanks, but I wasn't expecting the rage that tightened the skin around her eyes and drew down the corners of her mouth. "Are you kidding? Is this a joke? This isn't my thumb drive! Mine is red. I distinctly remember telling you it was red."

"You didn't—"

"Oh, dear God." She must have paled because age spots suddenly seemed more noticeable at her temples and the bridge of her nose.

She was taking this mix-up much harder than it seemed to warrant and I wondered what was really on the thumb drive.

"You'll have to go back," she announced.

"No way," I said. "I'm sorry, Sherry, but—"

"Then give me the key and I'll find someone else." She held out a peremptory hand, palm up.

"I can't do that."

"You mean you won't."

I didn't answer.

The anger in her eyes turned to calculation after only a few seconds. "Okay, what'll it take?"

"Sorry?" She'd lost me.

"How much? How much to go back to Rafe's and find my thumb drive? Tonight?" Reaching into her purse, she pulled out a checkbook and waited expectantly.

"You can't pay me to do it!"

"Certainly I can," she said calmly. "There's very little that money won't buy."

I crossed my arms over my chest. She studied my face for a moment, and I got a flash of what she must be like in a congressional committee meeting or at the poker table. Favors and back-scratching and bartering were coin of the realm in political circles. She and Uncle Nico would probably get along like Bonnie and Clyde. Come to think of it, she did kind of look like Faye Dunaway.

"Okay, then." She put the checkbook back. "If the carrot doesn't do the trick, it'll have to be the stick."

I didn't like where this was going.

"What if I told you there were documents on that thumb drive that would destroy Rafe's reputation?"

I shifted uneasily. "Like what?"

"Photos. I don't need to draw you a picture, do I? Sleeping with students isn't exactly the height of professionalism. And—"

"It happens all the time," I said, ignoring the pang I felt at this confirmation of Rafe's routine unfaithfulness, and trying not to envision what those photos looked like. *Ew.* "You and Rafe are both over twenty-one. Way over," I added cattily. "I'd think photos like that would do you more damage than Rafe."

"And," she continued as if I hadn't spoken, "evidence of payoffs to ballroom dance judges. That might reflect badly not only on Rafe but on Graysin Motion, don't you think?"

I did, indeed. "Rafe wouldn't do that."

"He was desperate to make this studio successful," she countered. "And he needed the money."

"What for?" I knew, of course, that Rafe was looking for money, and it lent a tiny bit of credence to her accusation.

She shrugged. "How would I know? He asked me to float him a loan, but I told him I had a firm rule about not doing business with friends. It's a surefire way to lose both your friends and your money. I leased him a car instead, so he could sell his Camry."

Staring at her, I wondered suddenly where Rafe's

new Lexus was. Had the police found it? Maybe not if it was leased under Sherry's name. I was about to suggest that she locate the Lexus and search it for the flash drive when something stopped me. Maybe my dislike of being blackmailed. I gnawed on my lower lip as Sherry rose.

"Think about it," she said. "I'm sure you'll realize that we both have a vested interest in making sure the documents and photos on that thumb drive stay private." Flicking a minute speck of dust or lint from one of her cuffs, she walked out, her stiletto heels *pock-pock*ing on the wood floor.

I sat trancelike for ten minutes after she left, my mind whirring with what she'd told me. I was ninety-eight percent sure she was lying about the bribes, but could I risk it? Sliding my desk drawer open, I fingered the key I'd dropped in there. Another visit to Rafe's condo was probably no big deal. The police undoubtedly had been through the place by now and wouldn't have a need to return. And whoever was there when I'd dropped in yesterday was long gone, surely. The cold, jagged edges of the key bit into my hand as I closed my fist around it.

The area around Rafe's condo was busier in the early evening than it had been at midday. People returning from work, I presumed, watching the sporadic trail of cars disappearing into the garage. That would work in my favor, I decided, crossing the street from where I'd parked my Beetle. I'd be one in the crowd. Anonymous. The condominium complex housed young professionals—singles and couples—and people pretty much kept to themselves. I let myself into the building with the key, holding the door open for a fit-looking woman wheeling a bicycle out, then took the elevator to the fourth floor.

As the elevator door closed behind me, I scanned the hallway. No one in sight. Good. I paced rapidly toward Rafe's door and leaned my ear close, listening for a moment. A shower ran in the next door unit and a phone rang somewhere down the hall, but I didn't hear anything from within Rafe's place. Dings from the elevator warned me it was coming up and might spit out someone on this floor. Jabbing the key into the lock, I pushed open the door and quickly closed it behind me, leaning against it. I surveyed the room without moving, noting immediately that the laptop was gone. The cops had taken it, I'd bet. That didn't bode well for my search for the thumb drive.

I pushed away from the door, intending to start my search around the coffee table where the computer had been, when the slap of bare feet on wood made me whirl to my left. A man stood in the dim hallway, towel wrapped around his waist, water dripping from his hair, knife held confidently in one hand and pointed at my stomach.

Chapter 9

I gasped and the key fell from my nerveless hand, clinking on the floor. The man took a step forward, moving into the light, and I recognized him: Tav Acosta.

"What are you doing here?" we said simultaneously.

Tav lowered the knife so it dangled at his side. I thought it was from the knife block in Rafe's kitchen, but I was too distracted by Tav's bare torso, glistening with water, to care much. A sprinkling of black hairs covered strong pecs and tapered across defined abs to disappear beneath the towel. His skin was smooth and unblemished, the color of caramel. He looked so much like Rafe that my mouth went dry. My gaze flew to his face, catching the flicker of heat in his eyes before a more wary look came over his face.

Seeming suddenly conscious of his lack of apparel, Tav gripped the towel with one hand—not the one holding the knife—and told me, "Wait here. Do not leave." He disappeared back down the hall and closed the door to Rafe's bedroom with a *thunk*.

I remained by the door for a moment, trying to remember how to breathe, then eased into the living room and retrieved the key from the floor. I wasn't about to compound my difficulties by getting caught searching the room, so I sank onto the sofa and picked up the dance magazine that had been on the floor. My fingers trembled as I tried to turn the pages and I set the magazine down, clenching my hands into fists. Who knew getting caught sneaking into one's dead former fiancé's condo was so unnerving?

Tav was back within four minutes, wet hair combed back, wearing chino shorts and a red-striped golf shirt. His feet were still bare. His expression was stern and the hint of suspicion in his eyes gave me a pang after our enjoyable lunch and conversation. "Talk," he said.

"It's not what it looks like," I said, as he sank onto the chair opposite me. "I—" Trying to come up with a reasonable excuse for being here, I bit my lower lip. I finally decided on the truth; hell, I didn't owe Sherry Indrebo anything. I spilled out the story of Sherry's request—demand—and watched Tav's face. It didn't reveal much. "So I'm here to find the thumb drive," I finished.

"Because you think my brother might have been bribing judges?" Tav sounded skeptical.

I couldn't much blame him; telling the story out loud made it sound pretty unlikely. I nodded unhappily. "Might," I emphasized. "I don't really think he was, but he did seem to be in a real financial bind lately, and maybe that drove him to ..."

"How much money could he win at a ballroom dance competition?" Tav asked. The way he relaxed back into the chair made me think that he believed me and I let out my breath, unaware until then that I'd been holding it. "It's hard to say," I said, "because there are so many prize categories. But if we'd taken home the top studio award and a few division prizes, maybe ten to twelve thousand—not a fortune by any stretch. The money in ballroom dancing is in teaching and competing with amateur students . . . or getting a gig on *Ballroom with the B-Listers*."

"Hardly seems worth bribing judges," Tav said, almost to himself. He stood and held out a hand to pull me up. "Let us begin."

"Begin?"

"Our search."

It wasn't until half an hour later, when we had gone over every inch of the living room and were pulling utensils out of kitchen drawers and checking the ice tray in the freezer for the thumb drive that I thought to ask, "Hey, what are you doing here, anyway?"

Tav looked up from where he was systematically removing spices and canned goods from the lazy Susan in a low cupboard and smiled. "When I picked up Rafael's effects, his keys were among them. The police had no objection to my staying here. A week in a hotel in this area would eat my profits for the month."

"Were you here yesterday morning?"

"No. My plane did not land until late last night and I did not get the key until this morning. Why?"

I told him about my visit yesterday and the intruder who had hidden in the closet and snuck out while I was in the bedroom.

"You thought it was me?" Tav said, a smile lurking in his brown eyes. "I am not much of one for hiding in closets."

No, he was more the type to grab a knife and confront an intruder. I washed my hands after sorting through the cleaning supplies under the sink and accidentally shifting a roach motel.

"Who do you think it was?" Tav asked, brow furrowed.

We headed toward the bedroom and began rifling through the drawers and closet, and I gave him the thoughts I'd already hashed out with Danielle. It felt weird to be in Rafe's bedroom, which still smelled like Rafe, with a man who looked so much like Rafe but wasn't Rafe. I remembered the last time I'd woken up in here, dawn just creeping through the slatted blinds and striping the cherry chest of drawers and Rafe's chest and arms as he snored softly. A *plip-plip* sound had drifted in from the kitchen as the automatic coffeemaker kicked on. The smell of coffee followed moments later. The scent had half awakened Rafe and he'd turned to embrace me, his beard stubble rasping my face as he kissed me. I'd still had a ferocious case of beard burn when I walked in on him and Solange later that afternoon. I couldn't face the bed with its rumpled sheets, so I drifted into the bathroom to search while Tav tore apart the bed, seemingly unaware of the conflicted thoughts and images chasing one another through my head.

We gave up forty minutes later without having found my love letters—Rafe must have trashed them—or the flash drive. Either the police had taken it along with the computer, Rafe had put it somewhere else (possibly planning to return it to Sherry), or someone else had lifted it. I discounted the possibility that Sherry Indrebo was wrong about where she'd left it; she didn't strike me as a woman who got details confused.

"I will ask the police about it," Tav said, offering me a glass of water in the kitchen when we'd finished.

Leaning against the sink, I swallowed it in one long gulp—rifling someone's condo was hard work—and said, "Just don't make them suspicious."

"Never fear." He grinned.

"Did they give you Rafe's car keys, too?"

Tav nodded.

"Is the Lexus in the garage?" I didn't see how Rafe's car could be in its slot below the condo building when he'd been shot at the studio.

"No. My rental is parked in his space. Why?"

I explained my thinking and he disappeared into the bedroom momentarily, emerging with Rafe's key ring in his hand. He lobbed it at me and I caught it. "You're giving me Rafe's keys?" I felt a spark of warmth at his trust.

"It is not his car, correct? So I have nothing to lose if you turn out to be a clever car thief."

"Oh." His prosaic logic deflated me.

"Search the car if you come across it, or return the keys to Ms. Indrebo," Tav said.

I pocketed the keys. "I should go."

"Let me buy you dinner. I would offer to cook for you, but my brother did not keep the refrigerator well stocked." Pulling the fridge door open, he gestured at the mostly bare shelves that featured only a bottle of salad dressing, a carton of take-out Chinese, and some yogurts. "You can tell me about your compulsion to chase after aging punk rockers. I hear Rod Stewart is between wives again."

I punched him on the shoulder. "Just for that, you can pick up the check."

*   *   *

Over a delicious seafood dinner at a casual restaurant two blocks from the condo complex, I confessed to my initial assault on the mysterious limo and my conviction that its occupant knew something about Rafe's death. "Or, if not his death exactly, something about why he was so worried these past weeks, why he needed money." I sawed a small slice of bread from the crusty loaf the waiter had brought and ate it dry, watching jealously as Tav ripped off half the loaf and slathered it with butter. Watching my weight like a jockey was part of the price I paid for being a professional dancer.

"The limo's license plates started with DPR," I said, "which means it belongs to a diplomat."

"From Argentina," Tav said, setting his knife down slowly, his attention caught. "PR is the country code for Argentina."

"How do you know that?"

"I was at the embassy earlier today, dealing with issues related to shipping Rafael's body back to Argentina. The cars all had plates starting with SPR or DPR."

"S for staff, D for diplomat," I said. "See, it proves that limo had something to do with Rafe."

"I must return to the embassy tomorrow," Tav said. "Perhaps I can ask around and find out why someone from the embassy might be meeting with Rafael."

"That'd be great." Our food arrived then and we ate our meals—sole for me, crab cakes for Tav—in silence for a few minutes. I broke it to ask, "So what happened between you and Rafe that you didn't keep in touch?"

Tav looked up from his plate, his dark eyes serious. He seemed to be looking at something past me, but after a moment, his expression lightened and he focused on me.

"It wasn't so much what happened between me and Rafael as what happened between our parents. My father took up with Rafael's mother, Suzette, when I was only three. She was in Argentina to study tango—she was a dancer, too—and it was love at first sight for her and my father." His grimace betrayed what he thought of that. "He divorced my mother to marry her. I split my time between the two households, spending the school year with my mother and my summers with my father, Suzette, and Rafael. When I was nineteen and Rafael was sixteen, my father and mother decided that they were meant to be together after all and he divorced Suzette to remarry my mother. You can see that Rafael came by his womanizing honestly," Tav said with a wry smile.

"What a plate of emotional spaghetti," I said.

He gave me a puzzled look.

"Everything all tangled up and stuck together."

"That's exactly how it was. Suzette returned to America—she was from Texas—and took Rafael with her. He was angry, so angry, with my mother and his anger leaked over onto me." Tav said. "I do not know if Suzette forbade him to keep in touch, or if he was not inclined to do so, but I did not hear from him for several years. Not until after Suzette died. Breast cancer."

"Rafe never told me any of this," I said, saddened by this evidence of our lack of true intimacy. "I mean, I knew he was semi-estranged from his dad and I knew his mom was dead, but I didn't know the details."

"Did he talk about me?"

I hesitated a moment, on the brink of a comforting lie, then said, "Never."

"Ah, well." He scooped some crab cake onto his fork and fell silent.

I half reached out a hand to him, but drew it back, glad he hadn't seen it. I felt like I knew him because he was so like Rafe in some ways; I had to keep reminding myself that I didn't know him at all.

"And you?" Tav interrupted my thoughts. He was smiling at me over the rim of his wineglass.

"Me?"

"Family? Siblings?"

"My parents divorced when I was fifteen. They both live in the area and I see them pretty often. My dad's remarried. Two sibs—a brother and a sister. No half siblings, stepsiblings, or ex-husbands. Rafe's as close as I ever got to marrying." On the verge of asking if he was married, I became aware that our conversation had shifted from investigating Rafe's murder to first date sorts of topics. Uncomfortable with the segue, I finished with, "So when do you think you can get hold of your embassy contact?"

"Monday." Signaling for the check, he pulled out his wallet.

I pushed a twenty across the table to cover my share and was slightly surprised when he accepted it without comment. Did that mean he needed help financially? Or was he an enlightened man who accepted women as equals? Rafe had always insisted on paying when we went out, even though we made roughly the same amount. It had seemed charming at first, gallant, but then had grown irksome.

Tav and I walked back toward the condo and my car in near silence, each absorbed by our own thoughts. We said good night on the sidewalk and I was halfway home when I realized we hadn't discussed Graysin Motion at all. I hadn't asked him to let me have a say if he decided to sell his half of the studio. I didn't want to end up with Mark Downey as a partner, or any other well-off student with more money than talent (and we had a lot of those), or a stranger who didn't know a foxtrot from a fox hunt. I banged the steering wheel and vowed to make it our first topic of conversation the next time we met.

As I turned onto my block, I slowed the car to a crawl, looking for Rafe's—Sherry's?—black Lexus. Traffic was relatively light this late in the evening and no one seemed too perturbed that I was creeping along at five miles an hour. In a three-block radius, I spotted a silver Lexus and a green one, and several black luxury cars, but no black Lexus. *Hmm.* I knew Rafe used to park his Camry on the street, but maybe he was more cautious with the Lexus? I made my way to the parking garage two blocks down from my house and parked on the curb across from it, unwilling to pay a fee to spend a few minutes in the garage looking for the Lexus.

Enough passersby strolled the streets at ten o'clock on a Friday that I didn't feel too isolated. I crossed the street and slid around the moveable arm blocking the garage's driveway. No attendant. The garage was a dark cave lit by strips of fluorescent lights and my footsteps echoed weirdly off the cement floors. With my arms crossed over my chest, Rafe's car keys clutched in one hand, I methodically walked up and down the aisles on the ground level. More than half the spaces were empty and I didn't spot the Lexus. I felt fairly stupid and vaguely criminal to be scoping out people's cars, and I wondered if the chance of finding Sherry's flash drive was worth it. It wasn't really about the flash drive, I realized; it was about the hunt. I'd already invested so much time in looking for the stupid thing that I hated to give up now. I'd give it ten more minutes, I decided, reaching the stairs.

The stairwell door screeched as I opened it and I surprised a couple in their fifties making out on the landing as I climbed to the second level. The gray-haired woman giggled and pressed her face into the man's chest. He smiled and waved, seemingly unaware that his other hand was cupping the woman's rear end. The smell of alcohol hung around them as I hurried past. I'd have to be dead drunk before I'd think it was fun or romantic to play kissy-face in a garage stairwell that stank of urine and cigarettes. On the second level, I began marching up the rows again, staying in the center of the driveway, as far as possible from the shadowed spaces between the cars. Coming around a massive concrete post, I spotted a black Lexus in the farthest corner. Finally! I broke into a trot, aiming the clicker at the car.

My heart beat a bit faster as I halted beside the car. I punched the remote buttons again without getting a flash of headlights or the beeping sound that signaled the car was happy to see its owner. Maybe the battery was dead. Making a visor of my hand, I peered into the side window. I could make out nothing but vague shapes at first, but then I recognized the bulky object on the backseat as a child's safety chair. *Oops.* I jumped back as if stung just as someone yelled, "Hey! What are you doing? Get away from our car!"

I whirled to see a young couple, him dark and scowling, her blond and obviously pregnant, jogging toward me. Their attire suggested they'd been at a semiformal dinner or reception.

Holding up Rafe's keys, I stammered, "I thought it was mine. So sorry! I must have left mine on the next level." I hoped the dimness hid the blush I could feel warming my cheeks.

The scowling man inspected the keys in my hand, walked all the way around his car suspiciously, and then escorted his wife to the passenger seat, giving me a wide berth.

"Drinking and driving is very irresponsible," the wife murmured as she passed me.

"I'm not— I haven't been—" I shut up. It didn't seem worth it. Turning on my heel, I headed back to the stairwell and up to the top level, my breaths coming faster than usual.

With little hope of success, I emerged on the third floor, held my arm out at shoulder height and clicked the remote. Nothing. I turned forty-five degrees and tried it again. A flash of brake lights in the row just to my right rewarded me. Hallelujah. My shoes *tap-tap*ped on the cement as I hurried toward the Lexus. It gleamed a dull black in the stingy light and the door opened smoothly when I pulled up on the handle. I hesitated, running my gaze over the interior, and glints from the passenger seat and footwell caught my eye. Leaning in, I saw that the sparkles came from glass bits strewn over the seat. I looked up, squinting, and realized the passenger side window had a hole stove in it, big enough to admit a hand.

The sight was unexpected and creeped me out. I jerked upright, banging the back of my head against the door frame, conscious of my mother's admonition to always check the backseat before getting into a parked car. I backed away two steps, rubbing my head. Could there be someone— The ding of the elevator interrupted my thoughts and I turned, expecting to see another couple looking for their car postmovie or postdinner. Instead, a uniformed police officer came toward me, face stiff with suspicion, flashlight describing an arc in front of her.

"I was just about to call you," I said, intensely relieved.

"Oh, really?" Her tone held polite disbelief and her eyes studied me, lingering on my hands as she said, "We had a report of a suspicious person casing vehicles in this garage."

I was indignant that the couple with the other Lexus had apparently called the cops on me over a perfectly innocent mistake.

"Is this your car, ma'am?"

"Umm." I winced inwardly, foreseeing an awkward explanation. I dove in. "Well, not exactly. It's my ex-fiancé's, my business partner's. He—"

The flashlight beam raked the broken window. "Mad at him, were you?"

"I didn't do that! It was like that. He was killed last week and—"

"Step away from the car and keep your hands where I can see them." At the word "killed" her voice went all stern and coplike and I sighed, raising my hands, palm out, and dangling the Lexus's remote between a thumb and forefinger. The cop's hand went to her holster and she spoke softly into the radio affixed near her shoulder, never taking her eyes off me.

I sighed, anticipating a late night. "Do you know Detective Lissy?"

*   *   *

It was indeed a long night. By the time backup cops arrived and someone called Detective Lissy, and I explained how I came to have Rafe's keys and Lissy called Tav to verify my story, it was after midnight. Lissy, not surprisingly, wanted to know why I was searching Rafe's car. I'd had plenty of time to realize the question would come up, and I told him Rafe had some files related to studio business and I thought they might be in the car since Tav had looked for them in the condo and not found them. I blinked at him with great innocence when I finished my explanation. Lissy looked like he didn't believe me—why was I getting that response so much lately?—but said I could go.

I hesitated, then asked if he thought the murderer had broken into the car, searching for something. I didn't suggest the "something" might be a flash drive.

"The car's apparently been sitting here since the day Acosta died," Lissy said. "A target of opportunity for any petty thief. The stereo system's missing, so this is probably a random break-in, not connected to Acosta's death. Unless you know otherwise?" The lift of his brows said he'd be happy to take down my confession.

"You might want to give Sherry Indrebo a call about the car," I said casually, happy to supply him with a course of action that might distract him from poking around in my affairs. "She leased it for Rafe."

Lissy sucked his lips in and eyed me wearily. "What a good idea," he said. "I might not have thought of it on my own, what with having only twenty-seven years on the job."

"Just trying to help," I muttered as I moved toward the stairs, avoiding the forensics team who were now going over the Lexus with swabs and little vacuums.

"Well, stop it," Lissy said, getting the last word for the night.

I didn't spend too much time over the weekend dwelling on the car. Vitaly and I met to practice on both Saturday and Sunday and then spent two hours practicing Monday morning. I began to have a faint hope that we might not utterly disgrace ourselves at the Capitol Festival, which started Friday. The rest of the morning dissolved in back-to-back private sessions with two other students who were competing with me in the pro-am divisions. One was an older gentleman who had no illusions about his ability but loved to dance and had the money to pay for private lessons, coaching, and trips to competitions. The other was a thirty-something Department of Energy employee who danced, I thought privately, to inject some glamour and excitement into his cubicle-bound life. The Capitol Festival was his first competition. He'd either love it, or find the hours of waiting in a chilly ballroom interspersed by ten minutes on the dance floor a grind and give it up. Vitaly observed the sessions and offered some useful comments, managing to critique the other men without offending or embarrassing them. He was going to be an asset, I decided happily, going downstairs at noon to shower and change.

Before hopping into the shower, I made the phone call I'd been putting off: Sherry Indrebo. This time, her aide put me through immediately. "Tell me you found it," Sherry said, again skipping the small talk. I wondered how much time we could all save on a daily basis if we eliminated the how-are-yous and have-a-nice-days from our conversations.

"It's not there."

"What? Of course it's there," she said impatiently. "You didn't look hard enough."

"We searched the place from top to bottom."

"*We*?"

"Rafe's half brother. He helped me look."

"You told someone else?" Anger and disbelief jangled her voice. "What kind of moron are you?"

The kind that didn't appreciate being called a moron. "The police probably have it," I said with some satisfaction. "They took his laptop, too."

"I guess I'm going to have to handle this myself." She banged the phone down. I debated calling her back to tell her Tav was staying in Rafe's condo, but decided against it. It might do her good to come face-to-face with a man wielding a knife.

As I finished dressing, the doorbell rang and I jumped. The police again? Fighting off the cowardly urge to pretend I wasn't there, I walked to the door. The fuzzed outline of a man showed through the wavy glass insets beside the door. I opened it a cautious half inch to find Leon Hall on the stoop. His thick brown hair was mussed and anger or anxiety contorted his face. Before I could guess his intention, he stiff-armed the door and it bounced back, hitting the side of my face, my chest, and my knee. With an exclamation of pain, I stumbled back and he pushed into the hallway.

"Where is she?" He looked around. "She wasn't upstairs."

Hall's habit of charging in to look for people was getting wearisome. Did my place look like the local outlet of Hiding Places 'R' Us? My brow and knee hurt where the door had conked them and it made me cranky. "Get. Out. I'm calling the police." I marched toward the phone in the kitchen. A choking sound halted me and I turned to see Hall standing where I'd left him, hands at his sides, blinking rapidly. Holding back tears? I hesitated.

"Are you looking for Taryn?" I finally asked, compassion getting the upper hand over good judgment.

His jaw worked. "She didn't come home last night."

I bit my lower lip. Not good. "What makes you think she's here?"

"She said."

"What?"

"She called at dinnertime last night and told me she was rehearsing here, getting ready for that competition, and not to expect her until late. She never came home at all. When I went to wake her this morning, her bed hadn't been slept in."

His eyes shifted from side to side and I could tell he still thought Taryn might be here. Maybe he didn't so much *think* she was here as *hope* she was here. The alternatives were worse. It felt awkward standing here in the foyer and I invited him back to the kitchen, watched him lower himself heavily into a chair, and brought him a glass of water. "I was out last evening," I told him once he'd taken a swallow. I leaned back against the counter, ready to get a running start if he went on the attack again. "As far as I know, Taryn wasn't here."

"But she might have been?" He was reaching for straws, his bloodshot eyes searching mine. "With another instructor maybe?"

I had to shake my head. "Have you tried her cell phone?"

"You think I'm stupid? It goes straight to voice mail."

I thought of how I'd last seen her, sliding into the front seat of Sawyer's car. "Have you checked with Sawyer Iverson?"

He growled. "Taryn knows she's not supposed to see that poofter outside of dance practice. He's not good for her. His family has too much money. He doesn't know how to work." Hall pounded one anvil of a fist on the table, making it shudder.

I didn't feel the need to argue with him about Sawyer's work ethic, and his anger made me hesitate to tell him I'd seen Taryn go off with Sawyer Friday morning . . . and they certainly hadn't been planning to practice their cha-cha. After a moment's thought—he was Taryn's father and she was only sixteen—I told him about visiting the house and seeing Taryn drive off with Sawyer.

He didn't react the way I thought he might. "What were you doing at my house?" he asked suspiciously. He seemed to have a limited emotional range: suspicion and anger. Living with him must be exhausting.

"I wanted to talk to Taryn."

"What couldn't wait until her next lesson?"

I sighed, wondering how I painted myself into corners like this. Mentioning the pregnancy was going to make him go ballistic. "I didn't think Rafe got her pregnant and I wanted to ask her about it."

"You're saying Taryn's a liar?" Hall looked outraged and pushed his chair away from the table with a scraping sound.

I didn't think it would appease him if I told him that all teenage girls were liars. It came with the territory. I'd lied to my folks about completing homework so I could dance, to my friends about who was my BFF at any given moment to avoid hurting feelings, to Danielle about borrowing her favorite green sweater. I wasn't proud of the lies, but, looking back, I thought they were pretty much par for the course.

"Taryn's under a lot of pressure."

"Don't tell me about my own daughter!" He rose, glaring. "My daughter is not a liar." He swiveled his jaw from side to side. "I'm going to talk to the Iverson kid. If I find out he's done anything to hurt Taryn—"

"Have you called the police? Told them Taryn's missing?" I asked as he surged past me, intent on rending Sawyer Iverson limb from limb.

"They were useless," he said, continuing toward the door. "Said it's too soon to consider her a missing person, asked me if she had a history of running away, if I'd checked with all her friends. They don't give a damn that my baby's out there somewhere and she's only sixteen." Wrenching the door open, he tromped outside and slammed it so hard it bounced open again. I stood at the threshold watching him make his way to the street. The very set of his shoulders betrayed his anger and I saw people give him a wide berth as he bulled down the sidewalk.

Was it possible that Tuesday's scene with me and Solange was staged, that he knew damned well Rafe wasn't at the studio because he'd killed Rafe? But how would he have known about my gun? Taryn and Sawyer had been present when Rafe brought my gun up that night . . . but was it likely that Taryn had mentioned it to her father? Or that he'd broken into my house to steal it? It seemed too convoluted to me, which was too bad because I didn't much like Mr. Leon Hall and I'd've been happy to elect him Rafe's killer. The thought of Phineas

Drake and his implied willingness to set up someone came to mind, but I virtuously put it aside, locked the front door, and headed up the interior staircase to the studio.

Chapter 10

Music poured out of the small studio and I peeked in to see Vitaly rehearsing with one of the competitive students. I gave him a thumbs-up, which he returned behind his partner's back, along with a slight grimace I took to be a comment on her waltzing. Maurice was instructing his senior group in the ballroom and I smiled to see two new elderly gentlemen circling the floor with Mildred and Edwina. Hoover, watching from his spot under the window, scratched an ear vigorously with his hind paw. It felt almost normal today, the most normal it had felt since Rafe's death. I hummed a snatch of tango music and walked into my office to see Solange rifling my drawers.

I stared at her a moment, anger building, before she noticed me. "Can I help you find something?" I asked icily.

She started and looked up, eyes widening. In a split second, though, she had recovered. "Oh, there you are!" She said it as if she'd been looking for me for hours.

Like she expected to find me in my desk drawer?

She came around the desk toward me, moving fluidly

in blue leggings, a matching workout bra that bared her tight midriff, and a whiff of sheer skirt. Her hair was caught up in a casual knot and skewered with a couple of combs. "I was just . . . There was a man here looking for his daughter. I was going to write you a note about him. It's the scariest thing," she added, scanning my face to see how I was reacting.

"Getting caught searching someone's desk?"

Annoyance flashed across her face and her voice was indignant as she said, "No! Having your sixteen-year-old daughter go missing. It's got to be every parent's nightmare."

I had to agree with her on that.

"I mean, think of all the dreadful things that could happen. Abduction, rape, murder, sold into white slavery . . ." She shuddered.

I couldn't tell if she was acting or genuinely worried about Taryn. "Well, I saw her go off with her dance partner Friday noonish, so I don't think she's in that kind of trouble." She might well be in more trouble when her father caught up with her.

"Really? Thank goodness for that." Solange edged toward the door. "Well, I guess I don't need to worry about that note anymore. Gotta get into the ballroom—Maurice asked me to help with his class."

"Solange."

Stopping on the threshold, she looked a question at me. Something like defiance or malice lurked in her eyes.

"Where were you Monday night?"

Her expression soured. "I've already gone over that with the police and I don't see that it's any of your business, Stacy."

"Maybe not. But I don't know why you're ashamed to tell me."

"I'm not ashamed! If you must know, I was at a friend's birthday party. At Technophile. Dozens of people saw me. I didn't get home until after two." She whisked out the door before I could question her further.

I drifted over to my desk and sat, thinking. Technophile was only three blocks from here. It was the current "hot" place in Alexandria, packed to the rafters every night of the week, including Sunday. I was pretty sure Solange could have slipped out at some point, walked to the studio, shot Rafe, and made it back to the party without being missed. Just because she could have, though, didn't mean she had. And what had she been looking for in my desk? Opening the drawer she'd been poking through, I stared into it, using my index finger to move aside some pencils, sticky note pads, a pair of scissors, and a couple of unlabeled CDs that were probably backup files. Nothing exciting.

A thought crossed my mind: Could Sherry Indrebo have hired or coerced Solange into searching the office to find her missing thumb drive? Maybe she suspected I'd found it and was keeping it for my own purposes. If that were so, why was Solange rifling through my desk and not Rafe's? I stared at his desk. Maybe she'd looked in Rafe's first. I shut my drawer more forcefully than necessary and the photo of me and my first ballroom partner hoisting a trophy slapped face downward. I righted it, taking a moment to smile at my gap-toothed grin and the self-conscious expression on Bobby's ten-year-old face. Last I heard, he sold hot tubs outside Newport News.

Opening the folder with all the paperwork related to

this weekend's competition, I went over everything from the hotel and meal arrangements to the heat times, sending my clients reminder e-mail about what to bring and what time their events took place. I was convinced scheduling and logistics at a ballroom dance competition made D-Day planning look like a walk in the park. Vitaly came in after half an hour and I went over it all with him, too. "You'll meet Sherry this evening," I told him, sliding him a page with Sherry's heats highlighted.

He lounged on the love seat, sipping bottled grapefruit juice. "For the regularities," he said, noting my glance at the bottle. "Is this Sherry dancing better than that one?" He nodded his head toward the small studio and, presumably, the partner he'd just been practicing with.

I nodded reluctantly. "Sherry's pretty good," I said. "You can see she's competing in the gold divisions."

"*Da*. Good. She is having money?" He looked up from under the blond hair flopping across his brow.

"Lots," I assured him.

"Good," he said again. "Vitaly is liking this studio with the many rich womens. Perhaps Vitaly is buying." He beamed at me.

"What?"

"Rafe is no longer. *Pfft*." He flicked the fingers of both hands open like little starbursts. "Vitaly is hearing that Rafe's share is for selling."

"Where did you hear that?" I stalled, not sure how I felt about the possibility of Vitaly buying Rafe's half of the studio. I couldn't do much better for a dance partner, but I didn't know a thing about him as a businessman.

Vitaly shrugged and rose. Vowing once again to talk to Tav today about his plans for the business, I wrote his name and number on a purple sticky and passed it to Vitaly. "That's Rafe's half brother," I said. "He's the one you need to talk to."

Vitaly left with a flash of his new teeth and I ran downstairs to get ready for my early-afternoon workout with Danielle. We tried to meet twice a week at the health club on King Street, about half a mile from here. Nondancers don't realize how demanding a sport ballroom dancing is; I trained as many hours as a Redskins lineman did, I'd bet. In addition to the time I spent teaching or practicing, I took a weekly ballet class and a biweekly jazz class, weight-trained at least four times a week to give my arms and legs some definition, and did Pilates for my core, which was critical for balance and posture.

Jogging to the gym because it was quicker than finding a parking space, I pushed through the glass doors just as Danielle emerged from the locker room. "Back and chest today," she announced. We went into the weight room, a huge space crammed with Nautilus and Cybex machines, weight benches, racks of dumbbells, stacks of mats, and exercise balls. Mirrors lined two walls and windows looked out to the parking lot from the wall opposite the door where we stood. Early-afternoon exercisers crowded the room and the sounds of conversation and groans of straining weight lifters drowned out the TVs.

While we bench-pressed, Danielle told me her boss's wife had been in the office that day and she had hopes that they were getting back together. "She keeps him in line," Danielle said.

"You still need to talk to him and let him know that

hounding you for a date is way out of line." I racked the bar.

"I hate those kinds of confrontations," Danielle confessed, taking my place on the bench. "It's much easier to tangle with an out-of-line boss on someone else's behalf."

"Man up, sister-mine," I said.

"*Hmph.*" She cut off any more elder-sister advice I might have been planning to offer by asking if Phineas Drake and Uncle Nico had framed anyone yet. I'd called her when I'd gotten home from the police station and she'd been fascinated to hear about Phineas Drake swooping in to liberate me.

"Not as far as I know," I said, using ten-pound weights to do biceps curls. My goal was lean and defined, so I used light weights and did lots of reps. "But Taryn Hall is missing."

"You don't think maybe she's gone off for an abortion or something, do you?" Danielle suggested when I told her about my meeting with the girl and Leon Hall's invasion earlier this afternoon.

I hadn't thought of that. "I hope not," I said. I had no idea where one would even go to get an abortion. But I suspected a resourceful—and desperate—woman could find out easily enough. "I'm sure the police will take action if she hasn't shown up by tonight."

"Hey," Danielle said, glancing up at the TV mounted over the water fountain. "Isn't that your congresswoman?"

"My congresswoman?" I followed her gaze to see Sherry Indrebo being interviewed on the Capitol steps. Wearing a charcoal-gray suit with a maroon blouse and a serious expression, she faced a wall of microphones and reporters. Still clutching my dumbbells, I moved closer so I could read the closed captioning.

"Allegations of fund-raising improprieties and of inserting an undercover spy into her opponent's staff have surfaced in regard to Congresswoman Sherry Indrebo's reelection campaign."

"I guess the thumb drive turned up," Danielle observed, reading the text alongside me.

"The congresswoman denies any wrongdoing and says she has no intention of resigning. She says she will continue to serve her constituents and is staying focused on the upcoming vote in the House Armed Services Committee, which could decide the army's helicopter acquisition strategy for years to—" A commercial broke in before the scrolling type could catch up with what had happened in the interview, replacing Sherry with a mother applying a stain treatment to grass-stained jeans. I didn't figure any product made would get the stain out of Sherry's reputation if the allegations proved true.

A livid Sherry Indrebo burst into the ballroom at six o'clock, vibrating with anger in stretchy pants and a workout top showing sinewy arms and prominent collarbones.

"I will ruin you, Stacy Graysin," she said between gritted teeth, stalking toward me like a barn cat focused on a mouse. Her face was gaunt, her lips drawn into a thin line. She didn't give Vitaly, standing behind me by the stereo, a glance. "You found my flash drive and sold it to the *Washington Post*. I hope they paid you a lot because—"

"Hey! I had nothing to do with it," I said. "I didn't find it." I tightened my grip on the CD cases I held, ready to fling them at her if she pounced. "And if I had, I'd have given it to you." Probably after I checked it for anything incriminating about Rafe bribing judges. At any rate, I wouldn't have sold it to a reporter. I didn't even know any reporters.

She bit out a laugh. "Ha! Then how did the *Post* come up with the documents that were on that drive?"

"I don't know, but it wasn't me."

"Politicians is having many enemies," Vitaly put in, moving forward. "In Russia, peoples is shooting politicians." Reaching for Sherry's hand, he lifted it to his lips. "But our politicians is not so beautiful as American politicians."

I stared at him in astonishment as his lips brushed the back of Sherry's hand. I thought I caught the barest hint of a wink as he released her hand. "I am Vitaly Voloshin," he proclaimed, "and we must practicing so we are winning the competition this weekend, yes?"

"Yes," Sherry said, anger melting from her in the face of Vitaly's charm and flattery. She stood straighter and cast me a sidelong look. "Don't think this is over, because it's not," she said, moving toward the middle of the floor with Vitaly.

Under the pretense of putting a CD into the stereo, he glided back to me and whispered, "You are not leaving Vitaly alone with this—" He used a Russian word that I didn't attempt to translate. The way he snapped his white teeth together made it clear what he thought of her.

By the time the session ended, with Vitaly announcing loftily, "You are not totally disgracing Vitaly this weekend," we were all drained. I escaped into my office as Sherry, lacquered hair drooping, trudged to the door.

I had to be grateful to Vitaly for exhausting her to the point where she couldn't harangue me anymore. As soon as she had gone and I had turned off all the lights and locked up, I nipped downstairs to the convenience store on the corner, paid for a *Washington Post*, and brought it back to the house with me. The story about Sherry Indrebo was on the second page and I zeroed in on the name of the reporter: Kevin McDill. It had occurred to me that perhaps McDill had gotten the flash drive not from someone who found it after Rafe died, but from Rafe himself. I wanted to talk to the man and find out. If he'd met with Rafe, maybe he could tell me something that might point to why Rafe was murdered.

A phone call to the *Post*'s switchboard hooked me up with McDill the following morning, Tuesday, and he agreed to meet me for breakfast. He insisted on a hole-in-the-wall Mexican diner not too far from the *Post*'s offices on 15th Street. I arrived ten minutes late, having gotten turned around when I exited the Metro at the McPherson Square stop. The diner smelled of cilantro and refried beans as I pushed through the smudged glass doors. What sounded like a Spanish love song played from the kitchen and a handful of Latinos, all men, sat at a counter eating burritos, drinking coffee, and arguing loudly but amicably with one another in Spanish. The man I took to be Kevin McDill lounged at a tiny, chrome-rimmed table in the corner, newspaper open, mug of coffee steaming in front of him.

I approached and stopped three feet away. The paper stayed up. The *Wall Street Journal*, I noted. "Mr. McDill?" I finally said.

"Yeah." A gravelly voice spoke from behind the newspaper.

"I'm Stacy Graysin."

"You're late."

Impatient with his rudeness, I pulled out the chair opposite him and sat.

After a moment, the paper dipped slightly and a pair of bushy brows and eyes framed by reading glasses appeared over the top edge. "You said you wanted to talk about the Indrebo story." He had skin the color of old walnuts and dark eyes with slightly yellowed corneas. He was older than I'd expected, in his sixties.

"That's right. I was wondering where you got the documents you referred to in your story."

"You want information from me?" He hacked a laugh and I figured he'd been a smoker back in the day. "That ain't the way it works."

"I just need to know who you got the thumb drive from."

Laying the paper on the table, he eyed me cynically. A toothpick stuck out of the corner of his mouth and it jumped up and down as he talked. "What makes you think I've got a thumb drive? I don't compromise my sources, Miz Graysin."

He folded the newspaper and I got the feeling he was headed out. I reached across the table and put a hand on his forearm, bared by rolled-up sleeves. "Wait. Can you at least tell me *when* you got the thumb dr— the information? Was it this week?"

After a moment's thought during which the toothpick wiggled mightily, he said, "I don't see what that would hurt. I acquired the information last week. The story only broke yesterday because we had to get corroboration on some of the details. And that, Miz Graysin, is all I'm prepared to tell you." He stood, revealing a thick trunk and short legs. Something in my expression grabbed his attention because he paused, looking down at me, reporter's nose all but twitching at the faint scent of a story. "Why are you so interested, anyway?"

I hesitated, unsure whether it would help or hinder my investigation to have him poking around, too. I decided it couldn't hurt. "I'm just wondering if there's any tie between Rafe Acosta's murder and your story."

His thick brows climbed, wrinkling his forehead like a bloodhound's. "Why would you think that? What's the connection?"

He seemed genuinely intrigued and I began to wonder if Rafe had, in fact, gone to him with the thumb drive. Maybe I had added two and two and come up with five. Math never was my strong suit. Surely a seasoned reporter like McDill would've recognized his source's name when it popped up in a murder story? "You don't think it's a bit coincidental that Rafe was murdered a couple days after giving you the political story of the year?"

"If—and I say 'if'—I had interviewed Mr. Acosta, the fact that he was killed shortly thereafter could be nothing but coincidence. And, believe me, sweets, the Indrebo scandal will be superseded within a month by a politico selling influence some way he shouldn't or sleeping with someone she shouldn't. It's just the same old, same old."

I rose, tired of craning my neck to look up at him. We were the same height. "She left—" The connection suddenly hit me and I almost dropped into the chair again.

When Rafe found Sherry's thumb drive stuck in his computer, was his immediate thought "reporter"? No. Much as I hated to think he would stoop so low, he must have tried to sell it back to Sherry, perhaps after looking at the contents so he knew what it was worth to her. She'd refused to buy it—why?—and he'd looked for another market. I wasn't sure if legitimate news reporters could ethically pay for source information, but I knew Sherry's opponent would have no such restrictions. Rafe had taken the flash drive to the enemy camp, so to speak, and the contender for Sherry's seat, or someone on his staff, had bought the drive and then turned it over to the *Washington Post*. It all tumbled into place as neatly as three cherries lining up on a slot machine.

"I'm sorry I bothered you, Mr. McDill," I said. "Thanks for your time."

His reporter's instincts now thoroughly aroused, he blocked my path. "I'm missing something, aren't I?" His eyes searched my face. The world-weary air had dropped from him and I could feel the energy vibrating off him, like a Thoroughbred loaded into the starting gate.

I moved around him with a forced smile. "Nothing important." I hurried toward the door, not even stopping for an egg and potato burrito to appease my growling stomach.

"I'm going to find the connection, you know," he called after me.

I didn't doubt it.

The Metro car sped into a curve and I gripped the underside of the molded plastic seat to keep from leaning into the woman on my right. My brain chewed on the idea that had come to me while talking to McDill and I barely noticed the trees leafing out in spring green as they flashed past the window, or the silver-blue of the Potomac surging under the Metro rail. If I was right, and Rafe had tried to sell the flash drive back to Sherry Indrebo, then why hadn't she paid him off? Constitutional dislike of being blackmailed? Confidence that she could get the drive another way? Conviction that he was bluffing about selling it elsewhere? Had she threatened him? Confronted him at the studio Monday night, pointed a gun at him—my gun—and told him to hand it over, not knowing it was already too late and he'd sold it to her opponent? Had he laughed at her or jumped her, and gotten shot?

I shook my head. Sherry had been at the studio that day; she could, conceivably, have snuck down to my bedroom and stolen my gun. Where had she been Wednesday night? She'd said she was going to a dinner, but had the police checked to see if she was really there? As the train slowed for my stop, I let go of the murder puzzle momentarily and wished sadly that Rafe had confided in me. I knew he'd needed money, but I hadn't known how badly. What could possibly have been so important to him? I couldn't ever recall him talking about a dream or a passion that he was saving money to finance. Dancing was his passion. The studio. Once upon a time, me. I was ninety-nine percent convinced that his need for money had sprung up recently, most likely about a month ago when he started hounding me to expand Graysin Motion's offerings, turn the studio into a recital mill. Maybe he owed someone money—like a gambling debt—and they killed him when he didn't pay up. That sounded good until I remembered that the murderer had used my gun. I found it hard to believe that a bookie's enforcer would go looking for a gun in my bedroom.

I muttered, "Damn," and the woman beside me inched as far away as she could on the narrow seat. If Rafe hadn't confided in me, and he hadn't confided in Tav, who might he have told about his money woes? Why, his main squeeze. Solange. It was time to have a heart-to-heart with the Samba Queen.

Chapter 11

Solange wasn't at the studio when I got back, so I called her. She was surprised to hear from me, but when I told her I needed to talk about her teaching schedule for Graysin Motion, she agreed to meet me. Her notion of twenty minutes was considerably longer than mine and I had given up on her and was pushing the dust mop around the ballroom, working up a gritty sweat, when she finally showed. Doing the cleaning ourselves to save the cost of janitorial services had been one of Rafe's cost-cutting ideas. In a gold lamé halter top and cream linen shorts, Solange looked like a model ready to saunter down the runway and I looked like Cinderella, pre–fairy godmother.

The comparison put me in a crabby mood, but I refrained from griping about her lateness. You catch more lions with zebra meat, Great-aunt Laurinda always said. Whatever that meant. "Thanks for coming," I said. "I appreciate your being willing to help with the classes."

"It's what Rafe would have wanted me to do," she said.

Gag me. I went over the schedule with her, assigning

her the Tuesday-afternoon youth class and the Thursday-evening ballroom cardio, an exercise class that drew a mostly female crowd. Solange slanted me a sideways glance out of her long-lashed blue eyes. "Making sure I don't have a chance to steal any of your competitive clients?" she asked acidly.

"Absolutely," I said. I wasn't about to set her up with Mark Downey or the other men who competed with me in pro-am competitions. Talented, well-off male amateurs were rarer than blue diamonds and twice as valuable to the studio.

My candidness surprised a wry smile out of her. "That's honest, at least." She tossed her auburn mane over her shoulder. "You know I could walk out of here with any man I wanted to."

"I remember."

That threw her off balance and while she stuttered for an answer, I said, "You were close to Rafe these last few months, Solange. Do you know what was worrying him, why he needed money?" Walking ahead of her to the bathroom, I grabbed a bottled water from the fridge, pushing aside Vitaly's six-pack of bottled grapefruit juice. "Want one?"

"Diet Coke?"

I handed her a cold can. We stood awkwardly in the hall, not moving to the office or back into the ballroom.

"You know," she said, "I might be willing to teach here on a more permanent basis." One long nail tapped against the aluminum can: *ting, ting, ting*.

Was she offering to trade information for a job? I'd give her a permanent job when a donkey won the Kentucky Derby. Having Solange around all the time would be like Han Solo asking Darth Vader to be first mate of the *Millennium Falcon.* "We'll have to wait and see how things settle out," I hedged. "I don't know what Tav's plans are and I don't know how stable our client base will be now that Rafe's not here. But I'll certainly keep you in mind."

Her face twisted with dissatisfaction, but then she said, "Rafe got a call almost a month ago, early— before six."

She just had to work that in so I'd know she'd spent the night. I kept silent, sipping my water.

"A woman. I could tell by the way he was talking to her." Her nostrils flared and I could see the idea of Rafe having a relationship of any kind with another woman rubbed her the wrong way. "When he got off the phone, he told me he had to go out."

"Did he say who she was or why he was meeting her?"

She shook her head. "No. When I asked, he jumped down my throat, said we didn't own each other." From her expression, the memory was clearly still raw. She regretted sharing it with me immediately, though, adding airily, "Of course, we made up—he took me to Atlantic City for the weekend. That's when he asked me to marry him."

Tears leaked from the corners of her eyes and I thought maybe she'd really loved him, even though I didn't for a moment believe he'd proposed. "It must be hard."

She looked at me with only half the usual hostility. "The worst. And I don't suppose I'll get my money back, either."

"What money?"

"The three thousand dollars I loaned him. It's all I

had in my savings account. He told me he'd pay me back, but it doesn't look like that's going to happen now, does it?"

"Did he say why he needed it? Did it have anything to do with the woman who called?"

"If I thought for a moment he spent it on that—" The cords in her neck stood out and she looked like she'd have happily plunged a dagger into the unknown woman.

Question was: Would she have been angry enough to put a bullet into Rafe?

Solange left and I heard voices on the landing outside as she exchanged greetings with someone. I wasn't surprised, then, when the door pushed open almost immediately. The figure that came through the door, though, surprised me: Taryn Hall. She was wan and her hair and her step both had less spring than usual. She still held herself with that perfect posture that made her such an elegant dancer and she managed a smile when I gasped, "Taryn."

"The ghost of Taryn past," she said, lowering a tote bag from her shoulder.

"Are you okay? Your dad—"

"Yeah, I'm fine. Making it, anyway. I've already been home and talked with my dad. I'm sorry I landed you in it yesterday by telling him I was here. I didn't expect to be gone so long, but the car broke down and we just got back this morning."

"'We'? You and Sawyer?"

She nodded.

"Why didn't you call your dad?"

She gave me a look, one hundred percent teenage

girl. "You've seen what he's like. Sometimes it's just easier not to tell him things."

"But you told him about the pregnancy."

She was shaking her head before I finished. "No way! He found the EPT box in the trash. He does things like that," she added bitterly. "Goes through my trash." She swayed and I caught her arm.

"Have you eaten?"

"Not since—I don't know—eleven last night or so?"

"Let's get some food into you. Come on." I guided her down the hall to the interior door that led to my living quarters. She followed me downstairs and stood gazing out the back window into my tiny courtyard.

"It's pretty," she offered as I pulled eggs from the fridge. "Peaceful." She sounded wistful, as if peace were beyond her grasp.

"Sit," I commanded, putting a glass of cranberry juice on the table. "I'll scramble some eggs."

Sitting, she leaned her elbows on the table to support her chin. "I've never been down here before." Her gaze swept the kitchen with its dated maple cabinets that needed refinishing, the newer but mismatched appliances—black stove, white fridge, stainless-steel microwave—the deep porcelain sink with a mixing bowl and a plate in the dish drainer beside it. "Where's the dishwasher?"

I laughed. "My great-aunt Laurinda lived alone. I guess she didn't think it was worthwhile installing one." And I couldn't afford one.

The eggs sizzled on the griddle and I slid them onto a plate, added a piece of toast, and plunked it in front of her. I made a similar plate for myself.

"Thanks," she mumbled as I sat.

"What are you doing here?" I asked when she'd had

a chance to eat a little. I'd cleared my plate in record time, ravenous after my trip to D.C. and my talk with Solange.

"I thought I'd get in a little more practice before we leave for the competition tomorrow. Sawyer should be here in a few minutes."

"You're still going?" *Your dad's letting you?* I thought but didn't say.

"I talked my dad into letting me compete this one last time. He hates to waste money and I told him it was too late for our entry fees to be refunded. He's coming with me, though," she added glumly.

"Are you sure you're up to it?" She didn't look well to me and since eating a mere three bites had turned a pale greenish color.

"I'm pregnant, not terminal. It'll be my last competition for at least a year. Maybe I'll never dance again."

Despite the melodramatic utterance, I wasn't tempted to laugh or even smile. Having a baby would change her life forever. She'd dance again, of course, if she wanted to, but I guessed she was probably thinking about all the things it was unlikely she'd ever do if she kept the baby: attend her senior prom, enjoy spring break in Cancun, date casually, go to college. It wasn't that she *couldn't* do those things, but it would be much harder. My heart ached for her.

"What's your mom think about all this?" It struck me that I hadn't seen Mrs. Hall around in a while. I used to see her when she dropped Taryn off for lessons, but since Taryn had turned sixteen and started driving herself, I hadn't run into her mother.

Shoving a curd of egg around her plate with a fork, Taryn mumbled, "She left. Last year."

"Oh." Not knowing what to say and not wanting to pry, I stacked our plates and carried them to the sink.

"She ran off with someone," Taryn said in a louder voice. "Just walked out on me and my dad. No 'good-bye,' no 'keep in touch,' just gone." She flung her arm out on the last word, tipping the glass so cranberry juice washed over the table and dripped to the floor. "Oh, I'm so sorry!" Taryn jumped to her feet.

I lobbed a roll of paper towels toward her and she caught them, beginning to blot up the juice. "I'm sorry to hear about your mom," I said, grabbing a sponge and joining her.

" 'sokay," she said, not looking at me as she tossed a sodden mass of paper towels into the trash can and pulled more off the roll. "That's why I'm giving the baby up for adoption. Better to abandon it now when it doesn't know the difference than to wait. That's where Sawyer and I were yesterday—South Carolina, interviewing a couple who want to adopt the baby."

"Is Sawyer the baby's father?" I asked gently.

She didn't answer directly. "I shouldn't have said what I did about Rafe. I wasn't thinking straight. My dad— It's no excuse, but Rafe always seemed like he could cope with anything, that he could deal with my dad or anyone else."

Her sixteen-year-old's perspective on Rafe's invincibility was touching. On the dance floor, he could cope with anything. Off it . . . Well, given our breakup, his scramble for money, and the bullet in his head, I didn't think he rated an A-plus in coping. "Surely you knew that the truth would come out, that Rafe would deny being the father?"

She hung her head. "I told you, I wasn't thinking. I

guess I was hoping my dad wouldn't find out, that some-thing would happen—"

She broke off, realizing that something *had* hap-pened. Her expression warned me just in time and I lunged for the bowl in the drainer and thrust it toward her as she threw up.

She felt better almost immediately afterward and in-sisted on returning to the ballroom in case Sawyer had shown up. He wasn't there yet, but Tav Acosta was and she gasped when she saw him, apparently struck by his resemblance to Rafe. I introduced them and Tav chatted with her politely for a moment before signaling that he wanted to talk to me privately. Sawyer came in as Tav and I headed for my office and I left Taryn in Sawyer's care.

"What's up?" I asked.

Before answering, Tav closed the office door and turned to face me. I arched my brows, surprised.

"I've just come from the embassy," Tav said. He stood, formal and severe-looking, yet somehow very attractive, in a gray suit with a white shirt, his back against the door. "The license plate you gave me belongs to the lim-ousine that the deputy ambassador uses. His name is Héctor Bazán."

His dark eyes scanned my face as if expecting a reac-tion, but the name meant nothing to me. I shrugged.

"Bazán is a big-time player, a multimillionaire indus-trialist who contributes regularly to the right campaigns. There have been rumors that some of his money came from drugs, but he has never been indicted. The journal-ists and others who repeat those rumors tend to disap-pear."

"Are you suggesting Rafe was involved with drugs in

some way?" I asked. I couldn't believe it. It might explain his money woes, but I hadn't seen any physical signs that he was doing drugs—no bloodshot eyes or lassitude or runny nose.

"No." He waved the idea away impatiently. "Bazán and my father have been business associates for years. His ranch shares a border with ours."

"Oh. So you think Rafe was just catching up with a family friend." The idea was a letdown. I'd been so convinced there was something sinister about the limo and its occupant.

"Hardly. Although he is my father's contemporary, Héctor married the girl Rafael was engaged to."

"Rafe was engaged before?" *Before me*? He'd never mentioned it. I was belatedly realizing that there were many, many things Rafe had never mentioned. What had we talked about besides ballroom dance, and judges, and other competitors, and the studio? I couldn't think of much.

"Yes. When he was in college. Her name is Victoria. They dated in high school before Rafael and his mother returned to Texas. They must have kept in touch because she went to university in Texas and they got engaged. I remember my father talking about it and insisting that the wedding would take place in Argentina, on our ranch, despite the fact he hadn't seen Rafael in several years by then. And then, next thing I knew, Bazán was introducing her around the neighborhood as his wife."

"What happened?"

"I do not know." Tav looked troubled. "Rafael never talked about it. But I find it concerning that you have seen Bazán's limousine outside; I am not much of a believer in coincidence."

"You think Rafe took up with Victoria again when he discovered she was in town? And that her husband found out?"

Tav's silence answered me. "Bazán is a ruthless man," he said after a moment. "One does not get to where he has gotten without playing what you call hardball. And Argentinean men can be very possessive about their women."

After Rafe's shenanigans with Solange, I didn't find it all that hard to believe he had another woman on a string. But I didn't see how Bazán, no matter how ruthless he might be, could've been the murderer, as Tav seemed to be hinting. "The killer used my gun," I reminded Tav.

"I cannot explain it," he said with a quintessentially Latin shrug. "All I know is that Bazán is capable of killing. One of his gauchos—cowboys—was found beaten to death three or four years ago. The police blamed it on a migrant worker who was never found and quickly closed the case. The other gauchos, they tell a different story. Very softly, it is true, but word has gotten around. They are afraid of him."

I crossed to the window and looked out, half expecting to see the black limousine idling across the street. The space was open. I turned around. "Maybe it's worth mentioning this Bazán to the police. You should do it since I'm sure you have more credibility with them than I do." Which wasn't saying much—Daffy Duck probably had more credibility with them than I did.

"He will have diplomatic immunity," Tav said.

That gave me pause. The police probably wouldn't be interested in a suspect they couldn't toss in jail unless they had rock-solid proof he did it. I wondered what kind of investigatory resources Phineas Drake had available.

"There is a party at the embassy this evening." Tav broke into my thoughts. "I have been invited. Perhaps you would like to go with me? It is almost certain Bazán will be there."

"You must really be somebody to rate an invite to an embassy party."

"Correction: My *father* is somebody." The smile that lit his eyes said he didn't mind.

Even though I had to pack and take care of last-minute things before leaving for the competition in the morning, I wasn't about to miss the chance to finally come face-to-face with the mysterious limo man. "What time and what do I wear?"

After Tav had left, hurrying to a business meeting, I realized I had once again forgotten to mention that I'd like a say when he got around to selling his half of Graysin Motion. I didn't know if he would have to wait for probate or other legal processes, or who might be interested in buying into the studio (besides Mark Downey and Vitaly), but I wanted to vote on any and all potential buyers. After a moment's thought, I dug Phineas Drake's card out of my desk drawer and phoned. A sultry-sounding receptionist answered and told me he was in court. I hung up rather than leave a message, getting cold feet about giving Bazán's name to Drake. Who knew what he would do with it? True, Bazán sounded like he belonged behind bars, but I didn't want to start an international incident by having my uncle and his lawyer frame him for Rafe's murder if he wasn't involved.

I wandered into the ballroom a few minutes later, watching Vitaly work with Taryn and Sawyer. When the latter got frustrated with his samba rolls, Vitaly clapped his hands together. "We is breaking now."

Sawyer and Taryn drifted to the corner where their dance bags sat and pulled out water bottles. They talked quietly, Sawyer reaching up at one point to smooth a sweaty strand of hair from Taryn's face. Vitaly, half-drunk bottle of grapefruit juice in hand, came over to me to discuss the couple. He was disappointed when I told him Taryn was going to stop taking lessons at the studio.

"Is pity," he said. "She is having talent. And her partner is being better than average," he added, studying the pair across the room.

"She's very good," I agreed. "I hope they do well this weekend."

Vitaly, who I was beginning to believe had been a member of the Russian Imperial Guard in a former life—he ran lessons with almost military discipline—clapped his hands to bring Taryn and Sawyer back to the middle of the dance floor. They waltzed in a big circle around him and he urged Sawyer to "Smiling!" and tilted Taryn's face a fraction of an inch. Putting a hand to his abdomen, he grimaced, and I saw that sweat beaded his upper lip. Before I could ask if he felt all right, Vitaly said, "Excusing me," and bolted from the room. A few seconds later, the bathroom door slammed.

The dancing couple stuttered to a stop. Slightly embarrassed by Vitaly's obvious digestive difficulties, I moved toward them and motioned to indicate they should continue. They circled the floor another couple of times, but it was clear from Taryn's pallor and her occasional stumble that she was exhausted, so I halted them and told them to go home. "Eat. Get some rest today and a good night's sleep. Friday's the big day and it'll be a busy one."

Sawyer glanced at his partner, but spoke to me. "I'm not sure we should compete. I think it's too much for Taryn in her . . . now that she's . . . with the . . ."

Taryn stamped her small foot. "Don't you dare try to tell me how I feel, Sawyer Iverson, or make decisions for me. I'm tired, not ill, and I'll be fine by Friday."

Sawyer backed up a step in the face of her ferocity, still looking uncertain. His thumb and forefinger tugged at the small gold hoop piercing his earlobe. Her face softening, Taryn placed a hand on his arm. "Let's just dance and have fun this weekend, okay? We've worked really hard for this."

Sawyer acquiesced with a nod and they walked from the room, his arm around her waist. I found his concern for her touching. Whether or not he was the baby's father, he was clearly willing to help her through this difficult time and I hoped their friendship endured. I left the ballroom and paused in the hall, hearing retching from inside the bathroom. I didn't know Vitaly well enough to intrude, but he sounded really ill. I knocked lightly on the door. "Vitaly? Are you okay?"

After a moment, the toilet flushed and he opened the door, paler than a funeral lily, slightly hunched over as if in pain. His blond hair looked even lanker than usual.

"Do you want me to drive you home?" I asked. He lived in Baltimore, so it would take a chunk out of my day, but he clearly wasn't well enough to drive himself.

"Vitaly is calling John," he said, holding up his cell phone. "John is coming."

"Maybe some peppermint tea would help?" Mom used to dose us with peppermint tea anytime we had tummy troubles. "I've got some downstairs."

"Vitaly is—" His eyes widened and he whirled, shutting the door in my face.

Chapter 12

Vitaly's partner, John Drummond, arrived forty-five minutes later. A tall, solid-looking man in his late forties, I guessed, with deep-set brown eyes, he gently escorted Vitaly down the stairs, thanking me for the plastic bucket I supplied for their drive back to Baltimore. I sighed as they drove off; if Vitaly didn't recover quickly, it would be disastrous for Graysin Motion's showing at the competition. One of the awards was "Top Studio" and we didn't have a prayer of winning it if our female students couldn't compete in the pro-am divisions. And without Vitaly, they couldn't compete. I sighed again and returned to the ballroom, beginning to think the studio was jinxed. This week had been one disaster after another. I contemplated crawling into bed and not getting out again until a new week arrived. I let the blinds down in the ballroom to keep the room cooler. I was trying to hold off on using the air conditioner until June; the utility bills almost doubled when I cranked up the AC. Crossing to the stereo, I turned it off and noticed Vitaly's almost empty grapefruit juice bottle atop the cabinet. I picked it up, intending to throw it away, then paused.

He'd drunk the juice, then gotten violently ill. Surely there was no connection. Did juice spoil? Could someone have put something in Vitaly's juice to make him sick? I tried to block the word "poison" from my mind, but it seeped through. I knew my thoughts would never have headed in this direction if I hadn't just been thinking about jinxes and the week's string of mishaps. I was letting my imagination run away with me, I told myself firmly. Locating the cap, I started to screw it onto the juice bottle.

"Stacy."

The soft voice startled me so that I jerked and dropped the bottle. It clunked to the floor, dribbling its remaining contents onto the wood. With an exclamation, I turned to see Mark Downey in the doorway.

"I'm so sorry," he said, hurrying forward. "I didn't mean to startle you."

"Well, you did," I said more tartly than I intended. Grabbing a tissue from the box on the stereo cabinet, I sopped up the grapefruit juice droplets.

"Since when do you drink grapefruit juice?" Mark asked, stooping to pick up the bottle and plunk it in the trash can.

"I don't. Vitaly does. I think it made him sick."

"Yeah, it's too bitter for me, too. I'm an orange juice man myself," Mark said, smiling.

I started to tell him what I really meant, then stopped. He'd think I was paranoid. "Did you need something?" I asked instead.

"Not really." He reached into a pocket and pulled out a small envelope. "A friend got called out of town unexpectedly. He had tickets to *Lord of the Dance* tonight and he gave them to me. Any chance you'd like to go?"

"I'm sorry," I said, not really sorry. I'd seen *Lord of the*

Dance before and didn't in any event want Mark to think our friendship was going to move out of the ballroom. Ours was a business relationship, teacher-student, and I could see I was going to have to remind him about the boundaries. I had to do this with one student or another at least twice a year. Most of the male pros I knew—Rafe included— had to do it more or less weekly as their female students tended to develop inappropriate romantic attachments with the first simulated caress during a rumba or the intoxication of a turn series. I'd talk to Mark after the competition, when things had settled down a bit. I didn't want to hurt his feelings now and have it affect his dancing this weekend. "I've already got plans for the evening," I told him.

His smile froze, but then he restored the tickets to his pocket. "Yeah, it was kind of late notice. Maybe another time."

I carefully avoided answering him as I dropped the juice-sodden tissue in the trash can.

"Are the police making any progress on Rafe's case?" he asked as we moved into the hall.

"Not unless you consider arresting me progress," I said.

"What!" He put a hand on my arm to stop me and scanned my face worriedly.

"Well, they didn't really arrest me," I conceded. "They hauled me down to the station for questioning, though, and scared me good."

"They're idiots," he said, releasing my arm with a small laugh. "Give me a call if they lock you up—I bake a mean German chocolate cake and I'm sure I can slip a file into it, or maybe some plastic explosives."

"You cook?" Maybe I needed to reconsider my rule about getting involved with students.

He shook his head. "Bake. And only German chocolate cake. It was my mom's favorite and I baked one for her birthday every year. My dad didn't know a measuring spoon from a garlic press and my sister was too busy memorizing words to bother—she was into spelling bees big-time—so I elected myself."

"That's nice."

Shrugging, he pulled open the door to the outside landing and the wind ruffled his sandy hair. "Mom seemed to enjoy it. So, see you tomorrow?"

"You bet. You are going to walk away from the comp with the Top Student prize."

"I'll do my best to make you proud." With a light kiss on my cheek and a grin, he descended the stairs two at a time.

Tav and I approached the historic building that housed the Argentine embassy on New Hampshire Avenue as a waning spring sun cast long shadows across the treelined street and rush-hour traffic clogged the roads. I was a little nervous, never having attended an embassy function of any kind before. Even though Tav had assured me that all the embassy personnel spoke flawless English, I worried that other guests might speak only Spanish. In his tuxedo, Tav looked like a movie star from the 1940s and I was too conscious of the hand he placed at the small of my back to guide me through the wrought-iron fence that surrounded the three-story white brick mansion. I craned my neck to see more wrought iron curving around toe-hold balconies on the second floor and a couple of window air-conditioning units jutting out like warts from windows on the top floor. Argentina's blue-and-white-striped flag with the starburst sun in the middle undulated in the evening's gentle breeze. Uniformed guards checked our IDs and invitation before nodding us toward social secretary types, who directed us into a receiving line.

We shook hands and murmured pleasantries to tuxedoed or military-uniformed men and stunning women in designer gowns. I wasn't quite sure what the guest of honor, a rotund man with a luxuriant mustache and small hands, did, but he greeted me with a vigorous handshake and a huge grin. I smiled back and moved ahead of Tav into the reception rooms, the hem of my emerald-green dress whispering against my ankles.

Surveying the room, I noted more men than women, a buffet table clad in a tablecloth that echoed the blue of the Argentine flag, and a combo of six musicians playing big band tunes for a handful of dancers at the far end of the room. My foot tapped in time with the beat. Tav stood close behind me. I could feel his heat against my back and our faces were disturbingly close when I tilted my head back to ask softly, "Do you see him?"

Scanning the assembled guests, Tav urged me forward slightly so we weren't blocking the entrance. "There," he said, nodding discreetly toward the far corner of the room, where a clump of dark-haired men in formalwear carried on an animated discussion with raised voices, expansive gestures, and the occasional bark of laughter. "The one facing us with the blue bow tie and cummerbund."

I studied Bazán surreptitiously. Probably no more than five-eight or five-nine, he still, in some indefinable way, seemed bigger than the taller men around him. Maybe it

was the barrel chest or broad shoulders and bull neck. Or
it could've been that he was much stiller than the other
men, with an economy of motion that made his few gestures seem stronger. He had broad features, tanned skin,
and dark eyes under droopy lids; I could totally see him on
a horse riding the range or the steppes or the pampas—
whatever they called open grassland in Argentina.

It took me a moment to realize he was studying me as
closely as I was studying him. Our eyes met and I looked
away, flustered. I chastised myself for being so obvious.
I'd make a really bad spy. "Bazán caught me looking at
him," I confessed to Tav.

"What man would not be flattered by your interest?"
he said, pivoting to impose his body between me and
Bazán.

"He didn't look flattered," I said dubiously. "Maybe
we should go talk to him and get it over with."

Tav smiled and I felt a little jolt zing through my body.
"It won't be necessary. He'll come to us before the evening is out." As he talked, he nudged me toward a buffet
table laden with goodies that made me want to forget
dancing and eat until I qualified for a career as a plus-
size model. I helped myself to a handful of carrots, some
strawberries, and a few barbecued shrimp.

"How can you know that?"

"He will have seen the guest list for tonight's party
and noted my name. I mentioned that our ranches shared
a border, did I not? He will come over to greet us out of
respect for my father."

"Goodness." I wasn't sure my father's neighbors
would recognize him on the street, never mind go out of
their way to chat with him at a party. Maybe that was the
difference between renting a suburban town house and

owning a ranch. I watched enviously as Tav bit into a puff pastry that oozed chocolate and raspberry. The rest of his plate held other desserts, including a minicheese-cake, a strawberry-kiwi tart, and sopapillas dusted with powdered sugar.

"How can you mainline sugar like that?" I asked, searching his plate in vain for a vegetable or any item that didn't come from the "rot your teeth" food group.

"I have a sweet tooth," he said, licking a trace of confectioner's sugar from the corner of his mouth. "And, luckily, I have a fast metabolism."

"You'd be easy to hate," I informed him.

He laughed. I crunched ostentatiously and noisily into a carrot. A voice from behind Tav said, "Good evening, Acosta. What brings you to D.C.? I was surprised to see your name on the invitation list for tonight's reception. Is Arturo in town?"

Tav turned to reveal Héctor Bazán standing there, even more intimidating up close. The men shook hands. "No, my father is at home. I am here to make arrangements for Rafael's body to be returned for burial. You will have heard about his death?"

"Indeed," Bazán said, his gaze panning me from my upswept hair, to the shoulders bared by my strapless emerald dress, to the red-painted toenails peeping from my high-heeled, bronze-colored sandals. "I read the reports and have discussed the case with the detective in charge. Even though Rafael opted for American citizenship, I took an interest for your father's sake."

"That was kind of you," Tav said.

"The police seem to think Rafael's business partner did it."

With an amused glance at me, Tav said, "I do not believe

you have met Stacy Graysin, Héctor. She was my brother's dance partner and co-owned the studio with him."

Irritation flickered in Bazán's eyes for a moment before he took my hand and gracefully dropped a kiss on it. "I regret my unintentional rudeness, Señorita Graysin," he said, smiling. "Obviously, you had nothing to do with Acosta's death. The police are imbeciles."

"Thank you for the vote of confidence," I said, reclaiming my hand. The man had a certain rough charm and an intensity that I figured many women would find attractive. I was not completely immune to it myself, even after what Tav had told me about him. "And thank you for inviting me tonight. I've never been to an embassy party. It's fascinating."

"They pall after a very short time, believe me," he said.

"I wanted to say hello to Victoria," Tav said, "but I don't see her. Is she here?"

"Unfortunately, no," Bazán said smoothly. "She is visiting friends. She will be sorry to have missed you."

"I will be in town for a while yet. Perhaps I will still get a chance to see her. When does she get back?" Tav's expression was guileless, expressing only the casual interest of a neighbor. Being a good liar obviously ran in the family.

"Her plans are flexible," Bazán said, after the briefest of hesitations. His narrowed gaze assessed the nature of Tav's interest. "I'm not sure exactly when she'll be home—a week? Ten days? But I'll be sure to tell her you send your greetings." Before Tav could respond, he turned to me. "Octavio said you dance?"

I nodded.

"Perhaps you would do me the honor?" He nodded

toward the dance floor, where four or five couples cha-chaed with varying degrees of ability and enthusiasm. "You don't mind, do you, Acosta?"

Taking Tav's acquiescence for granted, Bazán led me toward the dance floor, a smooth expanse of parquet at the far end of the long room from the buffet tables. Bazán led me around the floor and had a brief word with the keyboard player. Within seconds, the band segued to a beat suitable for the Argentine tango. Unlike its American counterpart, the Argentine tango is largely improvisational and I was surprised that Bazán had apparently requested it. It's much easier to do standard figures with a partner who you don't know than to improvise. Bazán clasped my right hand in his left and settled his right hand just above my waist, pulling me into a close hold. There was something familiar about his scent, but I couldn't place it.

"You are familiar with the Argentine tango?" he asked, leading me into a *paso basico*, the basic step. "It is not as predictable as your American version. You strike me as a woman who appreciates unpredictability."

What the hell does he mean by that? I wondered, following him easily. His timing was just a shade off the music's beat, and he moved with more power than grace, but he was a better than average dancer.

"Occasionally," I agreed.

"That must have been part of what attracted you to Rafe Acosta," he said. "His . . . unpredictability."

I arched back slightly in his hold, trying to read his face. His eyes held a hint of mockery. "Actually, Rafe was pretty predictable," I said. Up until the last few weeks. "He took dancing very seriously and trained hard." And slept—predictably—with any woman who caught his fancy.

As we traveled counter-clockwise around the floor, I spotted Tav engaged in conversation with a handsome couple about his age. He seemed oblivious to Bazán and me. I felt a bit piqued at his indifference, but quickly squelched the feeling. Tav was Rafe's half brother and would be returning to Argentina in a few days. Letting myself be attracted to him spelled "disaster" in at least eight languages.

"I, too, am a hard worker," Bazán said, reclaiming my attention. "Perhaps I could be a competitive dancer." He laughed, as if the idea were preposterous, but I got the sense of an ego that believed it could excel at any challenge. "I could take lessons at your studio."

"Absolutely," I said. "Drop in when your wife gets back from her trip."

His hand tightened painfully on mine. "What do you know about Victoria?"

I gave him a startled look. "Nothing! I've never met her." I tugged at my hand and his grip loosened.

Steering me around an elderly couple who moved like they'd been dancing together for fifty years, he studied my face. "So who do you think killed Acosta?" he asked. "Perhaps it was a random thing—he surprised a thief or some such?"

His tension communicated itself to me through the stiffness in his shoulders and a certain immobility in his jaw. "I have no idea," I said truthfully. "Although I can't think why a thief would be in our ballroom. Hopefully, the police will realize I had nothing to do with his death and get on with finding the real killer."

"Indeed," Bazán said with a tight smile. I got the feeling he was going to say more, but something behind me caught his attention.

"The ambassador needs me," he said. "I'm afraid I must cut our dance short, Miss Graysin. May I call you Stacy? Perhaps we can finish this another time."

"Of course," I murmured as he escorted me to Tav's side, nodded, and strode off toward the beckoning ambassador. The disturbance in the air caused by his movement brought a whiff of his scent back to me and this time I identified it: cigar.

"He's the one," I whispered to Tav as we moved away from the couple he'd been speaking to. "The man from the limo."

"What were you talking about?" Tav nodded sideways toward the dance floor.

"I'm not quite sure," I admitted, filling him in on our conversation.

"I would really like to talk to Victoria," Tav said.

"Did you believe Bazán about her traveling?"

Tav's gaze followed the diplomat as he exited the room. "No, I do not think I did."

"Maybe Rafe knew where she was. You said they were engaged once. Maybe they were running off together." My stomach felt hollow and I had to force the words out. Maybe Rafe had never loved me. Maybe our whole time together was a sham. When he thought Victoria was unavailable, he settled for me, but when he found out she was here, nearby, they rekindled their romance. I blew out a sigh as if expelling the idea. It completely left Solange and his other brief flings out of the equation.

Tav and I batted around a few ideas about how Victoria might tie in to Rafe's murder. I suggested she might have killed him and was now in hiding, and Tav countered with Bazán as the murderer, having found out that his wife and Rafe were carrying on a torrid affair. He had killed Victoria, too, Tav theorized, and hidden her body. Both our theories foundered on logistics: neither Bazán nor Victoria was likely to know I had a gun, never mind have the opportunity to sneak into my bedroom to steal it.

The band struck up "Fly Me to the Moon," perfect foxtrot music, and I looked up at Tav. "Let's dance."

He shook his head, a rueful smile playing across his handsome face. "You forget—I do not dance."

"I'm a teacher." I took a step toward the dance floor. Teaching Tav to dance would be fun, and I had to admit that the thought of him pulling me close had more appeal than it should.

He grabbed my hand to restrain me, his hand callused and hard against mine. "This"—he gestured to the crowded room—"is not the ideal location for a first lesson."

"There's a dance floor and music." I tugged at his hand. "Come on."

"I do not choose to look like a fool in front of so many people," he said, standing as if rooted to the floor. "Would you want to learn how to play soccer with a hundred people looking on?"

He had a point. "I don't want to learn to play soccer under any circumstances," I said, letting go of his hand.

He grinned, crinkling the skin at the corners of his eyes and looking so dangerously attractive that I caught my breath. "But turnabout is fair play, no? If you are to teach me to dance, than I must also teach you something."

I returned his smile, thinking that he could teach me anything he wanted to, although I'd prefer that the activity not involve a ball, teammates, or onlookers.

Chapter 13

The excitement of the competition swirled around me
Friday morning as I descended in the hotel elevator
from my twelfth-floor room in downtown D.C. Dressed
in a short scarlet dress with narrow horizontal panels of
flesh-colored mesh and thousands of stones twinkling
across the bodice and skirt, I was ready for the Latin
rounds that kicked off at seven o'clock. I'd been up since
four, doing my makeup—including false eyelashes—and
hair. I had pulled it back into a complicated twist, secur-
ing it with rhinestoned clips and gel. The getup was
probably more appropriate for a nightclub than a hotel,
and the businessman who got on at the fourth floor had
trouble not staring. The lobby, though, bustled with sim-
ilarly dressed women, some wearing silk robes over
their brief Latin costumes and others shuffling around
in flip-flops or slippers. Temperatures in the ballroom
were generally kept at levels a penguin would find chilly
and Latin costumes especially tended to be skimpy, so
robes or other cover-ups were useful for preventing
frostbite. A student in a tux did relevés to warm up as he
chatted with a friend by the registration desk.

It was a familiar scene and I let a smile burst over my face. I loved this. The competitive spirit that electrified the air, the fit bodies, the glitz of costumes, and the female students feeling glamorous with their fake lashes and cat's-eye black liner, moving with an ease and sensuality that they normally hid behind tailored suits or mom jeans in the cubicles or minivans that defined their usual existence. Nondancers, a minority of the hotel's clientele this weekend, eyed us surreptitiously, disconcerted, curious, or envious of the gathering that looked and sounded like a convocation of noisy tropical birds. I didn't imagine their dental conventions or library association meetings looked much like this.

I grabbed a coffee, a yogurt, and a hard-boiled egg from a cart in the hall by the ballroom, needing fuel for the dancing, but keeping it light because the sleek contours of my dress would be unforgiving of a large meal. Entering the large ballroom, I spotted the event organizer on a dais that stretched the width of the room and waved. Graysin Motion's table—each studio competing in the event had a floor-side table at which competitors could relax between heats—was midway down the dance floor on the far side and I made my way to it, exchanging greetings with pros I hadn't seen since the last competition. Vitaly was already at the table chatting with a student. He'd called me last night and said his tummy troubles were under control and he'd be able to compete.

"Vitaly is never saying die," he had told me over the phone, sounding as energetic as a soggy string mop.

The dark blue silk robe he wore with VOLOSHIN embroidered across the back gave his skin the pallor of a day-old corpse, but he managed a smile when I got to the table. Maurice showed up moments later, an elderly student on each arm. They were the pair I'd heard arguing the day Rafe died. The lanky one wore a stunning silver gown I suspected was vintage Valentino and the plumper one had on a hot-pink number with enough ruffles to make it fit in at the Copacabana. At her side walked the harlequin Great Dane, a green vest around his middle that read SERVICE DOG. His cropped ears were pricked forward and he sniffed interestedly at everyone who crossed his path. The threesome sat at the table and the dog rested his chin on it, his nostrils working as if trying to figure out where the food was.

"Service dog, my eye," the woman in silver said. "You're not blind or crippled, Mildred, even if your knees creak like a rusty gate when you dance."

Mildred patted the dog's head and he lolled his tongue happily. "Hoover is a service dog. He keeps away people who annoy me, don't you Hoover-love?" She made kissy noises at the dog and he licked her face. "Give Edwina a little sugar. Sweeten up her sour attitude."

The dog obligingly moved toward Edwina, who rolled her chair backward and swept her skirts out of the way of his huge paws. "Don't let him drool on my gown. It's Valentino!"

"See, it works," Mildred said triumphantly, patting her thigh so the dog lumbered back to her.

"Hmph."

I shot Maurice a look and he shrugged his shoulders in a "what can you do?" gesture.

The students competing with us in the bronze Latin heats trickled in and the competition kicked off only a few minutes behind schedule. My student was a fiftyish man with all the rhythm of a two-by-four, but he loved the Latin dances and jiggled from foot to foot as we waited in the holding area just off the dance floor, near the table laden with computers, scorecards, and schedules. Judges ringed the floor, clipboards at the ready, as the announcer called out the competitors' numbers and we filed onto the floor with eight other couples, including Vitaly and his student. Samba music boomed out of large speakers and someone hastily adjusted the volume to something less than shuttle liftoff decibels as we began to dance.

Heats lasted only a minute and twenty seconds with dancers filing off the floor and new ones hurrying on in a choreography almost as complicated as the cha-chas and jives that livened up the dance floor. At this early hour, few spectators besides other competitors ringed the floor or sat in the lines of chairs carefully set out by the hotel. We danced for ourselves and the judges alone, and I felt my student relax into the music. I whispered words of encouragement or step reminders as the music flowed around us. We stayed on the floor, moving from one heat to the next, as the judges made notes on their scorecards and runners took the cards from the judges and ran them up to the score collators seated behind computer terminals. By the time I left the floor, Taryn and Sawyer were seated at our table alongside Sherry Indrebo with a man I guessed was her husband, and Leon Hall. The latter kept his eyes fixed on his daughter, much the way I imagined a U.S. marshal might keep an eye on a convicted felon he was transporting. All that was missing were the handcuffs.

"Have you guys warmed up?" I asked brightly.

"We should probably stretch," Sawyer said, seizing on the excuse and rising.

"There'll be room in the hall," Taryn said. She slipped gracefully between the tables, which were situated too close to one another and headed for the door, the turquoise chiffon of her dress fluttering behind her.

Her father foiled their plan to snatch a little privacy by plodding after them. Sherry and I watched them go.

"He acts like he's her jailer," Sherry observed, unconsciously echoing my thoughts. She pulled her cashmere robe more tightly around her slim figure. "You'd think she was six instead of sixteen. By the time I was that age, I'd already worked on my first political campaign and traveled to D.C. by myself for the inauguration festivities."

The story impressed me and I realized I didn't know much about Sherry. "Have you always been interested in politics?" I asked.

"Always. It's my life." Sincerity rang in her voice. As if embarrassed about her response, she immediately turned to face the dance floor and studied the jiving couples as if she were going to be quizzed on them later.

Her husband, a distinguished-looking man in his late sixties or early seventies with steel-gray hair, squeezed her arm. A cane hung over the chair arm on his left side. "I told Sherry the first day we met that she could get elected to Congress. I've always been one to put my money where my mouth is, so I backed her and she was on her way to D.C. the next November. It's been a win-win situation for the American people and Sherry."

"And you," Sherry said, a note of petulance in her voice. She shrugged off her husband's hand.

I tried to remember his name. Ruben? Rudy?

He seemed unperturbed by her pettishness, letting his hand drop to the table. A heavy gold ring set with a dark red stone winked dully from his ring finger, drawing attention to a large-knuckled hand more suited to farming or blacksmithing than steering a Fortune 500 company. "We'll be living in the governor's mansion before we're through."

"Or the White House?" I suggested, half joking.

"Never say never," he agreed.

"Ruben." Sherry frowned at her husband like he'd said something indiscreet.

A flicker of movement from the far end of the ballroom caught my eye and I looked up to see a slim, dark-haired woman staring at me. Wearing jeans and a denim jacket, she turned away when she saw me looking her way and hurried out of the room. My brows drew together; she looked vaguely familiar, but I couldn't place her. Obviously not a dancer—probably just a fan, or a relative of a dancer trying to figure out where to sit. It could be confusing. I dismissed her from my thoughts and rose to join my student as our next heat was called.

The day progressed pretty much as usual, although I found myself missing Rafe more than I'd realized I would. I kept looking for him to share a glance or a raised brow about a judging result or a misstep by one of our fellow pros, but he wasn't there. Vitaly's ongoing commentary was more trenchant, and occasionally amusing—"He is looking like the hunching back of Notre Dame with that weak frame"—but I didn't have the connection with him I'd had with Rafe. Having to break the news of his death to the few pros and friends who hadn't heard about it put a damper on my day, too. Our students did well in the day's heats, though, and came off the floor glowing when the judges handed them ribbons during the rapid-fire announcement of winners at the end of each division.

Late that afternoon, as the day's competition was wrapping up so dancers could grab a quick meal before the evening's heats started at seven, I finished a conversation with the woman selling off-the-rack ball gowns and Latin costumes and cut through a darkened conference room that adjoined the main ballroom via one of those folding walls. A shuffling sound in the corner made me realize it wasn't empty and I found myself gazing at Sawyer and Taryn, locked in the kind of clinch that convinced me Taryn's baby would probably sport Sawyer's strong nose and high forehead. I took a surreptitious step backward, planning to ease myself out of the room before they came up for air, but halted when I caught sight of another figure staring at the oblivious couple, his rage visible even across the shadowy room. Leon Hall.

"Taryn Adrienne Hall!" he bellowed, charging toward the couple, who split apart guiltily. "Why are you kissing that . . . that poofter?"

Sawyer straightened his spine and took a half step to shield Taryn from her father's wrath. He looked young and spindly, and I knew Hall could mow him down in half a second. "Sir, I—"

The clue-bird landed on Hall with the heavy weight of a vulture and his expression of astonishment was almost ludicrous. "You're not queer, are you? Taryn lied to me! You told me he was light in the loafers." Hall growled at Taryn, caught midway between confusion and fury. "That's the only reason I let you do this ballroom dancing thing and spend all that time practicing with him. Why did you lie to me?"

I thought he'd just answered his own question, so I kept my mouth shut, moving forward quietly so I could intervene if necessary.

"Daddy, I—"

With the inevitability of the sun rising in the east, the rest of the truth dawned on Hall. "You're the father! You're the bastard who knocked up my baby!" With a roar, he charged toward Sawyer, who held his ground for a split second and then scrambled toward the door.

I wished I had my cell phone so I could call hotel security, but there was nowhere to put it in my Latin costume so it sat uselessly on the table in the ballroom. "This way," I called to Sawyer, hoping to direct him out the door I'd come in, but apparently he didn't hear me because he dodged around a couple of chairs and vaulted onto the conference table, sliding across it on his hip before Hall could change direction. Sawyer dashed through the door into the main ballroom as Taryn called, "Don't kill him, Daddy. I love him!"

Her words added fuel to Hall's fire and he ran after Sawyer with Taryn and me following, hoping to prevent a maiming. Dancers floated across the floor to the strains of a Viennese waltz and Sawyer plowed through them, knocking a woman in yellow chiffon aside as the rest of the dancers stuttered to a halt. One pro I knew slightly, a tall man in his thirties, stepped in front of Hall, holding his hands out to stop him. "Hey, buddy, this is a dance—"

Hall knocked the pro aside and the man windmilled his arms to keep his balance. Several people pulled out cell phones and began to take photos or video of the chase. I hoped some of them were calling the police because I had no doubt Hall meant to inflict serious damage on Sawyer if he caught up with him. Sawyer had

made it to the far side of the ballroom and was headed
for an emergency exit when he caught his foot on a table
leg. The table, laden with glasses and pitchers of ice water for thirsty dancers, tilted and its contents splashed to
the ground, strewing broken glass and ice cubes across a
twelve-foot radius. Stumbling forward, Sawyer recovered without hitting the ground, but it gave Hall the necessary seconds to catch up with him. With a huge lunge,
Hall flung himself toward the younger man, catching the
tails of his tux.

The fabric made a ripping sound but didn't totally
give way, and Sawyer crashed against the emergency
door, triggering a loud alarm that added to the general
chaos. He fell, half in and half out of the door, with Hall
clutching at his feet. Daylight and a fresh breeze swept
into the room.

A quavery voice yelled, "Sic 'em, Hoover," and suddenly the Great Dane was there, unclear on the concept
of "siccing" but happy to join in this fun game that involved people rolling on the floor. He nosed first Sawyer
and then Hall, who turned his head aside with a gagging
noise.

"Woof," Hoover barked, bowing over his outstretched
forelegs, his rump in the air with his tail whipping back
and forth. Skirting the tail, which had already knocked a
soda can from a nearby table, I flung myself onto Hall
and grabbed for one of his legs as he tried to simultaneously climb his way up Sawyer's legs and pound at him.
Kicking at the heavier man, Sawyer struggled to claw his
way out the door to safety. Hall had maneuvered his way
up Sawyer's torso and had one hand around his neck
when Taryn joined me and latched on to her father's
other leg. Together, we leaned backward, bracing our

thighs and hauling on Hall's legs. My shoulder muscles burned as he twisted and kicked. My hands slipped and I was reduced to clutching at the hem of his jeans, unable to get a good grip.

"Daddy!" Taryn cried, tears in her voice and her eyes. "Stop it!"

Just as my grip gave way, Hoover bounded over again, planting one saucer-sized paw onto Hall's back, making the man grunt and look over his shoulder, which allowed Sawyer to wiggle forward another couple of inches. Mildred appeared in her ruffly pink dress, a supersized Milk-Bone in her hand, and commanded, "Sit, Hoover."

Hoover sat, planting his rear end firmly on Hall's back, and disposed of his treat with two crunching bites. Five men hurried up—finally!—and two of them grabbed Hall's arms while another two secured his legs. The fifth took his cue from Hoover and sat on Hall's back. Immobilized, Hall hurled names and threats at Sawyer, who had struggled to his feet and limped over to where Taryn sobbed into her hands. He glared at Hall, his face rigid and white.

"Don't you talk about how much you love Taryn when you treat her like this." Sawyer hugged Taryn to his side with one arm. "I love Taryn and I'm going to take care of her and our baby whether you like it or not."

Despite the strain on his face, his ripped clothes, and the way his voice cracked on the word "baby," Sawyer had a certain dignity about him. I caught a glimpse of the man he was going to be and I thought Taryn could do far worse. Apparently, her father didn't agree.

"You're not good enough for my daughter, you lying sack of crap," Hall growled, his words muffled from having his face mashed into the ground by one of his captors. "Don't tell me I don't love her—I'd do anything for her."

"Like kill Rafe Acosta because you thought he was the baby's father? Like try to kill me? Like tell her she can't dance anymore? Yeah, you'd do anything for her except respect her choices."

From the sudden silence in the room, I suspected everyone had tuned in after Sawyer accused Hall of killing Rafe.

"He wouldn't—" Taryn began, eyeing her father with heartbreaking doubt.

Hall saw it and let out a groan, going still beneath his captors. I felt some sympathy for him, but it was all mixed up with my disgust at his ugly prejudices and my fear of the way his anger and frustrations immediately fizzed into assault and battery.

"He would," Sawyer said implacably. The bruise on his cheek and the livid marks on his neck bore him out.

Uniformed police officers burst through the ballroom doors then, and one of them drew his gun at the sight of the huge dog now standing over Hall, snuffling at his pockets.

"Shoot him," Hall urged. "He attacked me! He's dangerous."

"Don't you shoot my baby," Mildred warned, imposing her plump form between the officers and the hapless Great Dane. I was closer to the dog, so I grabbed his collar and pulled him toward me. "He's a hero," I told the confused-looking officers.

"He saved the boy," someone in the crowd called out, and a smattering of applause turned into a torrent. "Hooray for Hoover!" another voice called. Someone poured champagne into a shallow bowl and set it down where Hoover could reach it. He lapped at it thirstily, looking like he enjoyed it, and I hoped Mildred's budget ran to magnums of Dom Pérignon if Hoover turned up his nose at tap water in the future.

The police, apparently convinced Hoover wasn't a threat, cuffed Hall, and led Taryn and Sawyer away to interview. Onlookers faded away, unwilling to get caught up in answering police questions. I told a polite officer only what I'd seen and heard, keeping my thoughts to myself. Was it possible that Hall had killed Rafe and then shown up the next day, ranting and raving, in an effort to divert suspicion from himself? I didn't know if he was that wily; he seemed like a man who operated under the emotion of the moment, not planning things out in advance. I just couldn't see him sneaking into my bedroom to steal my gun, even assuming that Taryn happened to have mentioned that I had one. It didn't strike me as being standard teen-father dinner-table chitchat. I imagined the conversation:

"So, Dad, in dance class today I found out that Stacy Graysin has a gun."

"That's nice, honey. How did your geometry test go?"

The imaginary exchange just didn't work for me, but I couldn't completely discount the possibility that Hall knew about my gun. I wanted to talk to Taryn, find out exactly when she'd told him that Rafe was the baby's father, but she and Sawyer were nowhere to be found. Maybe the police had hauled them off to the station to sign statements or something.

Tired and bedraggled, I took the elevator up to my room, wanting a brief respite before the evening's competition, which was postponed until seven thirty because of the "unscheduled incident," as the announcer called it. Slumped against the back wall of the elevator, I noticed three broken fingernails, probably from trying to cling to Hall's jeans. Damn. I wouldn't have time to fix them before the evening's competition began . . . I'd have to rely on a little transparent tape. Most people didn't realize it, but ballroom dance judges had eagle eyes and would spot the smallest out-of-place detail, such as a broken nail or poorly applied lipstick.

The elevator doors *shush*ed open and I found myself at my floor, facing the denim-clad woman I'd noticed earlier. Up close, she was older than I'd first thought—in her early thirties—and pretty, with dark eyes fringed by long lashes, strong brows, and black hair falling to her shoulders. Her eyes opened wide when she saw me and the penny dropped. This was the woman in the strip of photos I'd found at Rafe's condo. My brain made another leap and I blurted out, "Victoria!"

Chapter 14

The dark-haired woman's chin jerked up at the sound of her name and she hesitated, on the brink of flight. Then her haunted eyes fixed on my face and she asked, "Is it true?"

The elevator doors started to close and I stopped them with my arm thrust through the opening. I hopped out before they could close again and confronted the shorter woman. "Is what true?"

"Rafe. Is he—?"

"Dead." I nodded, feeling a pang when her face crumpled. Where had she been for the last five days that the news hadn't reached her? On a Crusoe-esque island? In a cave?

"Oh, God," she breathed. "I didn't know. It wasn't until I arrived here today and heard people talking... What happened?"

She looked small and vulnerable huddled in her denim jacket, her shoulders braced against the pain, ringless fingers twisting around the strap of her purse. Her voice was lightly accented, exotic, and sexy, and I understood completely why Rafe had fallen for her.

A family of five trooped toward us and pushed the down button, the tween-age girl staring at my dress curiously. "Let's go to my room," I suggested.

Victoria Bazán nodded. "Yes. I came up here looking for you."

She followed me down the hall and stood silently as I inserted the key card into the lock and pushed open my door. "Excuse the mess," I said, ushering her into the room with its two double beds, one of which was buried under costume jewelry, hair accessories, and backup costumes spread carefully on the coverlet. The bathroom counter held a litter of lipsticks, eyeliners, glue-on beauty patches and rhinestones, foundation, blush, false eyelashes, black mascara, and enough hair spray to tame the locks of a roomful of beauty contestants. People don't realize how logistically difficult professional ballroom dance is and how much stuff pros—women, mainly—have to cart around.

My dress for tonight's professional competition hung on a padded hanger in the closet, swathed in plastic. I motioned Victoria to the only chair in the room not covered with clothes and pulled the dress from the closet. "I hope you don't mind," I said, "but I've got to change while we talk. I'm dancing again in twenty-five minutes." I ducked into the bathroom and left the door ajar.

"Sure," Victoria said. "Can you tell me what happened to Rafe?"

Swallowing, I recounted my tale of finding Rafe shot to death in the ballroom.

"Oh, God," Victoria said. "When he didn't come back when he said he would, I was afraid of something like this."

"Come back?"

"To the cabin."

She must have meant Rafe's hunting cabin in West Virginia. I'd never been there, despite his invitation. It sounded too primitive for my tastes. It had an outhouse, for God's sake.

"He said I'd be safe there, that no one knew about it, but it didn't have a television or computer and he made me give him my cell phone in case Héctor could use it to track me down."

I popped my head out of the bathroom to stare at her. "You can do that?"

"Apparently." She shrugged. "Héctor has many, many resources—all that money and intimidation can buy."

I returned to working on my face.

"He said he'd come back for me by Wednesday, that he had a way to get the money I'd need, but then he didn't come. I waited a couple of days, not knowing what to do, and then I walked to the nearest big road, about six miles away, and hitchhiked to the city. I was afraid to go to Rafe's condo or the studio for fear Héctor might have had them watched, so I came here. Rafe had told me about the competition and I thought I'd find him here." Her voice held more than grief; it ached with despair.

"You loved him?" I asked, glad she couldn't see my face.

"Once. And I could have loved him again, but that's not what was going on. He was helping me."

"With what?"

"Escape my husband."

I didn't know what to say to that, so I kept quiet, slipping my Latin costume off and draping the wisps of mesh and red satin on a hanger hooked over the shower curtain rail. I wasn't quite sure why she needed Rafe—wouldn't a good divorce lawyer have been a better bet?

"A woman does not just leave or divorce Héctor," she said as if reading my thoughts. "He is possessive. And I had knowledge of certain of his ... activities. He would never let me go. But I couldn't bear it any longer—his secrecy and cruelty. I had to leave!" The last was a passionate cry.

"Cruelty?" It wasn't a word that came up in conversation often.

Suddenly, she was in the doorway, T-shirt lifted to just below her breasts, exposing an expanse of trim midsection marred with ugly bruises. I gasped. "He hits you?"

"Among other things." She rolled the shirt down and disappeared from the doorway, her tone making it clear she didn't want to discuss what "other things" meant.

"So Rafe was helping you ... what? Get together enough money to go back to Argentina? Find a job here?" After outlining my lips with a red pencil, I filled them in with a dramatic garnet red. I felt superficial applying makeup and worrying about the placement of my hairclips while the woman in the other room revealed her pain and marital secrets, but I *had* to get ready. A glance at my watch told me I had only nine more minutes to get downstairs.

"He was helping me buy a new identity and get together enough money to hide."

That sounded a bit extreme to me. Surely a shelter could help, or she must have relatives to turn to. My silence prompted another outburst, the Argentinean accent more noticeable. "You don't believe me! Disap-

pearing was the only way. Do you think I want to start
over again? Work as a waitress or some such to support
myself? Never see my mother again? No! But Héctor
will kill me if he catches up with me and he won't hesitate to hurt anyone he thinks is protecting me. Rafe said
he knew where he could get me a gun, but then he was
killed. Staying hidden is my only protection."

Wait a minute . . . "Rafe said he'd get you a gun?" I
stepped out of the bathroom in my bra and undies, wanting to read her face.

She nodded, puzzled. "Yes." She sat in the uncomfortable straight chair, hands clenching and unclenching on
the wooden arms. That revelation opened up all sorts of
thoughts, but I didn't have time to question her further
right now. With mere minutes to go before I missed the
call for our first heat, I freed tonight's gown from its
plastic wrapping, dropped it over my head, and wriggled
it down over my hips. Turning with a swish of fabric, I
was gratified by the look on Victoria's face.

"You look beautiful," she said.

Since Vitaly and I hadn't had time to have matching
costumes made, he was going with a basic black tux and I
was wearing this white gown with black flowers splashed
across the fabric and accented with jet stones that gave
the dress a certain heft that weighed on me, but in a good
way. A few years back, chiffon and feathers had been all
the rage for smooth competitions, but feathers were out
now and stones were in, which I appreciated. Cap sleeves
showed off my toned arms, and a scooped neck and back
displayed cleavage and creamy skin. My blond hair was
still in the updo, but I'd decorated it with black-beaded
combs to match the dress. Faux diamonds dangled from

my ears and flashed from the choker at the base of my neck. It's basically impossible to pile on too much bling in the ballroom dancing world.

"Thanks," I said. I eyed her with concern, feeling somehow as if I'd inherited her from Rafe, like I needed to help her because he had been going to. A tightness inside of me that I hadn't been consciously aware of eased with the realization that Rafe hadn't been trying to raise money to run off with another man's wife, buy drugs, or pay off a gambling debt. It had hurt to think badly of him and I was relieved to find out he'd been scraping together money to help a friend. "Look, I've got to go down now and I won't be done until around eleven. There's so much more we need to talk about. Can you wait?"

"I have nowhere else to go," Victoria said simply.

"Order some room service," I said, wondering if she even had enough money to eat, "and charge it to the room. Watch a movie or something. Your husband has no reason to suspect you're here, and we can talk about what to do after I'm done dancing."

"Rafe talked about how kind you were," Victoria said with a small smile.

"Did he?" For some reason, the thought made me very sad.

Downstairs, Vitaly waited for me, his skin practically twitching with impatience. "You are being very late," he said, grabbing my hand and pulling me toward the ballroom. He peered at me sideways as we hustled into the room, now filled with a full gallery of spectators. "But you are looking completely satisfactory."

Wow . . . satisfactory. "I was aiming for beautiful," I

said with mock disappointment, "or maybe elegant and sophisticated."

He grinned, displaying his perfect teeth. "You are accrediting Vitaly."

Did that mean I was a credit to him? Or that I owed my appearance to him? I decided it didn't matter as we stepped onto the dance floor and that indefinable change came over him, an electric charge that made him snap with energy and charm. A healthy round of applause greeted all of us and the announcer called out, "Quickstep." As the music started, I focused on the dancing, forcing all thoughts of Victoria's situation and Rafe's murder from my mind. Dancing with Vitaly was a pleasure, with none of the tension that had spoiled things between me and Rafe. I let myself flow with the music, responding to Vitaly's lead almost effortlessly, and was happy with how we performed.

When the evening's heats came to a close, however, I gave Vitaly a kiss on the cheek, turned down his and John's offer of a drink in the bar, and hurried upstairs to continue my conversation with Victoria. Slipping my shoes off in the elevator, I wiggled my toes, which sighed with relief. Competitions are murder on the feet. I traipsed barefoot down the hall to my room. The murmur of the television reached me as I fumbled for my key card. Pushing open the door, I called softly, "I'm back."

No response other than the annoying sales pitch of an infomercial. It took me mere seconds to check the room and bathroom. Victoria was gone. And so was my wallet.

I seethed for the better part of an hour, wanting to call someone and vent. I couldn't call Danielle because it was too late. She was meeting me for breakfast, though—she liked to watch me "do that dance thing," as she called it, when I was competing close to home—and I went over and over my encounter with Victoria in my mind so I could lay it all out for Danielle. Scrubbing off my makeup, I ordered a bowl of soup and a salad from room service—I was famished—and watched reruns of *Gilligan's Island* with my feet in a bowl of Epsom salts until I calmed down enough to fall asleep.

My alarm went off way too early and it took several layers of concealer to cover up the dark circles under my eyes. The gold pro-am heats were this morning—"gold" being the division for advanced students, some of whom were good enough to turn pro—and I donned the lime-green Latin costume with the fringe, for competing with Mark Downey. After calling my credit card company to report the stolen card and to arrange for a replacement, I scuffed into my slippers, tucked my shoes under my arm, and went down to breakfast, grateful I could charge it to my room since I had no money.

Usually, I can spot Danielle's red mop across a crowded room. In the dining room full of flamboyant dance costumes and hairstyles, however, it was her taupe sweater and charcoal pants that stood out. Over a bowl of oatmeal (me) and a plate of eggs Benedict with hash browns (definitely not me), Danielle exclaimed over yesterday's events.

"So this Taryn girl's dad tried to kill her dance partner?"

"Looked like it to me," I said.

"And then you met this Victoria person and she told you Rafe was helping her escape from her husband?"

I nodded, pouring skim milk over my oatmeal and

mixing in a spoonful of raisins. On a Saturday morning, the hotel didn't have much in the way of business clientele, so almost everyone in the dining room was involved with the competition in one way or another. I scanned for Mark Downey but didn't see him yet.

"Did you believe her?"

"About what?"

"Any of it." Danielle gestured impatiently with her fork. "Doesn't it seem a bit unlikely that she hadn't heard about Rafe's death? I mean, come on. No one's that out of touch in this day and age."

"She seemed surprised and upset." Was I a gullible idiot for buying her story about no TV, no phone? No, I'd heard Rafe talk about the cabin—it was primitive with a capital P.

"Yeah, just like she seemed helpless and confused . . . right up until she stole your wallet and disappeared on you."

I shrugged slightly, conceding the point. "I still think she was genuinely scared of her husband."

"Yeah, well, from what you've told me, he sounds like a nasty guy. But killing her because she wants to leave him? Doesn't the guy have any pride? He needs to man up and pretend he doesn't care. Have you considered the possibility that this chick killed Rafe?" Danielle gave me a serious look over a forkful of dripping eggs Benedict.

I'd considered every possible contender for Rafe's murder during my sleepless hours last night, from Victoria to Héctor to a time-traveling assassin from the future. "I considered it," I said, "but I don't know why she would. He was helping her."

"So she says," Danielle said significantly. "Maybe he was going to tell Bazán where she was."

"Why would he do that?" I frowned at her. "That wouldn't be like Rafe. And it doesn't mesh with him scrounging around for money." And selling Sherry Indrebo's flash drive to her opponent, I thought. "Listen to this, though: Victoria told me that Rafe knew a place to get her a gun."

Danielle's blue eyes opened wide. "You think he meant *your* gun?"

I nodded. "Yup. I think Rafe took my gun, planning to give it to Danielle. The jerk. I'd have loaned it to him, if he'd asked. Anyway, I think it's possible that he had it with him the night he was killed."

"So the murderer got the gun away from Rafe and used it on him? Cold."

"*Uh-huh.* But the important thing is that it means whoever killed him didn't have to know I had a gun, and didn't have to sneak into my place to steal it."

"That must make you feel better," Danielle said.

"Marginally. But it also means that anyone could've killed Rafe, even people I assumed couldn't have because they wouldn't have known about the gun. Like Leon Hall."

"So the killer really could have been a thief that Rafe walked in on," Danielle said, "and not someone he knew at all."

"I suppose that's possible," I said slowly. She'd hit on the one possibility I hadn't thought of last night. "But it doesn't seem likely. What thief would want to rob a dance studio? There's nothing worth stealing. He'd be better off knocking over a convenience store or even a fast-food joint. No, I still think it was someone Rafe knew, someone he planned to meet, or someone who knew he'd turn up at the studio eventually."

"You need to tell that Detective Lissy about Rafe having the gun," Danielle urged. She pushed aside her empty plate and drew her coffee cup closer. "Maybe then he'll stop considering you Public Enemy Number One."

"Good idea," I said. "As soon as—"

"Hey, Stacy, are you ready to rumba?" Alert and smiling, Mark Downey approached with a cup of coffee, seating himself at our table without asking. His form-fitting Latin costume had lime green accents to match my dress and his sandy hair flopped rakishly across his forehead. "Hi, Danielle," he added. "Good to see you again."

"Hi, Mark. Good luck today."

"Thanks. I'm thinking this may be my last competition as an amateur."

I smiled at him. Amateurs who won out in the gold division frequently made the jump to professional status, assuming they wanted a career of teaching and competing. "Let's do it," I said, giving Danielle a look that said we'd continue our conversation later. She accompanied us to the ballroom and took a seat at the studio table, chatting with a tense-looking Sherry Indrebo. She was husbandless this morning. She and Vitaly would be competing against Mark and me, and I knew that regardless of who won, we'd have a very unhappy loser on our hands.

I found myself looking at the older woman with her wiry muscles and tight body, clad now in an orange costume, wondering if she had it in her to shoot Rafe. She'd told me politics was her life; if she knew Rafe had sold her out to her opponent in the House race, just how mad would she have been? Livid, I imagined. If she and Rafe had met that night and Rafe had told her what he'd done, she could have snapped. Before I could work out the scenario any further, the announcer called us onto the floor and Sherry rose with a flutter of feathers and took Vitaly's arm with a practiced smile. Mark offered his arm to me and the competition got under way.

Mark and I won. Which is to say, we won the "Overall" title for the Pro/Am Scholarship—International Latin—Gold Division. The uninitiated would need the Rosetta stone or a code-breaking book to read ballroom dancing score sheets; suffice it to say that Mark and I were ranked number one in three of the five dances and no lower than third in any of them. Sherry and Vitaly took a second and a third and landed as low as fifth in the cha-cha. That really wasn't surprising considering they'd had only a couple of practices while Mark and I and several of the other pro-am couples had danced together for years. At any rate, Mark was ecstatic and I was pleased; our success might (hopefully!) attract more students to Graysin Motion.

Mark grabbed me around the waist and twirled me around, pressing a fast kiss onto my lips. "We did it!" He set me down and accepted congratulations from various other dancers, including Sherry, who looked like her cheeks ached from the effort of maintaining her smile. She disappeared immediately after congratulating Mark, not staying for the celebratory bottle of champagne Vitaly graciously purchased.

After a few minutes, Mark bounded over to where I sat at the studio's table, watching the Pro/Am Scholarship Open Nite-Club competition in which Graysin Motion had no entries. As couples demonstrated their West

Coast Swing, Mark leaned close. "I won out in gold," he exulted.

"I guess you'll be competing against me next year," I said, smiling.

The excitement drained slowly from his face. "Against you?"

"Why, yes. Didn't you say you were going to compete as a pro if you won out? I'm sure you'll have no trouble finding a partner . . . You're really good, Mark. It must have been because you had such a good teacher." I smiled again, although Mark's reaction didn't feel right.

"I thought that you . . . that you and I—I figured that when I was good enough, we would team up, be partners." His expression mixed disbelief and pleading.

Ouch. I should have forced myself to have that talk about boundaries earlier. I silently apologized to Danielle for getting on her about not confronting her boss when I hadn't even had the gumption to have a similar talk with a student. Vitaly, sensing something was wrong, discreetly led the others at the table away under the pretext of watching the dancers from another angle. I was liking him more every minute. Even though his English was iffy, he could read gestures and expressions in a way that let him understand more than some people who'd been speaking English since the cradle. Mark for instance. He reclaimed my attention by grabbing my wrist where it lay on the table.

"Stacy! I knew that while you and Rafe were dancing together there was no hope for me. You'd built a professional reputation together—I understood that. But with Rafe out of the picture—"

"He's dead!" I said, pulling my wrist away.

"I know. I didn't mean to disrespect your grief or imply that his murder wasn't a terrible thing. I'm not doing this well." He looked miserable.

"Mark, I don't want to take anything away from your achievement today, but you need to look for someone at your level to partner with."

"You're too good for me, is that it?" Anger was replacing his hangdog look.

"I've got several years' experience as a professional," I said as diplomatically as possible. "I'm at a different place in my career. I own a studio. I've got to dance with someone who can bring students into the studio, who I can win important competitions with to boost the studio's reputation. That's Vitaly."

"But you just started with him! It's not like you've had years, or even months, of training together. He'd understand if you wanted to give me a tryout—"

"No." I spoke the word forcefully.

Mark scraped his chair back, rocking the table as he jumped up. I grabbed for the champagne bottle before it could fall. People at the tables on either side watched us with open curiosity and the nearest judge turned around to glare at us. With an obvious effort, Mark controlled his temper. "I could work at Graysin Motion, then, and we could see how it goes. Maybe in a couple months—"

"No." I tried to soften the harsh word. "I don't think it's a good idea, Mark. Look, this is your big day. Let's get back to celebrating—"

"Screw you, Stacy," he spat, turning on his heel and hurrying out of the ballroom.

I let out a long breath. Mark's anger, his lack of control, the way he said Rafe was out of the picture . . . I wondered if Mark could've had a hand in Rafe's death.

Was his obsession with me, his fantasy that we would be professional partners, strong enough to lead to murder? If Mark had come to the studio that night, maybe looking for me, and run into Rafe and they'd had words . . . I almost jumped when I felt a hand on my shoulder. It was Vitaly, tracking Mark as he banged out the door. "He is one gigantic prickle," Vitaly announced, squeezing my shoulder.

"That's one way to put it," I agreed.

Chapter 15

I have never been so happy to see my house as I was Sunday night when I got home from the competition. The usual euphoria I had after competing had leaked out of me like helium from a three-day-old party balloon. The dancing itself, combined with the sprint and grapple with Hall, had left my body worn out, my feet throbbing. I was mentally worn out, too, from the emotional ups and downs of the weekend, including Victoria's appearing/disappearing act, the brouhaha with Taryn and Sawyer, dancing with a new partner—Vitaly and I hadn't won an overall title, but we'd won some of the individual dances, which was good enough for our first competition together—and Mark Downey's tantrum. After his blow-up Saturday, Mark had returned to dance his International Standard heats with me, but he was cold and uncommunicative and we didn't do nearly as well. If anything else had been needed to convince me not even to consider him as a professional partner, that did it. A pro's got to be able to divorce his or her personal life from the dancing. You've got to be able to smile and look like you're enjoying yourself, or be tender and romantic—whatever suits the character of the dance—even if you recently caught your lying son-of-a-bitch partner cheating on you.

Despite my weariness, I forced myself to lug all my costumes into the house; I couldn't afford to have them stolen—they each cost upward of $2,500. Holding the hangers high above my head to keep the garment bags from dragging on the ground, I plodded from my car to the back door and fumbled with my key in the lock. As the door eased open with a squeak, an impression of motion to my left had me half turning in that direction. Before I could spot anything, a hard forearm pressed against my throat and the man's other hand clamped over my mouth and nose.

"Quietly," a gruff voice whispered into my ear. "Let's go inside quietly." He bumped me forward with a rude knee to the back of my thigh.

For a split second, I was most worried about the dresses, still gripped awkwardly in my upraised hand, their weight making my arm go numb. Then common sense reordered my priorities and my mind seized up with images from news stories of horrific home invasions where whole families were beaten and/or shot; the serial rapist who was supposed to be operating on jogging routes in Arlington, but who might have changed his hunting grounds; and of Rafe, bloody and dead, in the ballroom upstairs. The man pulled his arm painfully tight against my throat, cutting off my airway, and I reluctantly stepped into the house. I automatically reached for the light switch with the hand not holding the dresses, but the man knocked my arm down with his elbow. "No lights."

Once inside, the arm across my throat eased up and he nudged me toward a chair. "Sit."

My arm trembling with fatigue, I asked in a disgustingly shaky voice, "May I put the dresses down?" Some part of me hoped that with two free hands, I might be able to escape my attacker. My gaze flitted to where I knew my knives sat in a block on the counter, even though I couldn't see them in the dark. And on the end of the counter nearest me was Great-aunt Laurinda's ugly ceramic rooster that I hadn't been able to bring myself to trash or donate; given the opportunity, I could grab it and smash it into my assailant's skull.

"On the table."

I laid the dresses gently across the kitchen table and wondered if I should lunge for the knives. As if reading my mind, my assailant, dressed entirely in black I realized now that my eyes were adjusting, stepped between the counter and me. "Sit."

I sat. Every muscle tensed. I would go down fighting. Instead of ripping my clothes off, though, or demanding that I hand over my valuables, the man turned away. I heard a faint click, then the whirr of the vent fan, a muffled "Damn," and then the light in the stove vent came on.

"Just a little light so I can see if you're lying to me," Héctor Bazán said, moving back toward the table. "But not enough to attract attention from your neighbors." He prodded a chair away from the table with his foot and sat adjacent to me, crossing his legs with one ankle on his knee.

Knowing my attacker's identity both relieved me—it wasn't the serial rapist—and made me more nervous. Hadn't I heard somewhere—maybe a movie?—that if a kidnapper let you see him it meant he was going to kill you? Not that this was a kidnapping, exactly, but maybe the same principle applied. I stared into Bazán's dark, expressionless eyes, easily believing now that he had killed a migrant worker on his ranch and maybe dozens of other people. He wasn't brandishing a weapon, but that didn't mean he didn't have one.

"Where is my wife?" Bazán asked conversationally.

I stared at him.

"Victoria. Where is she?"

"I don't—"

He slammed his hand on the table, making me jump. "I'm not in the mood for game-playing or lies. I know she was at the dance competition. I've had men watching Acosta's condo and this studio for two weeks now; one of them showed initiative in checking out the competition, thinking she might try to link up with Acosta there if she hadn't heard about his untimely demise. So where is she?"

"How would I know?" My voice squeaked. I cleared my throat and said more forcefully, "If she came looking for Rafe, she would've found out he was dead and left, right?"

Bazán studied my face, his gaze drilling into first my right eye and then my left. I tried to keep from fidgeting.

"You're lying," he said. "Just tell me. It'll be easier on both of us. And you'll be doing Victoria a favor."

I raised my brows and made a skeptical sound.

"Really. My wife is a sick woman, Miss Graysin."

I stopped myself from saying, "She didn't look ill to me."

"What story did she tell you?" His eyes scanned my face. "That I'm involved in mysterious criminal activities and won't let her leave because she knows too much? Or was it the one about me institutionalizing our child because of birth defects? We've never had a baby. Or—"

"She showed me the bruises," I said.

"On her stomach?" When I nodded, he said, "She was in a car accident two weeks ago and her stomach and chest got badly bruised when the air bag drove her purse into her torso. She had it on her lap, looking for a lip gloss, I believe." Mingled sadness and weariness pulled his mouth down. He didn't look threatening at the moment.

Not sure what to believe, I said, "I really don't know where she is."

"But you talked?" His eyes lit up.

Reluctantly, I nodded.

He grabbed my left hand with both of his. "Please. Tell me what she said."

His hands were callused and hard. "Not much. We were going to talk after I danced, but she was gone from my room by the time I finished. She stole my wallet."

"I will reimburse you," Bazán said instantly. "Unfortunately, it is not the first time something like this has happened. I need to find her before she gets herself in serious trouble, or ends up hurt."

"I wish I could help," I lied. I wasn't sure I believed anything Victoria had told me, but her husband hadn't exactly won my trust by breaking into my house.

He narrowed his eyes. "Surely she said something."

"Nope.

He slapped my face with his open palm, not hard, but it stung.

Surprise, as much as pain, made me cry out. No man had ever struck me. Even my father had never spanked me. I put my hand to my cheek.

"I don't have time for your flippancy. Tell me what Victoria said and where she went. It's for her own good."

"Go to hell."

The next slap was harder, almost knocking me from my chair. "She didn't say anything!" I yelled through incipient tears. "She was staying at Rafe's cabin, in West Virginia. Maybe she went back there." I was darned sure Victoria hadn't returned to Rafe's isolated man cave. "And before you ask, I don't know where it is. Somewhere outside a town called Canon-something."

"If you are lying . . ."

"I'm not." I stared at him defiantly. "Although I wouldn't tell you where she was, even if I knew."

"Then you'd be doing her a great disservice," he said, standing. "Victoria is a menace to herself."

"Not as big a menace as you."

"Acosta knew what he was doing when he dumped you," Bazán observed. "No man wants to live with a sharp-tongued wife. If you were my wife, I'd be tempted to cut it out."

He said it with so little emotion that it froze me to stillness. He crossed to the door. "I'll be back if I find out you've lied to me."

Scrambling to my feet, I lifted my chair and held it in front of me, not sure if I meant it as a weapon or a shield. "The police might have something to say about that."

He laughed, genuinely amused. "I've got two words for you: diplomatic immunity. Besides which, it's your word against mine. I don't think I need to worry very much about the police. You, on the other hand, have a lot to worry about." He opened the door, looked both ways, and stepped out, pulling the door closed behind him.

The chair dropped with a clatter, landing on my toe. I dropped cross-legged to the floor, massaging my toe and bawling my eyes out. I cried for at least ten minutes, knowing the tears were more about fear and tension release than pain. Shoving myself upward, I hobbled to the fridge and pulled a chunk of ice out, wrapping it in a dish towel and holding it against my toe. I followed that up with an aspirin and a call to the police.

Monday morning found me trotting awkwardly after Detective Lissy as he inspected the exterior of my house, peering at windows and doors. My toe hurt like the dickens and the nail was a lurid purple that told me it would fall off eventually. Dancing would be excruciating for a few days, at least. I thought evil thoughts about what I'd do to Bazán if the opportunity presented itself.

"But I told you he didn't break in," I said for the third time. "He waited until I unlocked the door and then pounced." The uniformed officers who came by last night had apparently misreported what I'd said, or Lissy was deliberately misinterpreting it.

"I'm not looking for evidence of a break-in," Lissy said damply. "I'm looking for proof someone waited out here. Cigarette butts, beer can, candy wrapper."

"He threatened me and you're looking for proof he's a litterbug?"

Lissy eyed me, his pale gray eyes assessing. "It'd be nice to have something to corroborate your story."

I held out my bare foot. "What about this?"

"You said you dropped a chair on it."

"Yes, but only because I picked it up to protect myself."

Lissy nodded, somehow managing to convey that he thought I was either an accomplished liar or a delusional conspiracy theorist who would shortly be accusing Bazán of being behind the Gulf oil leak and the subprime mortgage fiasco.

We had made our way around to the front of the house, not spotting a single thing that helped prove Bazán had forced his way into my kitchen last night and threatened me. The sun shone brightly from a cloudless sky and already my skin prickled with sweat. It was going to be a scorcher. Lissy flipped a page on his steno pad. "So you say Mrs. Bazán forced her way into your hotel room and then Mr. Bazán"—he consulted his notes—"'pounced' on you here?"

"She didn't force her way in," I said, frustrated. "I invited her in. But then she stole my wallet, which I already reported to my credit card company."

"But not to the police." Lissy's inflection made my omission sound suspicious.

In truth, I hadn't called them because I couldn't spare the time from the competition to hassle with the paperwork and I didn't think they had a prayer of recovering it. Some part of me, too, felt I deserved what I'd gotten for being so foolish as to leave a stranger alone in my hotel room. In hindsight, I should have taken the time to report the theft, if only to the hotel management. "I didn't want to bother the police," I said lamely.

"Mm."

We stood on the shallow brick portico outside my front door, which I noticed needed repainting. Its glossy forest green had dulled and was flaking near the bottom. One more expense. Maybe if I went at the knocker with some brass polish, that would spiff up the door. I pushed the thought aside.

"What is it, exactly, you want me to do, Ms. Graysin?"

Lissy asked, finger-combing his dishwater-colored hair from left to right.

"Arrest Héctor Bazán! At least talk to him, not just about last night, but about Rafe's murder. Now that we know that Rafe was helping Victoria Bazán—"

"We don't know this," Detective Lissy said. "You *say* that Victoria Bazán *said* . . . You see where I'm going with this?"

I ignored his interruption. "—it makes sense to think that her husband might have gone after him."

"With your gun?"

"Yes! I told you that Rafe told Victoria he could get her a gun. It's obvious that he stole my gun, intending to give it to her. Whoever killed him got the gun away from him somehow and shot him."

"Ms. Graysin, in policing we like to rely on a little thing called 'evidence.' And you don't have any." He held up a thin hand to forestall my protests. "I'm going to talk to Héctor Bazán and see what he has to say."

"What about his story? About his wife having mental problems and being in a car accident. He said it was just a couple of weeks ago, so you can look that up, can't you? See if he's lying?"

"As I might have mentioned before, I've been doing this job for twenty-seven years."

With that not-so-subtle reminder that he didn't need my help, he clomped down the steps and headed for his car.

I hurried after him. "Just one more thing, Detective," I said, my eyes pleading with him. "Did you check on Sherry Indrebo's whereabouts the night Rafe was shot?"

Lissy eyed me with something like fascination. "A

diplomat's not enough for you? Now you want to accuse a congresswoman?"

"I'm not accusing—"

"Who next? The Pope?"

"Was she—"

"Ms. Indrebo was at a fund-raiser at the Corcoran, in full view of assorted Republican movers and shakers and a photographer who has dozens of photos of her from when the party kicked off until they turned off the lights. Satisfied?" He yanked open the car door, rubbing at a smudge on the mirror.

Frustrated was more like it, but I thanked him and watched him drive away. Then I went inside and called Phineas Drake.

I spent the morning restoring order to my life and house after the competition weekend. I sorted through my costumes and put aside those that needed a trip to the dry cleaner, stowed my makeup and hair accessories, and cleaned the bathrooms and kitchen. With only minutes to spare before Drake arrived, I polished the knocker, kick plate, and doorknob on the front door with a crusty bottle of brass polish I found under the kitchen sink. I stepped back to admire the gleaming brass when I was done, liking the way they shone in the sunlight, but disappointed that their brightness actually made the door's paint look shabbier in contrast. *Drat.*

Drake's limo nosed up to the curb as I stood there and I hastily tucked the brass polish and rag into the house and gave my hands a quick sniff. They smelled a bit chemically from the polish, but not too bad. I hurried down the walkway as the chauffeur opened the door. Drake's secretary had said he could spare me only fifteen minutes on his drive to the courthouse and I didn't want to waste a second. I slid onto the slick leather seat and found Phineas Drake gazing at me, a tall glass foaming with a tan concoction in his hand.

"Protein drink," he greeted me, hoisting the glass a couple of inches. "Doctor says I have to lose a few pounds or I'm going to keel over before I'm sixty." He laughed and patted his hefty paunch covered by a tartan vest of blues and greens with a thin yellow stripe.

Since I'd already pegged him for past sixty, I didn't comment.

Running his huge hand down his beard when he finished drinking, he fixed his sharp eyes on me. "You said you discovered something about Acosta's murder this weekend?"

"Yes, and the police aren't taking me seriously, so I thought you . . . that you might be able to look into it."

"Tell me."

I gave him the unedited version of the weekend, from Leon Hall's attack on Sawyer, to bumping into Victoria in the hall and our conversation followed by her disappearance, to Bazán's attack at my house, to my theory about Rafe stealing the gun. I looked at Drake anxiously when I finished, trying to read his expression. The luxuriant facial hair made it tough, especially in the dimly lit limo.

"That's good—the bit about Acosta having your gun with him. That's the kind of creative thinking that makes a good criminal defense lawyer. Any interest in giving up ballroom dancing for the law?" He chuckled.

Was he saying he didn't believe me? "It's not 'creative thinking'—it's what must have happened," I said indignantly. "And, no, I can't see myself as a lawyer."

Working in an office all day, wearing rigid suits, responding to someone's beck and call. I shuddered.

"You're more the creative type," he said indulgently. "My wife's that way, too—scrapbooking is her thing. That and eBay."

Great. He clearly dismissed my career as a hobby on par with his wife's interest in scissors that cut wavy patterns and colored cardstock. I held on to my temper. "Do you have a way to check out Bazán's story?" I asked. "And maybe find out more about Leon Hall?"

"A diplomat, huh?" Drake said, looking thoughtful, calculating the angles. "If the police were convinced he did it, they'd stop looking at you, and they wouldn't have to worry about enough evidence for 'beyond a reasonable doubt' because the case would never see the inside of a courtroom. The State Department might PNG Bazán if the cops built a good enough case, but that's about it."

"PNG?"

"Make him persona non grata—boot him out of the country."

"That's not right," I said, appalled. "If he killed Rafe he should go to prison for the rest of his slimy life."

Drake shrugged, dismissing my outrage as too naive to bother with. The limo glided to a stop at the courthouse curb and Drake shifted his bulk toward the door. "I think it'd be useful to locate this Victoria gal again. She sounds like a wily one." His tone was admiring.

A shaft of sunlight penetrated the car as the chauffeur swung the door open. Drake got out, then bent over to peer in at me. "Don't worry your pretty little head about anything. Since the police haven't moved on you yet, chances are they won't, at least not without new evidence. I'll be in touch." Giving orders to his driver to take me back to the town house, he strode up the court-house steps, fending off reporters as he went.

Halfway back to the house, my cell phone rang. Tav Acosta.

"How did the competition go this weekend?" he asked.

His voice, rich and dark and lightly accented, sent a little tingle through me. I stomped it down. Business. This was only business.

I shrugged, even though he couldn't see me. "Some wins, some losses. Better than I thought it would, actu-ally, without Rafe."

We were silent for a moment, thinking about Rafe; then Tav said, "The police have released his body. I can take him back to Argentina."

"Oh." I was surprised by how sad I felt at the thought of him leaving. "When?"

"As soon as I can make arrangements with the airlines—probably two or three days."

"Oh. Well, it was nice meeting you. I hope you have a good trip back." The inanities were a defense against the surprisingly strong stab of disappointment I felt at the news he was leaving.

"That's not why I'm calling."

"Oh?" If I said "oh" one more time, I was going to slap myself. The limo jolted into a pothole and I bobbled the phone, missing what Tav was saying. "Sorry," I said. "What did you say?"

"I said I have had a couple offers for my share of Graysin Motion and I need to talk to you about them."

"Oh!" I slapped my face lightly and the chauffeur eyed me doubtfully in the rearview mirror. "Who from?"

"I'd rather talk about it in person. Do you have plans for this afternoon?"

"Nothing that can't wait."

"Good. Would you mind if I played tourist while we talked? I have not had the chance to see anything of your nation's capital—too busy working. I would really like to see the Air and Space Museum before I go back."

His tone was half-sheepish, as if wanting to visit one of the world's great museums was embarrassing in some way. With rare exceptions, every man I knew preferred the Air and Space Museum to any other museum on the Mall. I laughed. "You shouldn't miss it. I'll meet you there in an hour."

Chapter 16

A flowered halter top, denim shorts, low-heeled espadrilles, my yellow sunhat, and copious quantities of sunblock and I was ready to play tourist in downtown D.C. Yes, the Air and Space Museum was inside, but I bet Tav would want to stroll down the Mall and see a couple of the monuments while we were down there and since today was forecast to be record-breaking hot, I didn't want to end up sunburned.

Tav stood near the museum entrance, long, muscled legs displayed by olive-colored shorts. A sprinkling of crisp black hair curled from the open neck of his white polo shirt, and sunglasses hung around his neck. He greeted me with a kiss on the cheek and a smile. "Thanks for humoring me, Stacy. I know this is not the standard venue for a business meeting."

I returned his smile. "Much better than a stuffy office or conference room." We moved into the air-conditioned building with its megahigh ceilings hung with planes, and joined the clumps of people looking upward. I'd visited the museum several times over the years—no schoolchild in the greater D.C. area graduates without at least one field trip to the Air and Space Museum—but I had to admit that the history of flight and space travel pretty much left me cold. Planes were transportation, pure and simple, and I couldn't get excited about a Pratt & Whitney engine the size of my car, even though Tav seemed fascinated. His enthusiasm was engaging and it kept a long afternoon of studying the Wright Flyer, an Apollo capsule, and various other artifacts of flight from being tedious. The museum wasn't too crowded on a Monday afternoon in April, which made it possible to move freely and linger as long as we wanted—or longer—in front of exhibits.

"I wanted to be a pilot," Tav confided as we stood beside a plane labeled MESSERSCHMITT ME 262.

"Why aren't you?"

"I have always admired the American idea that you can be whatever you want to be," he said, studying the plaque that described the plane. "It is not always that simple. Family expectations, financial realities . . . sometimes dreams take a backseat. Besides"—he looked at me and grinned—"I wanted to be a professional football player, too, but so far La Selección has not come calling."

"My dad wanted me to study accounting," I said. "He thought it would be a more stable career than ballroom dancing. I'm sure he was right, but I don't regret being a dancer. It makes me happy—most of the time."

Tav touched my elbow to move me toward another gallery and a group gathered around a docent giving a talk about an Apollo capsule. "I cannot see you as an accountant, Stacy. Such a job would quench your joie de vivre."

His smile warmed me and I was pleased that he saw

me as a happy person because I was, basically, except when my ex-fiancé got murdered in my dance studio and the police thought I did it. "It's funny you should say that," I said. "Just today someone suggested I should be a lawyer." I went on to tell him about meeting with Phineas Drake and the weekend's many surprises.

"Héctor Bazán attacked you in your home?" His eyes narrowed with a cold rage I hadn't seen in him before.

"'Attacked' is maybe too strong," I said, pleased by his reaction. Finally someone was taking me seriously. "He didn't have a gun, although he slapped me a couple of times."

Tav cupped my chin in his hand and turned my face from side to side to see what injuries I'd suffered. I'd inspected my face closely this morning, but there was no hint of bruising. He ran a finger down my cheek, stopping at the corner of my mouth.

"I'll live." I laughed it off, disconcerted by the flush of heat that shot through me at his touch.

"I will pay a call on Bazán before I leave," Tav promised grimly.

"Detective Lissy said he'd question him, but I can tell he thinks I made the whole thing up."

From the set of Tav's mouth, I thought his approach was going to be more physical in nature. He confirmed that by saying, "If Bazán is responsible for my brother's murder—" He cut himself off, forced a smile on his face, and said, "Come on. You have had enough of things with wings. Do you mind if we walk to the World War II memorial? My grandfather flew Hawker Typhoons with the RAF's 164th Squadron and was part of the Normandy invasion."

"Really? I didn't know Argentina fought in World War II."

Tav ushered me out the door into the brutal heat and humidity outside. Who sucked all the oxygen out of the air and replaced it with water? It was way too early in the year for me to feel like I needed a scuba tank to breathe outside. Grateful for my hat, I led Tav down the wide, pebbly path toward the World War II memorial. It was past five now and most of the tourists had drifted off to refreshing hotel pools or cocktail lounges, while D.C. workers clogged the outbound roads with their air-conditioned cars. I was just as happy to spend a little more time on the Mall and not have to get on a crowded Metro car during rush hour.

"About four thousand Argentine volunteers fought in the war, some with British, Canadian, and South African air forces. Our government at the time was a bunch of cowardly fence-sitters, but eventually they declared war on the Axis, sometime in the spring of 1945, I think. Volunteers, though, joined the fighting much earlier. My grandfather—my mother's father—still had family in the UK, cousins and such, so it was natural that he would go there. He didn't come back from the war, which is one of the reasons my mother did not want me to join the air force."

"Who can blame her?"

He shrugged, stepping between me and a gardener letting his leaf blower drift off target as he eyed a couple of attractive joggers. I appreciated Tav's instinctive courtesy. Rafe had not been so sensitive to his environment, to those around him. I needed to stop comparing the two men. Almost brusquely, I asked, "So you've had some offers for Rafe's half of the studio?"

"Feelers, let us say. It is too soon to have formal offers. Until we are able to assess the value of—"

"From who?" I wanted to cut to the quick.

"From a Solange Dubonnet—"

"Damn!"

"—and a Nicolaos Papadakis."

"Uncle Nico?" Double damn. I nibbled on my lower lip. I wasn't sure which prospect disturbed me more—working with Solange or with Uncle Nico. Solange would undoubtedly want to be involved in the day-to-day operations and compete with me for the male amateur dancers. Uncle Nico's motives were a little murkier. Maybe he was just trying to be helpful to his niece? Not likely.

"I can't believe Solange made you an offer without even talking to me first. When did she first contact you?"

"Yesterday," Tav said with a lifted brow. "And she sounded very interested. Who is she?"

I explained about Solange, leaving out the part about finding her in bed with Rafe. I didn't want to tarnish Tav's memories of his brother. "And Uncle Nico—" How did I explain about Uncle Nico? "Uncle Nico's an operator," I said weakly. "He has many business interests. I'm not sure where a ballroom dance studio fits into his business empire."

"So you don't want me to accept either of the offers?" Tav asked.

I was silent, realizing it was totally unreasonable of me to ask him not to sell Rafe's share—his share—of Graysin Motion to either of two qualified buyers. At least, I assumed Solange could afford it, and I knew Uncle Nico could. We had reached the World War II memorial and stayed silent as we walked through the Atlantic

Pavilion and into the huge granite oval surrounded by columns. Even though the memorial was rigidly symmetrical, something about the stone pillars set in semicircles at either end made me think of Stonehenge. Fountains splashed in the central pool and a little girl escaped from her parents' grip to dash into the water, shoes and all. Tav laughed at the sight, but sobered as he read some of the plaques on the wall. Heat radiated from the granite, even as dusk laid long shadows across the ground. As we made our way counterclockwise around the memorial, I said, "I hope someone else wants to buy your share. I have to say that neither Solange nor Uncle Nico would be my first choice of partners."

"Who would be?"

I considered. Vitaly came to mind, but I had no idea what his financial situation was. And I really didn't know him that well. "I don't know," I finally said. "How does one find buyers for a business? Do you advertise?"

"You can," he said, "although I would think word of mouth would be the best method for a small, specialized business like the studio. You mention it at competitions, tell friends to spread the word."

"How long?"

He looked at me quizzically.

"How long do you have before you have to make a decision?"

"There is no hard-and-fast deadline," he said slowly. "Although buyers will not hang around waiting for a decision forever." We approached a cluster of pigeons that waddled lazily out of our path.

A light breeze stirred my hair and I lifted it from my neck. The scent of hot dogs drifted over from a cart where the vendor was closing down for the day. I was

about to verbalize an idea that was burbling in my brain,
but Tav spoke up.

"Are you hungry?" At my nod, he said, "Let us get
dinner—unless you have other plans?"

"Dinner would be nice, although I'm not dressed for
anyplace fancy."

"Nor am I." He gestured to his shorts with a laugh. "I
am sure we can find something."

We found a casual Peruvian place a short Metro ride
away in the lively Adams Morgan section of town and
enjoyed a savory meal with a bottle of wine before re-
boarding the Metro to return to Old Town. I tried to
tell Tav he didn't need to escort me home, but he would
have none of it. "I am not putting you on a train by
yourself at this hour," he said, although it was just past
ten, not two in the morning. Strolling from the Metro
stop to my house in near silence, our arms brushing occasionally as we walked, I found myself feeling more
content than I had in a long time. The thought jolted
me and I tripped on the uneven walkway half a block
from my house. Tav caught my arm and asked, "Are
you okay?"

His dark eyes searched my face. His hand was warm
on my arm and I blamed the wine for heightening my
senses and making me ultra-aware of his cedary scent,
the warmth that drifted off his body, the dark stubble
hazing his jawline. "Fine."

His gaze lingered on my lips and I swayed toward
him, a completely involuntary movement, like breathing
or blinking. Over his shoulder, I noticed a light flickering
strangely in the upper windows of a house down the
block. *My* house! There shouldn't be anyone in the stu-

dio at this hour. Straightening, I grabbed Tav's hand. "Come on."

"Wha—?"

"Someone's broken into my house."

Tav's gaze followed my pointing finger. His face set in grim lines. "That is not an intruder," he said. "It is fire."

Before he could stop me, I was pounding down the sidewalk in my flimsy espadrilles, desperate to reach my house. I vaguely heard him talking to the 911 operator, and then calling at me to stop, but I didn't wait. I could see that the light was flames, now, dancing at the windows of the ballroom, an eerie interplay of red and yellow and shadow. As I got closer, I could smell the smoke. It caught in my nose and throat, making me cough. I stopped on the sidewalk in front of the house, not foolish enough to try to enter. What could I do? Water from the garden hose wouldn't reach high enough to tickle the flames, much less extinguish them. Thank God I didn't have children or pets to rescue.

Tav trotted up beside me and slid an arm around my waist, pulling me in close to his side, as if to ensure I wouldn't go dashing into the house. I let my head fall onto his strong chest for a moment, comforted by his presence and solidity, before pushing away as the fire trucks came screaming down the street in a swirl of lights. Firefighters piled out and Tav tugged at me, walking me across the street where we could watch the scene without being in the way.

"It is just the upstairs," he said comfortingly.

I'd already noticed that and had been racking my brain to figure out what might have caught fire up there. Maybe there'd been a short in the stereo system or my computer? The firefighters had dragged a hose up the side stairs and kicked in the door before I could think to offer them a key. The wrinkly, cement-colored hose swelled as water pumped through it and the flames began to falter as the firefighters disappeared inside. A cop car arrived and a crowd began to gather, late diners or moviegoers drawn by the activity and strobing lights. It was only twenty minutes or so before the firefighters emerged, sweaty and smoke-stained, giving a thumbs-up to the firefighters still with the truck. I was about to join them and ask what had happened when an official-looking car pulled up and Detective Lissy stepped out. Great. Just great.

Chapter 17

Detective Lissy and Tav and I sat in my front parlor half an hour later. Lissy wore his usual expression of sour suspicion as he dusted the base of a lamp with a hanky, Tav looked alert and relaxed, and I perched beside him on the edge of the uncomfortable love seat, clenching and unclenching my hand on its scratchy arm. The room smelled like someone had lit a campfire in it and doused it with dirty water.

"But who would want to set my studio on fire?" I asked for the third time since the fire captain had told us the fire had been caused by an accelerant on the ballroom floor and had been largely confined to that one room, due to Tav's and my timely return. "You got lucky," the captain summed up, scratching her cheek. "The floor's toast, but the old boards are still sound. You've got some smoke and water damage, but the place is habitable. A floor refinisher and a good cleaning team will have you back in business in a couple of weeks." She smiled, crinkling the skin around her eyes. "You got lucky."

"You tell me," Detective Lissy suggested. "If I was a

superstitious man, I'd think you were jinxed, what with finding a dead body upstairs, being attacked—allegedly—by an Argentine diplomat, and having your place set on fire." He ticked each item off on an upheld finger. "Since I'm not superstitious, I have to ask myself what else could be going on. Where were you this evening, Ms. Graysin?"

"Are you suggesting I set the fire?" I asked. I could understand him suspecting me of Rafe's death, but this was ridiculous. "Two weeks without being able to hold classes will put a huge dent in my finances," I said. "Some of the students will go to other studios and they won't come back. Why in *hell* would I do that?"

"To make it look like someone's out to get you, to make us think there's someone else out there who might have killed Mr. Acosta," Lissy answered promptly. "First you tried to distract us with the story about Bazán attacking you—which he completely denies, by the way—then—"

"She was with me," Tav put in firmly, before Lissy could finish building his case. "From three o'clock on. There is no possible way she could have set the fire."

"With you, *hmm*?" Lissy said, eyeing Tav speculatively. His gaze went from Tav to me and back again. "Very interesting."

"It is not 'interesting' at all, Lissy, and I resent the implication," Tav said.

Not one whit perturbed by Tav's anger, Lissy said, "You two seem very cozy"—he gestured to us as we sat side by side on the love seat and I self-consciously moved my knee from where it had been in casual contact with Tav's, making Lissy smile with satisfaction—"and it's a common enough scenario."

"What is?" I asked.

"Man gets offed by scorned lover and her new man, and they inherit—"

"I was the scorner, not the scornee," I objected. "I broke it off with Rafe. And that was months ago. I only met Tav after Rafe was murdered. And—"

"You have a prurient mind, Detective Lissy," Tav said coldly. "Immigration records will show I only arrived in this country after my half brother was killed. You can check them."

"Be sure I will." The man stood, brushing at his immaculate slacks.

"My relationship—connection—with Stacy is purely a business one brought about by my brother's death, not causing it. Since I inherited his share of Graysin Motion, we will have unavoidable interactions until I can sell it." He didn't spare me a glance as he said it and I felt unaccountably hurt.

"Whatever you say, Mr. Acosta," Lissy said with fake amiability. "Just don't plan on leaving the area without letting me know about it."

"I am taking Rafael's body home later this week."

"We'll see about that," Lissy said, striding toward the door.

I followed him, mostly to make sure he left, because I wasn't exactly in gracious hostess mode. Flipping on the porch light, I opened the door for him and said, "Good night."

He stepped out, glanced at a moth beating itself against the light, and said, "Your door needs painting."

I awoke Tuesday morning with a headache—probably from the smoky smell—and a burning desire to get away.

I couldn't teach today, Tav was tied up with business stuff so we couldn't go over options for the studio, and I just couldn't face doing paperwork in my kitchen while a specialized cleaning crew tackled the studio. After I got hold of a floor refinisher, I decided, I would go somewhere . . . anywhere. Having made these very logical decisions, I couldn't force myself to get out of bed. I lay there on my back, staring up at the ceiling, feeling as congealed and lumpish as a bowl of oatmeal left out all morning. My arms and legs were heavy, refusing to respond to my brain's halfhearted order to move. A small spider industriously working on its web in the corner where the ceiling met the wall finally motivated me to move. If a stupid arachnid could be up and at 'em, so could I.

A shower and a couple of Excedrin somewhat improved my outlook, and a cup of coffee made me think getting out of bed wasn't the absolute worst idea since gaucho pants. I called the floor refinisher who had last polished the boards upstairs and he agreed to drop his current project and start on my floors for only fifteen percent over his usual rate. A real philanthropist. Waiting for the cleaning crew to show up, I dialed my sister's number and told her what had happened.

"I want you to come stay with me," she said immediately.

"Why?"

"Someone's out to get you. Maybe he won't stop at torching your floor next time. Maybe he'll come after you with a hatchet or a chain saw."

"I told you not to go see *Saw 53* with Coop," I sighed.

"They haven't made that many," she said, "although with a constantly replenishing population of ghoulish teenage boys, they may get there."

"I'm going on a road trip today," I said. "Wanna play hooky from work and come with me?"

"Where are you going?"

"West Virginia."

"West Virginia!"

From her tone, you'd've thought I'd said Antarctica, not a state fifty minutes away. The idea had popped into my head and I'd latched on to it with the desperation of a drowning person grasping for a piece of driftwood. "I'm going to visit Rafe's cabin."

"Why?"

Not an unreasonable question. "To see if maybe Victoria went back there. To see if Rafe left anything there that would explain what's going on, why someone murdered him. To just effing get away from here for a day."

Danielle must have heard the stress in my voice. "I'm in," she said. "Give me half an hour to call in sick and change."

I sped to her apartment forty minutes later, where she was waiting outside, dressed in cargo shorts, a beige camp shirt, hiking boots, and a hat that looked suitable for a Botswanan safari. "We're driving to West Virginia," I greeted her as she buckled her seat belt, "not doing a death march across the Gobi."

"You said the cabin was remote," she said, "so I'm prepared." She patted a fanny pack. "Compass, map, water bottle, matches, mosquito repellent."

I laughed, feeling better than I had since spotting the flames in my ballroom. "What, no food?"

Her eyes widened with dismay.

"Don't worry," I said, putting the car in gear before she could get out and make sandwiches. "I'm pretty sure they have convenience stores, and maybe even fast-food joints, in West Virginia."

Two hours, three wrong turns, and a couple of Big Macs later, we were headed up a deeply rutted drive to what I hoped would be Rafe's cabin. I'd downloaded directions before meeting Danielle, but the roads were mostly marked with numbers instead of names and we'd had to backtrack a couple of times since leaving Capon Bridge and ending up on gravel and then dirt roads. Forest crowded in on both sides of the narrow road, pine trees or fir trees—I never could remember the difference—scraping the car's windows. It was cooler here than in Old Town and I rolled down the windows an inch or two to breathe the nature-scented air. The piney, loamy, sun-warmed scent of the woods beat the heck out of the charbroiled polyurethane stink of my house and the smoggy, warm asphalt smell of Old Town.

"Are you sure we're on the right road?" Danielle asked just as we popped out into a small clearing.

"Yup," I said, more relieved than I wanted to admit to see the small log cabin centered in the clearing. I was afraid we'd been headed for parts of the country that even Daniel Boone and his buddies hadn't explored. "This must be it."

I opened the door and climbed out, stretching my arms over my head. The cabin, not unexpectedly, was unprepossessing, being not much larger than the average suburban garage and made of splintery looking logs. Firewood was stacked beneath a tree a few feet from the front door, and a rickety wood building I assumed was the outhouse listed near the tree line behind the cabin. A faint trail led off into the woods behind the outhouse, beaten down by...what? Rafe on his hunting trips? Deer? A bear? Skittering sounds spoke to the presence of squirrels or other rodents and a crow cawed loudly from somewhere to our left. I wasn't much of a nature girl and either the vastness of the woods or the empty cabin was making me nervous.

"Let's check it out," I said before I could lose my nerve. I fumbled what I hoped was the key—it had been on the key ring Rafe gave me—from my purse and advanced toward the cabin, my feet scuffing through layers of dried pine needles and crackly leaves. Reaching the door with Danielle just behind me, I discovered the key wouldn't be necessary: Someone had cut through the shank of the padlock that secured the cabin.

"That's not good," Danielle observed, peering over my shoulder.

I poked a finger at the door and it swung inward. Something rustled inside the cabin. I jumped back, bumping into Danielle. "What was that?" I whispered.

"A squirrel?" Danielle suggested, her voice thinner than usual.

"It sounded bigger than a squirrel." I eyed the crack between the door and the rough jamb. Nothing bounded, slithered, or hopped out. *Hmm.* "Stand back." Danielle complied with alacrity. Inching forward, I stiff-armed the door and jumped back as it smacked against the interior wall. Light illuminated the whole of the one-room cabin and I watched as a ringed, black-tipped tail disappeared out a shattered pane in the window at the back. "A raccoon," I said with a nervous giggle. "That's all it was. A raccoon."

Danielle giggled, too, and said, "I had a plush raccoon when I was little. Mr. Mufty."

"I remember. Whatever happened to him?"

She shrugged and nudged me over the threshold. My gaze swept a card table with two folding chairs pushed neatly underneath it, a double bed with rumpled sheets, a camp stove, a cupboard, and a pair of jeans hanging on one of three pegs above the bed. Rafe had brought a cooler with him as a fridge when he came to hunt and, I presumed, bed linens and such. A scrap of something shiny green caught my eye and I bent to pick up a granola bar wrapper. "This must be what attracted our Mr. Mufty," I said, showing it to Danielle.

"The appeal of this place escapes me," Danielle said, wrinkling her nose at a slightly musty smell. Raccoon scat, perhaps? I crossed to the window and glass shards sparkled at me from the floor. Had the raccoon punched out a pane to gain access? It didn't seem likely.

"Why would someone break a window and then cut the lock?" I asked. "Or vice versa?"

"Maybe it was two different someones," Danielle said. "And Someone Number Two came better prepared than Someone Number One. He brought a bolt cutter," she clarified when I looked confused.

"Or maybe it was high winds or a bear that broke the window," I said, finding it hard to believe there was a raft of people lining up to break into this primitive cabin. I could see there was nothing here—not so much as a notepad or receipt to hint at who had been here when or what they'd been doing. Maybe I could find a trash bag out back that would be full of clues.

"What, you think they have trash pickups here at 111 Back-of-Beyond Court every Tuesday?" Danielle said when I floated my great idea by her. "I'm sure Rafe packed out his trash and tossed it in some Dumpster in Capon Bridge, like at that seedy motel we passed."

"Maybe Victoria was less responsible," I countered.

Danielle rolled her eyes but dutifully traipsed after me as I went back outside and circled the cabin. Lots of vehicle tracks, but no trash bag. We studied the tracks and I thought it would be useful if a CSI team would come by with their plaster of paris, or whatever they used, and make casts so we could identify the cars and trucks that had been here since the last rain, which couldn't have been much more than four or five days ago, judging by the softness of the dirt and the mud lurking in shady spots. Danielle and I agreed there were at least three separate sets of tracks; two looked like they were from pickups or SUVs and one was smaller and narrower, more like the tracks my Beetle made.

"Hunting buddies?" Danielle suggested.

"Not a bad thought. Is anything in season at this time of year?"

"Beats me."

We stood in the clearing, studying the ground, and then looked at each other out of the corners of our eyes. "We really suck at this investigating thing, don't we?" I said.

"I think we'd better keep our day jobs," Danielle agreed and we laughed.

A twig cracked behind me and I started to turn, thinking our raccoon buddy might have come back looking for handouts, when a voice said, "Put your hands up and turn around slowly."

Danielle and I shot each other scared looks and raised our hands to ear level. We shuffled around to find ourselves facing an athletic-looking woman in a tight brown T-shirt, those camouflaged pants that the military wears, and high-top trainers. She had medium-length brown hair flecked with gray and the no-nonsense attitude of a prison warden or junior high teacher. She also had a gun, a very large pistol, pointed at me and Danielle.

"This is private property," the woman said, her gaze flicking over us, summing us up. "What are you doing here?" Her voice was crisp, authoritative, and I wondered if she was a ranger.

"Not hunting," I said, in case she thought we were shooting deer or turkeys out of season. Danielle gave me a funny look.

"I never thought you were," the woman said drily, looking me up and down.

What—my lemon-and-lime tiered skirt and matching peasant blouse didn't qualify as hunting togs? I narrowed my eyes at her. "This is my fiancé's cabin," I said, not mentioning the ex part or the dead part. "What are *you* doing here?"

"Oh, good Lord." She lowered the gun and I heard Danielle let out a deep breath. "You're Graysin? Anastasia Graysin?"

"Stacy," I said automatically. "Hey, wait, how do you know my name?"

"I'm an investigator," she said. "I work for Phineas Drake." The gun hand went behind her back and reappeared without the gun. She stepped toward me, hand outstretched. "Mary Pearce."

I shook her hand, introduced Danielle, and asked, "Where's your car?"

"On that gravel road, just past the turnoff for this place. I hiked up. I heard your car and stepped into the woods, thinking I'd see what you were up to." Mary's eyes scanned the clearing. "I can't say I found much."

"Did you cut the padlock?"

She shook her head. "Nope. It was like that when I got here. So was the window. That big coon gave me a scare, though, I can tell you. He huddled in a corner and growled at me the whole time I was in the cabin. Not that it took long to search it—there's squat-all in there."

"What were you looking for?"

"A lead on Victoria Bazán. Drake wants me to find her."

"Do you have any identification?" Danielle asked suddenly.

With an amused smile, Mary pulled a business card and a driver's license from one of the deep pockets on her camo pants. "Here." She handed them to Danielle, who studied them and gave the license back with a nod, passing me the business card. It read PEARCE PRIVATE IN-VESTIGATIONS and had the usual assortment of contact info.

"Have you got any leads on Victoria?" I asked.

Mary scratched at a mosquito bite on her arm. "Nothing definitive," she hedged. "You?"

I shook my head. "I haven't seen her since she ran off with my wallet Saturday night. Oh, if you'll be talking to Mr. Drake sometime soon, you might mention that someone set a fire in my dance studio last night."

"You think it was Victoria?"

The thought startled me. "It never crossed my mind."

There didn't seem to be much else to say, so I looked at Danielle and we moved toward the Volkswagen. "Want a lift back to your car?" I asked Mary.

She shook her head. "Nah. I might stick around here for a bit, see if anyone else shows up. Looks like the place has been busier than a costume store in October, so I might get lucky."

"You'll let me know if you find anything?"

"I'm sure Drake will be in touch."

Huh. I wondered if they taught that kind of hedging in PI school, along with how to pry info out of reluctant witnesses and padding expense accounts.

"Nice meeting you," Danielle said as we got in the car and started off. Rather than make an eight-point turn in the small clearing, I drove around the cabin and headed back down the one-lane road. Mary Pearce stood in one spot and watched us, not moving until after we were out of sight.

"Do you think she was on the up-and-up?" Danielle asked.

"She must be. How else would she know my name and Victoria's, not to mention Phineas Drake's?"

"I guess you're right." Danielle settled back into her seat and occupied herself trying to pick up a radio station. "There was just something about her."

"She was tough."

"Yeah."

"Maybe it was the gun."

"Maybe it was her pointing it at us."

We drove most of the rest of the way home in reflective silence. As we approached the outskirts of Alexandria, Danielle said, "I talked to Jonah."

My gaze flitted from the road to my sister's profile. It didn't reveal anything. "Good for you. And . . . ?"

"And he actually apologized."

"Probably scared you were going to report him for sexual harassment."

"No, he was really sorry. He said he kind of lost it

when his wife left him and that he didn't have a good excuse. He said it would never happen again."

I wasn't necessarily buying Jonah's "I see the error of my ways" routine, but I only said, "As long as you feel comfortable at the office again."

"I do," Danielle said, fiddling with the radio tuner. Country music blared out.

"It probably wouldn't hurt to have Coop pick you up from work one of these evenings and stage a makeout session on your desk or something."

"Sta-ceee!" She thwapped me and I grinned.

Chapter 18

After dropping Danielle at home in the early afternoon so she could change and go into work, having made a miraculous recovery, I sat at a stoplight and drummed my fingers on the steering wheel. I should go home and see what progress the floor refinisher and the cleaners were making, but the idea had little appeal. I decided now was as good a time as any to have a heart-to-heart with Solange about her interest in the studio. Accordingly, I flipped a U-ey at the light, to the accompaniment of honking horns, and headed to Pentagon City, the upscale mall just up Route 1 from Old Town, where Solange worked part-time at a department store makeup counter. I hoped she wouldn't be too busy to talk on a Tuesday afternoon.

I was in luck. When I got to the counter, Solange, wearing a pale pink smock and looking as disgustingly gorgeous as ever, was organizing makeup boxes in a bored way. She started when she saw me, then plastered a smile to her face. "Stacy! What are you doing here? Don't you need to be scrubbing smoke stains off the studio's walls or something? Such a shame!" Her sympathy was as fake as her smile.

"Cleaning service," I said briefly. "We'll be back in business late next week. And speaking of the business, where the hell do you get off trying to buy Rafe's half of it from Tav?"

Solange leaned forward and indicated an older woman at a nearby cosmetics counter. "That's my boss. I really can't stand here and chitchat. If you want to have a conversation, it has to look like I'm selling you something. I could give you a makeover. Heaven knows you could use one. You look like you've been digging ditches." She wrinkled her nose at my makeup-free face, tousled ponytail, and rumpled skirt.

"Oh, all right," I said, hitching myself up onto the black and chrome stool she indicated.

"We'll start with a cleansing routine," she said a bit louder, for the benefit of her boss, I assumed. Nudging a countertop mirror out of the way with her elbow, she set out a variety of bottles, pots, compacts, and pencils.

"Let's start with why you want to buy into the studio," I said from the corner of my mouth as she swabbed my skin with a soaked cotton ball. The chill was refreshing.

"Since I've been out of action with my ankle, I need a built-in client base to get me back on track," she said. "Graysin Motion's got it. And it's time I got my own place instead of playing second fiddle at someone else's studio. This way, I feel like I'm carrying on Rafe's legacy."

Gag me.

"Look up." After smoothing foundation over my face, she dotted concealer under my eyes and blended with a wedge-shaped sponge. "Quite the under-eye circles," she commented.

"It's been a rough week. You know Graysin Motion—"

"We'd have to change the name, of course."

Fury shimmered through me. She must have felt it, because she took a quick half step back. "But not right away. There is *some* name recognition for the studio in the ballroom dance world."

"You know Graysin Motion needs a male pro. Two women could never make a go of it."

"I've never had trouble attracting men," Solange said with a smirk, "and that includes male students."

"You know women make up at least three-quarters of a studio's client base and income," I insisted.

"So we'll hire a couple of male pros. I've got someone in mind."

"Graysin Motion barely supports the current staff. We can't both take enough salary to live off of and also pay for another male instructor on top of Maurice. My arrangement with Vitaly is stretching the studio's finances to the limit."

"Maybe you should get a part-time job," Solange said, gesturing with an eye shadow brush to the expanse of cosmetics counters with a shoe display peeking up behind the Chanel counter and lingerie visible just past Lancôme's GIFT WITH PURCHASE poster. "It's not the end of the world."

The idea caught me like a fist in the stomach. "I'm a ballroom dancer, not a store clerk," I blurted.

Solange's lips thinned and I thought hurt flickered in her eyes before she turned away to select a mascara wand.

"I'm sorry, Solange; I didn't mean it like that. It's just that I've worked too hard at making a go of Graysin Motion to go back to waiting tables"—been there, done that—"or walking dogs." Ditto.

"Close your eyes." She slicked liquid liner at the base of my lashes and swept shadow across my lid. "I'm sorry you're so negative about the idea of being partners. That's going to make things much more awkward."

I snapped my eyes open. "Awkward? How can you expect it to be anything *but* awkward, under the circumstances?"

"You mean me and Rafe?"

I nodded. "Are you going to use that?" The blush in her hand was a virulent shade of fuchsia.

"It goes on sheer. Trust me." She swirled the fat brush in the compact and leaned in to dust it across my cheeks. "Don't you think it's time for you to get past it, Stacy? I mean, it's the oldest story in the book: Boy meets girl, boy gets girl, boy moves on when girl doesn't meet his needs. In this day and age, with people living into their eighties, for God's sake, the whole concept of monogamy is slightly ridiculous, don't you think?"

"No."

She heaved a put-upon sigh. "That's the kind of attitude that's going to make it tough for us to run the studio together."

"We're not going to be running the studio together," I said, sliding off the stool. I didn't care if she was done with the "makeover" or not. "It's my studio. Where are you going to get the money to buy Tav out, anyway? Didn't you say you were broke, that you loaned your last couple thousand to Rafe?"

"I've got the money sorted," Solange said, unperturbed. "Did you want to purchase any of the products?"

I grudgingly bought an eyebrow pencil for three times what a similar product would have cost me at Target, and said good-bye, wondering about the self-satisfied smile on Solange's face. As I exited the store, I noticed a couple of older women giving me sidelong looks and felt like telling them it wasn't that weird for a young woman of employable age to be spending the afternoon in the mall. I wandered the mall, casually window-shopping, reluctant to leave the air-conditioned halls for the sweltering heat outdoors and equally reluctant to return home and confront the ruined studio. A teenage couple passed me and the boy nudged the girl, who glanced at me and sniggered. I looked at my blouse, worried I had splashed ketchup on it when eating lunch or something. Nada. Giving way to the inevitable, I made my feet point toward the garage exit. Two storefronts from the door, I caught a glimpse of myself in a boutique's mirror.

Gaah! Solange had made me up to look like a hag, or a cross-dressing hooker with no mirror. The foundation she'd used was two shades too dark for my skin and orangey, contrasting strangely with my pale neck. The "concealer" she'd used had actually darkened the circles under my eyes, aging me dreadfully. Liner winged in a wavy line toward my temples, and harshly drawn brows arched in half-moons over eyelids coated a metallic aqua. The garish blush burned in clownlike circles on the apples of my cheeks. No wonder people were giving me strange looks. Wishing I had a scarf in my purse, I loosened my hair from its ponytail so it fell curtainlike across my cheeks and then hurried to my car, grateful for the garage's dimness. Solange would get half my studio over my dead body. I'd go to Uncle Nico and beg him to buy Tav's share, promise him unlimited favors, before I let her set foot in my studio again.

*	*	*

I arrived home to find Maurice leaving a note on my back door. He waited while I parked the car and looked at me with concern when I approached.

"I'm not sure that's a good look for you, Anastasia," he said. "I can understand you need a change of pace after this past week, but perhaps something less . . . colorful?"

"Solange," I explained as I unlocked the door. "Just let me wash this off and I'll be right with you." Leaving him chuckling in the kitchen, I hurried to my bathroom and cold creamed the makeup off, leaving my cheeks scrubbed red and my eyes irritated. Too tired to care, I rejoined Maurice. He'd made tea and was seated at the kitchen table.

"You're a god," I told him, sinking into a chair and sipping the steaming tea. I choked and coughed, unprepared for the healthy slug of bourbon he'd doctored it with.

"You looked like you could use a pick-me-up."

"And how." I took a more cautious sip and looked at him. Calm and debonair as ever, he leaned back in his chair, long fingers wrapped around the warm mug.

"I stopped by to see how you are doing. It looks like they're making good progress on the studio." He tipped his chin toward the ceiling.

"Are they? I haven't been up there. I just couldn't face it. I saw it last night, after the firemen put the fire out, and looking at the floor, all crackled and blackened, I felt like someone had flayed me."

Concern lit Maurice's eyes. "It's ugly and frightening," he said. "Do the police have any idea who did it?"

"Lissy seems to think it might've been me, despite the fact I've got an alibi."

"The man's an utter fool. Do you think this is tied in with what happened last week?"

I snorted lightly, almost amused by the delicate way he referred to Rafe's death. "I don't see how."

"Maybe someone is set on forcing you out of business," Maurice said. "A competitor or someone with a grudge."

"Come on," I objected, pushing my empty mug aside. "The arson, maybe. But killing Rafe? It'd take a psycho ballroom dancer to think that was the best way to up his—or her—odds at a competition."

"I've met more than one psycho in my years on the ballroom circuit," Maurice said half-jokingly, "and people have killed for less understandable reasons. But that's not what I mean. What if someone has a grudge against you, personally, and is doing whatever he can to hurt you."

"Why not kill *me*, then?" A shiver tickled down my spine as I said it.

"It was a stupid idea," Maurice said, collecting the mugs and taking them to the sink. "I'd be happy to sleep here for a couple of nights, despite the smell"—he forced air noisily out of his large nose—"if you would feel more comfortable."

I was touched. "Thanks, Maurice," I said, rising to hug him. "If I get nervous, I can go to Danielle's or my mom's. But I appreciate the offer."

"I'll be back first thing tomorrow," he said, "and we can talk about where we're going to hold classes in the interim. The YMCA may have space we can use, and one of my ladies mentioned that her church would be happy to let us use their basement."

"You're approaching this a lot more intelligently

than I am," I told him ruefully. "I don't suppose you'd like to buy Rafe's share and be my new partner?"

"Alas, dear Anastasia," he said, "but no. I'm past the age of wanting the responsibilities that come with owning a business. Dancing and teaching—yes. Billing and recruiting students and worrying about insurance and taxes and payrolls—definitely no."

"It was just a thought."

I closed the door behind him.

The doorbell dinged at a ridiculously early hour the next morning—six thirty, I saw when I cracked an eye open. I pulled the sheets up over my head, ostrichlike, hoping whoever it was would go away. *Ding-dong! Ding-dong!* With a sigh, I flung my legs over the side of the bed, thrust my arms into the sleeves of my ratty green terry-cloth robe, and shambled toward the door. Peering through the peephole, I was surprised to see Taryn Hall and Sawyer Iverson standing there.

I pulled open the door. "Is anything wrong?" I asked. The fresh breath of morning wafted in.

"We came to say good-bye," Taryn said, and Sawyer nodded. "You've been so kind to us . . . well, we didn't want to disappear and not have you know what's going on."

"Come in."

They crossed the threshold and Sawyer looked around curiously.

"Coffee?" I offered. "It will only take me a moment to make some."

"No, thanks," Taryn said, patting her abdomen. "I'm off caffeine."

Remind me never to get pregnant if you have to give up coffee.

"Do you have a soda maybe?" Sawyer asked. "Mountain Dew?"

"Didn't you have some in the fridge upstairs?" I asked. When he nodded, I said, "Let's go up and get some."

I led the way up the staircase to the locked door leading to the studio. Undoing the dead bolt, I pushed it open. The smell of charred wood overlaid with cleaning solvents and sawdust smacked us.

"Shit!" Sawyer blurted. "Uh, sorry, Miss Stacy. What's that smell?"

"You didn't hear?" I told them about the fire. "The only thing damaged was the ballroom floor, so it's perfectly safe to be up here." I ducked into the bathroom and opened the fridge. It seemed less crowded than usual and I stared into it for a moment, the cool air chilling my bare feet, and realized all Vitaly's grapefruit juice was gone. *Huh.* I tried to remember if he'd taken them with him when he got sick. I didn't think so. I sighed. It must be time to post a little reminder about the honor system. Pulling out the lone Mountain Dew, I crossed the hall to where Taryn and Sawyer hovered on the ballroom's threshold, looking at the floor stripped mostly bare by the refinisher. It looked naked, defenseless without its shiny coats of polyurethane, and I hugged my robe more tightly around myself.

"Geez," Taryn said.

"You're lucky you didn't burn up in your sleep, Miss Stacy," Sawyer said, pulling at the hoop in his ear.

"Sawyer!" Taryn punched his shoulder.

"What? All I said was—"

"Let's go back down," I said, interrupting the squabble and handing Sawyer his soda.

The teens sat side by side at the kitchen table, perched on the edges of their chairs, obviously ready to go. I busied myself dumping Kona coffee into the machine and adding water. When the strong scent began to filter through the room, I joined them and said, "So, what's this about good-bye?"

"I'm taking Taryn down to South Carolina today," Sawyer explained. "She's going to live with the people who are adopting the baby until it's born."

"What's your dad think of that?" I asked Taryn.

She shook her head and I wasn't sure if she meant he didn't know or he wasn't in favor of the plan.

"He kicked her out," Sawyer said, putting an arm around her shoulders.

"I think he was really hurt that I thought he might have killed Rafe," Taryn said in a small voice. "When we got home from the competition, he marched me down to the Holborns' house—they live down the block—and Mr. Holborn told me they were playing poker the night Rafe got killed, until past midnight. Daddy told me I was disloyal, and a liar. He called me an 'ungrateful whore' and . . . and—" She began to weep quietly and Sawyer stroked her hair.

I sighed inwardly, not knowing what to say. I looked at Sawyer. "And you?"

"I'll come back and finish high school. I graduate in June, you know. Then I'll get a summer job in Sumter—my folks are okay with that—and then we'll see."

"I need to finish high school; I'm hoping I can earn my GED over the summer," Taryn said. "And then we both want to go to college, but I won't have any money, so I may have to work awhile first." The resolute look on her face made me think she'd carry through.

"We're going to look into all the financial aid options," Sawyer put in. "And my folks say they might be able to help Taryn some. They really like her and they're pissed about the way her dad's treated her."

"Marriage?"

They both shook their heads. "Not now," Taryn said, reaching up to squeeze Sawyer's hand where it rested on her shoulder. "We're too young. Maybe later." She gave the youth a shy smile.

"Well, if you end up back in this area, you could always come teach at Graysin Motion," I said.

"Really?" Taryn's eyes sparkled. "Thanks, Miss Stacy."

Sawyer rose and helped Taryn to her feet. A lump formed in my throat at the sight of his tenderness with her.

I walked them to the door. "Good luck." I hugged Taryn tightly. Sawyer, looking teenage-boy awkward, leaned down to give me a hug. I waved from the portico as they climbed into Sawyer's Honda and drove away. Somehow feeling both sad and inspired, I headed back into the house to get dressed, giving a cheery wave to a neighbor heading off to cubicle hell.

After showering, dressing, and breakfasting, I marched upstairs, determined to get some work done in my office. I had students to contact, arrangements to make for temporary lesson locations, calls to make related to Blackpool, and a host of other tasks I'd ditched yesterday for the abortive trip to West Virginia. Throwing open the windows in my office, I hesitated only briefly before crossing the sanded floor of the ballroom to open all the windows in there, too. At one window, the sheers were nothing but burned strips of fabric and I pulled them down easily, leaving them in an ashy pile on the floor. The familiar scents of Old Town—car exhaust, the Potomac, and the sweet fragrance of blooming fruit trees—began to chase away the odors of fire and restoration.

A clanging noise behind me made me whirl, but it was only the cleaning team clanking their metal buckets up the stairs. "You need to see about the lock," the white-overalled supervisor said after we exchanged good mornings. "It doesn't latch properly."

"That's because the fire department had to bust the door in," I said. "I'll call a locksmith today. Thanks."

With a nod, she herded her team into the ballroom while I returned to my office and got to work. I took a break at noon to attend my ballet class—rarely had I needed to dance more—and was walking home, pleasantly tired and sore, when a familiar white limousine glided to the curb beside me. Phineas Drake. The rear window purred down and I was surprised to see not the lawyer, but Victoria Bazán.

Chapter 19

I stopped dead, causing the man behind me to bump into me. He shouldered past with an annoyed grunt.

"Miss Graysin. Stacy," Victoria said. "Do you have time to talk to me for a minute? Mr. Drake loaned me his limo so that we could have a chat."

"You stole my wallet," I said from the sidewalk.

"I'm sorry." Her dark eyes pleaded with me.

"Oh, all right," I said ungraciously, curiosity more than anything else propelling me to the limo's door.

Victoria sat on the back bench usually occupied by Drake, dressed in jeans and a white shirt, her dark hair loose. A suited man I didn't recognize sat beside her, short hair and a stern face making him look like Hollywood's idea of a federal agent. He gave me a sharp glance as I climbed in, then returned to contemplating the view out the side window.

"My minder," Victoria said.

That didn't exactly clarify things, but I sat opposite them, feeling compelled to apologize for my sweaty leotard and tights. "Ballet class," I explained.

Victoria waved my apology aside. An awkward silence fell, as if she didn't know where to start, so I prompted: "You were going to tell me what the heck is going on. How did you hook up with Drake?"

She laughed mirthlessly. "He caught up with me last night when I tried to use your credit card at a hotel in Richmond. His investigator, a woman named Mary—"

"Pearce. We've met."

"She found me and . . . kidnapped me!"

"Really?" I said, politely disbelieving.

"Well," Victoria amended, "she fingerprinted me and made me go with her to see Phineas. He's something else," she said, admiration and disgruntlement mixed up in her voice.

It hadn't taken her long to get on first-name terms with the lawyer, I noted. "What did he do?"

"He told me that my fingerprints were on the gun that killed Rafe—"

"What!"

"Stop interrupting," she said pettishly. "I guess I didn't tell you the whole story the other night. Rafe tried to give me a gun on Wednesday when he drove me up to the cabin. He handed it to me, so my prints were on it, but I didn't want it, so I gave it back to him."

"Really?" I let my disbelief bleed into my voice.

"Yes, really!" Her voice dropped to a whisper. "I was afraid. Afraid I'd kill Héctor. I didn't want to be tempted."

"How did Phineas Drake know your fingerprints were on the gun?"

"He faxed my prints to the police."

I was sure that even if her prints hadn't been on the gun, he'd have found a way to incriminate Victoria anyway. Phineas wasn't above lying or manufacturing evidence, in my opinion. But Victoria had lied, too, at least by omission. I didn't know whether or not to believe her, so I made a "go on" motion.

"Phineas said he could use the prints on the gun to prove I'd killed Rafe. I wouldn't end up in jail because of diplomatic immunity, but I'd be deported to Argentina, where Héctor would find me within minutes. I'd be dead within two hours of landing at the airport."

"I'm assuming there's an 'or' in here."

She nodded. "Or I could talk to your DEA"—she nodded toward her minder—"and provide details about Héctor's business dealings, and they would help me reestablish myself somewhere else, maybe in Canada or Australia."

"The witness protection program?"

"Something like that."

"So your husband's a drug dealer?"

"He has many business interests," Victoria waffled. "He—" She stopped as her minder shook his head sharply. "You're safer not knowing the details."

The sincerity in her voice made me shiver. That's all I needed—an Argentinean drug lord thinking I was clued in on his smuggling routes or something. "I don't want the details," I said hastily. "What does all this have to do with me, other than I assume you're going to return my wallet?"

"Phineas has your stuff," Victoria said. "Part of the deal is that he's sharing my fingerprints with the police. Since I can't be tried here, anyway, and I'll be set up somewhere else, it can't hurt me and it will get you off the hook for Rafe's murder."

I leaned back against the cushy leather, stunned. "But . . . did you kill Rafe?"

"Of course not!" Victoria's eyes flashed.

"If the police think you did, they'll stop hunting for the real killer."

"Phineas seemed more concerned with ensuring the police don't arrest you than with hunting down the murderer," Victoria said.

"So the murderer gets to wander around, scot-free? I don't think so." I didn't try to hide my indignation.

Victoria shrugged. "Take it up with Drake."

"I certainly will."

The minder tapped his watch and Victoria grimaced. "Time's up." She looked forlorn, and I tried to place myself in her shoes: betraying her husband to the cops, going into exile alone, leaving behind her family and friends. Her situation had echoes of Taryn's, but at least Taryn had Sawyer. Both women were object lessons on how one bad decision—not pausing for a condom, saying "I do" with the wrong man—could totally alter the course of your life.

"Take care," I told Victoria.

She smiled ruefully. "Always."

As I stood in a semicrouch to climb out the door the chauffeur had opened, the man beside Victoria spoke for the first time. "Is it true you're a champion ballroom dancer?" he asked, leaning forward to look at me around Victoria.

Startled, I nodded. He had rather attractive blue eyes when he wasn't concentrating on looking grim and threatening.

"Cool. Can my girlfriend and I come for lessons? She

wants to learn the West Coast Swing like they do on *Ballroom with the B-Listers*."

"Sure," I said, bemused. I pulled a slightly dented business card from my bag. "Here."

Alone on the sidewalk, I hitched my dance bag onto my shoulder and headed for home, intending to have a heart-to-heart with Mr. Phineas Drake.

Mr. Drake was in court, his secretary politely informed me when I called. She'd let him know I was interested in a meeting. I could hear "brush off" in her voice, but I thanked her and hung up gently, rather than slamming the phone down like I wanted to. Picking the phone up again immediately, I dialed Tav Acosta's number.

"I just talked to Victoria Bazán," I announced before he could even say hello. "Drake has set it up so the police think she killed your brother, but I don't think she did, so the killer's going to get away with it."

To his credit, Tav didn't say, "What the hell are you babbling about?" Instead, he said, "I am on my way over. Give me forty-five minutes."

Feeling antsy, I returned to the studio, where the whir of the refinisher's sander practically deafened me. The cleaning crew had gone and I was impressed with how much lighter the walls looked, now that they had removed the film of smoke and chemicals. Spotting me, the refinisher shut down his machine and pulled off the white mask that covered the lower half of his face. "It's coming along," he observed. "I'll do the first coat of polyurethane tomorrow and another couple coats by the end of the week. Let it cure over the weekend and you should be good to go early next week."

"Thanks," I said, relieved that we could resume classes in the ballroom so soon.

"Oh, here." He dug in his pocket. "I found this wedged between the baseboard and the floor when I removed the baseboards. It probably got pretty wet, but it doesn't look burned. I don't know if you can get anything off it, though." He handed me a small red item with a metal piece at one end.

It took me half a second to recognize it as a flash drive. My fingers closed over it. "Thanks," I managed.

I was sitting at my desk, newly showered and changed, turning the flash drive over and over in my hand, when Tav arrived. I hadn't worked up the nerve to see if there was anything on it, and I hadn't yet called Sherry Indrebo . . . I wasn't sure why. Maybe because it felt like a last link with Rafe; he must have had it on him the night he was killed. That alone made me think I should be careful with it. I slid it into my jeans pocket and rose to greet Tav. He kissed me on both cheeks, Continental style, and a little buzz hummed through me.

"What is this about Victoria?" he asked.

We sat on the love seat, where I could look down at the street, and I told him everything Victoria had told me. I ended my summary: "So she's off to Canada or someplace and Bazán gets to run around doing his thing until the feds get together enough evidence to throw him out of the country, I guess, or turn him over to your country's authorities, and whoever killed Rafe gets a 'get out of jail free' card."

"Victoria's fingerprints were on the gun?" Tav frowned.

"Yes, but I kind of believed her explanation. I don't think she killed him."

Tav tapped his fingertips together. "I have known her family a long time. It is hard for me to believe she could shoot Rafe in cold blood, or to believe that he would do anything that would prompt her to kill him in the heat of the moment."

"If Victoria didn't kill him, then who did? Bazán?"

"Possibly." Tav nodded, and sunlight streaming through the window made his hair glint blue-black. "Say Bazán had some inkling that Victoria had turned to Rafael for help. He comes here, looking to get the truth out of Rafael. Rafael feels threatened—"

"Who wouldn't?" I put in, remembering Bazán's quiet menace.

"—and pulls the gun. Either they struggle for it and it goes off accidentally—"

I snorted and finished, "Or Bazán grabs it from him and kills him."

We fell silent, picturing the scene. After a moment, Tav said, "Is Bazán the only one with a motive for killing Rafael?"

"I liked Leon Hall for it, because he thought Rafe got his daughter pregnant. But it turns out he's got an alibi." I told Tav about Taryn and Sawyer stopping by on their way to South Carolina.

"What kind of man kicks a sixteen-year-old out of the house?" he asked, his face darkening. "Not one who deserves the title 'father.' "

"And I wondered—" I stopped.

"What?"

I told him the questions Mark Downey had raised in my mind with his behavior at the competition.

"I met him, yes? The man with the light brown hair?" I nodded.

Tav looked doubtful. "He seemed intelligent; surely he would realize, since you and Rafael were going to sever your partnership after the competition in England anyway, that killing my brother would be an unnecessary risk. Did many people know you and Rafael were splitting up your dance partnership?"

"Everyone," I said, impressed and relieved by his logic. "And there could be someone else." I fingered the flash drive through the denim of my pocket. "I'm not sure what Rafe's relationship with Sherry Indrebo really was. The floor refinisher found a flash drive. I think it's the one we were looking for, the one Sherry wanted me to find." I pulled it out of my pocket. "Rafe must have had it with him that night."

Tav took it from me. "What is on it?"

I shook my head. "I don't know. Maybe nothing, what with the fire and the water and all. And it doesn't have its cap."

Eagerness lit his eyes. "We can check." He stood in one fluid motion and moved toward Rafe's computer.

"Are you sure—?" I didn't know why I was so hesitant, why I felt like Pandora about to open the fateful box.

"Why not?" He powered up the computer and tapped his fingers impatiently as the machine booted. I moved to peer over his shoulder as he slid the thumb drive into a USB port. He double-clicked on the drive's icon. I held my breath.

An error message popped up. I let my breath ease out as Tav's shoulders sagged slightly. He switched the flash drive to another port with the same result. "I guess it is damaged," he said finally. Pulling the drive out of the port, he pressed it back into my palm, his fingers warm on my skin. I slid the drive into my jeans pocket.

"That's that, then," I said, partially relieved that we hadn't accessed incriminating documents or photos.

"Maybe not," Tav said thoughtfully. "Congresswoman Indrebo does not know the device is damaged. If you told her you found it . . ."

"I could—what? Trick her into saying something incriminating? I just can't see her shooting Rafe. Besides, she was at a fund-raiser that night. Dozens of people saw her, Detective Lissy told me."

"There is that," Tav admitted. "All right, then, we will focus on Bazán."

"We?" Did I look like Emma Peel or that cop Grace Something played by Holly Hunter? My hair hadn't looked that ratty since I was twelve.

He gave me a serious look. "The police will stop investigating as soon as your Phineas Drake hands over Victoria. They will mark the case 'closed' and move on."

"Maybe that's for the best," I heard myself say. Now that I wasn't a suspect . . .

"You do not mean that," Tav said, his brows snapping together.

I sighed. "No, I guess I don't. Sure, let's go get Bazán. What did you have in mind—rappelling over the embassy walls at midnight, kidnapping him under the noses of the guards, and waterboarding him until he confesses?"

Tav grinned. "You have been watching too many spy movies. I thought we would invite him for a conversation, someplace public, and see what he has to say."

"He won't come."

"He might if he thought you could tell him something about Victoria."

"Like what? I'm not going to rat her out and tell him she's working with the DEA."

"No, but you could tell him about searching Rafael's cabin, or maybe that she used your credit card in Richmond. What could that hurt?"

I gave it some thought. I didn't see what it could hurt, but I had no faith that I had thought of all the eventualities. I told Tav that and he laughed. "Sure, you laugh," I said, "but my dad tried to teach me chess when I was younger and I was always lousy at it . . . I never thought far enough ahead. 'If I put my rook here, he'll move his knight there, and I'll take his pawn, and he'll . . .' *Blecch*!" I shuddered at the memory.

"Well, I am pretty sure Bazán is not a chess grand master, so it should go just fine," Tav said.

I smacked him with a throw pillow.

We agreed Tav would approach Bazán and he left, saying he was close to signing papers on a new import venture. "It might require me to spend more time in Washington," he said.

He seemed to be watching for my reaction and even though I felt a bubble of anticipation well up, I kept my voice even as I said, "You should hang on to Rafe's condo, then."

I met up with Maurice in late afternoon to teach a class in the basement of the Presbyterian church one of his students attended. With tables folded and stacked against the wall, the linoleum-floored space worked well enough and I left at the end of class thinking we might have picked up some new students from the congregation. That was good since my voice mail held several calls from students commiserating about the fire and saying they hadn't intended to take more classes, anyway. I felt a momentary flutter of panic at the financial abyss gaping in front of Graysin Motion, but pushed it aside. The last message on my voice mail was from Vitaly, saying he would meet me at the studio tomorrow for a practice session. "We are needing many more practicings before Blackpool," he reminded me. As if I needed reminding.

My phone rang as I deleted Vitaly's message. "Bazán has agreed to meet," Tav said. "He is on his way to the consulate in San Francisco and says he will give us ten minutes if we meet him at the airport."

"Now?" I felt flustered, unprepared.

"Now."

Chapter 20

I arrived at Reagan National Airport twenty minutes later and sprinted up from the Metro to the National Hall, which was crowded with shops, restaurants, and travelers in varying stages of excitement, frustration, and bored resignation. Turning right, I found the bookstore where Tav had said we'd meet Bazán. I spotted Bazán immediately, browsing a rack of nonfiction. A dark-haired young man fidgeted at his side and I pegged him as an assistant of some kind. Tav didn't seem to be here yet, and I didn't want to approach Bazán alone. I was about to phone Tav when Bazán looked around and saw me, beckoning me over. He then said something to the aide or flunky and the young man scuttled off as I approached.

Bazán raised the book he'd been examining. "Have you read *This Republic of Suffering*, Miss Graysin? Or may I call you Stacy?"

"Sure," I said. "And, no, I haven't read it. I'm more of a fiction reader." Truth to tell, I wasn't much of an anything reader, outside of ballroom dance publications and the occasional fashion mag. A book about suffering didn't exactly sound like the upbeat and escapist fare I preferred on the rare occasions when I bought a book.

"It's written by the president of Harvard University," he said. "It's about how the unprecedented number of deaths in your Civil War changed the nation. Do you do much thinking about death, Stacy?"

Not until recently. "No."

His dark eyes studied my face. "You should."

Why did that sound like a threat? And where the hell was Tav? This meeting was his idea.

"Death comes to us all. And, despite the author's contention that a massive number of deaths in a short period presents special challenges for a nation, it probably doesn't matter much to the individual whether he—or she—dies alone and unnoticed by history or as part of a mass die-off that history notes, like the Black Death, the Holocaust, or war." He slotted the book back onto the shelf.

"Aren't you going to get that?"

"I've read it." He faced me squarely and I felt like I was confronting a wall or some other immovable object. A boulder, perhaps. A muscle twitched at the corner of his eye, making me wonder if he was nervous or stressed. "Where is my wife?"

Mindful of Tav's instructions, I said, "I don't know where she is right now, but she tried to use my credit card at a hotel in Richmond last night. The credit card company called me."

His brows drew together. "Richmond? What in the world would she be doing in Richmond?"

A Japanese man in a suit jostled me as he reached for the latest Lee Child thriller. I shrugged. "I have no idea," I said. Not sure how else to keep the conversation going,

I added, "I went out to Rafe's cabin, where Victoria stayed, to see if I could find anything."

"And?" Anticipation lit his dark eyes.

"Someone had searched the place. Maybe a couple of someones."

"My men found nothing when they went out there," he said, waving a dismissive hand. "In fact, I can hardly believe Victoria stayed there, if what my men said about the place is true. She's what you Americans call 'high maintenance.' Wooden cabins with no electricity are not her style."

I was disappointed with how easily he admitted to searching the cabin. He didn't sound like a man with anything to hide. Something over my shoulder caught his attention and I turned to follow his gaze, hoping to see Tav. Bazán's aide stood at the door, pointing to his watch.

"I must catch my flight," Bazán said, shifting his weight to move past me.

"Wait!" I put a hand on his arm, feeling the slabs of muscle even through his suit. My mind revved as I sought desperately for some way to jolt him into betraying himself, into telling me the truth about the night Rafe died. "The police found Victoria's fingerprints on the gun that killed Rafe," I blurted.

He froze in place and I could feel the shock run through him, an involuntary tremor in his muscles. A split second later he surprised me with a bark of laughter. "Ha! So Victoria killed him? I could have told him not to turn his back on her. That woman would slip a knife between your ribs as soon as kiss you." Shaking my hand off his arm, he straightened his sleeve. "I'll have someone show her photo around Richmond, but she's probably long gone from there. I can make it worth your while to let me know if Victoria tries to use your credit card again. Call me." Without waiting for me to reply, he strode toward his assistant and they headed for the security checkpoint.

I immediately phoned Tav, but got his voice mail. Hoping he'd still show up, I browsed the books, trying to decide if I'd learned anything from Bazán. His shock when I told him about Victoria's fingerprints on my gun almost convinced me he hadn't killed Rafe. Or maybe he was surprised because he *had* killed Rafe without knowing Victoria had previously handled the gun. I tried to piece together a timeline.

If Victoria was telling the truth, Rafe tried to give her my gun the afternoon he died. She handled it, getting her prints on it. Bazán could have discovered she was gone that evening and guessed she was with Rafe, either because he'd had her followed or because he knew about their prior relationship. Heck, Victoria could even have told him—in a note?—that she was leaving him for Rafe. He confronted Rafe at the studio that night, I theorized. Rafe pulled out my gun, Bazán wrested it from him and shot him. Maybe his prints were on the gun, too, or maybe he'd had the foresight to wear gloves. Or maybe Bazán was right and Victoria really had done it. My head ached. I rested my forehead briefly on the book turned face out on the shelf in front of me. Straightening, I shined the cover guiltily with my shirttail, hoping I hadn't gotten sweat or makeup on it. It was a mystery by someone named Brad Parks and the cover intrigued me. On impulse, I took it to the cashier. Paying for the book, I looked around one last time for Tav, and then headed for the Metro.

My phone rang just before I got on the escalator and I stepped away from it to answer. Tav greeted me with apologies, told me the Metro car he'd been on had stopped underground for no discernible reason, and he hadn't been able to call me. He sounded frustrated. "Did you see Bazán?"

"Oh, yeah." I gave him the *Reader's Digest* version of our conversation.

"So we are no further forward then we were," he said, sighing. "And if Bazán is leaving town, who knows when we will get the chance to speak with him again."

A woman edged past me onto the escalator, pushing a stroller with a toddler in it, and juggling a slice of pizza on a paper tray, a can of soda, a diaper bag, and a rolling suitcase. "Let me help you," I said. "Gotta go," I told Tav when the woman smiled gratefully and passed me the diaper bag and pizza.

The Metro was crowded with late rush hour travelers and I had to stand all the way to my stop. I'd bobbled the pizza on the ride down the escalator and gotten a smear of pepperoni grease on my blouse so I smelled like a pizzeria. Trudging down the hot sidewalks to my house, I greeted my quiet entryway with relief and headed to the kitchen to sponge at the orangey stain on my shirt. I gave up and stripped it off, tossing it on the laundry room floor. Anxious to see if the refinisher had made more progress, I headed upstairs after grabbing a clean blouse out of the dryer. I had it halfway buttoned when I reached the top of the stairs and heard faint strains of quickstep music and a woman's voice saying, "The lock-step should go like this."

Solange.

Maurice must have let her in; he'd had a private session scheduled for earlier this afternoon. Furious that she had the nerve—the gall!—to waltz in and use my studio after all that had happened, I banged through the door and stomped to the small studio. The door stood open and I reached down and unplugged the stereo. The couple stuttered to a stop when the music died, Solange facing me.

"What the hell are you doing here?" I spat. "Out. Now."

"My partner and I are getting in some rehearsal time," she said, not one whit embarrassed by my appearance. "And since we're—I'm—going to be part-owner of the studio soon, it seemed foolish to wait on all that paperwork. That look's a little blatant, don't you think?" She nodded at my partially buttoned shirt, which, I saw, was displaying way too much cleavage and half of my sheer, flesh-colored bra.

My fingers fumbled with the buttons as my stomach roiled at the thought of sharing the studio with Solange. I couldn't do it. If Tav sold out to her I'd start over again, change the name . . . anything rather than work with the scheming bitch.

Solange's partner turned around and I gasped. "Mark?" My hands dropped to my sides.

Mark Downey's gaze grazed my chest and then he tilted his chin up as if daring me to say something. "Now that Solange's ankle is doing better, she and I have entered the Emerald Ball in LA next month—too bad it's too late for an invitation to Blackpool this year—and we need a place to practice. Surely you wouldn't be so petty—"

Oh, yes I would. I was prepared to scale new heights of pettiness, not that I thought it was petty to kick this conniving couple out of my dance studio. My mind snagged on something Solange had said. "What did you mean 'we' are going to be part-owners of the studio?"

For the first time she looked flustered, her eyes darting from me to Mark. "I just meant that we—you and I—were going to be partners."

"No, you didn't." I advanced on her.

"We might as well tell her," Mark said, stepping into my path. He looked smug. "I'm Solange's financial backer. We're going in together to buy Rafe's share. We weren't going to say anything until after it was a done deal—I was afraid you'd try to put a wrench in it since you didn't seem to want me involved—but what can you do, after all? Solange got a list of all your students and their contact info—you really ought to practice better computer security—and we've already talked to some of them."

"That's what you were doing in my office?" I asked Solange. "Stealing our client list?"

She looked furious with Mark for mentioning it, but nodded curtly.

Another thought came to me. "You went to Rafe's, too, didn't you, to search his laptop? The day after he died?" I suppose I shouldn't be surprised that he'd given her a key.

Her eyes narrowed. "That was you that came in? Shit, you almost gave me a heart attack."

Mark tossed a lock of limp hair out of his eyes, reclaiming my attention. I couldn't believe I'd danced with him, taught him for three years, and I hadn't seen what he was really like. This was turning into a nightmare. "You'll be sorry you passed up the chance to partner with me," he said in a low voice.

Something in his eyes made me back up a step and a horrifying thought came to me. "I'm only sorry I ever accepted you as a student. You can do better, Solange," I said.

"I've been out of action too long with my damned ankle," she said, rotating it. "The established male pros are already committed to other partners. I think Mark is worth taking a chance on." She sent him a smile.

"You'll be taking a chance, all right," I said, narrowing my eyes. "He shot Rafe and poisoned Vitaly in order to become my partner. Now he's using you to—"

"You're insane," Mark said. "Don't listen to her, Solange. She's losing it."

He sounded confident, but a furtive look in his eyes convinced me I was on the right track. "Did the police check your alibi for the night Rafe was shot? Probably not, because they were convinced I did it. And I'll bet they find your fingerprints on the grapefruit juice bottles—"

"I got rid—" Mark stopped himself, but it was too late.

I think my mind had made the connection between Vitaly's sudden illness and the missing grapefruit bottles subconsciously. Someone—Mark—had deliberately removed them after Vitaly fell ill. "You did . . . you killed Rafe."

"I was thrilled when someone bumped him off, but it wasn't me," he said. "You should have turned to me then, let me help you through the rough time, taken me on as your partner. I wanted to be there for you. But, no. You paired up with Voloshin. So I put a little laxative in his juice. Big deal! I thought with him out of action, you'd surely ask me to fill in. But he didn't stay down long enough. And then, with the fire, I thought you'd be forced to turn to me for help to keep the studio afloat. I was going to come to you in a couple of days and offer to pay for the repairs. I knew how happy you'd be. Stacy, I love you—just give me a chance." He lunged forward and grasped my hands, a pleading look on his face. "We've had a good thing going for three years. Don't throw it away because I made a little mistake."

"We haven't had anything going, Mark!" I exclaimed, trying to free my hands. "You were my student. That's all."

"I could feel more than that when we danced," he insisted, drawing me closer. His warm breath fanned my cheek. "You deny it, but you felt something for me. The way you pressed against me, the way your hand clasped mine. If it hadn't been for Acosta—"

"You're totally delusional," I said. "Let me go!" I struggled against him, but he was far stronger than I was and caught me in a bear hug with my hands trapped to my sides. I whipped my knee up, aiming for his groin, but only smacked his thigh because he held me too close. He let out a soft *uh*, and shifted position slightly. I stomped on his foot, but my espadrille made little impact.

"Don't make fun of me," he growled. His lips made a slimy trail up my neck. "You can love me back if you just try. I—" His grip suddenly loosened and he staggered back from me, then dropped to his knees. Blood dripped from the back of his head and he groggily reached a hand to his skull.

Solange stood behind him, dance pump gripped tightly in her hand, the heel bloodied from where she'd whacked it against Mark's head.

"Thanks," I said, gasping.

"The ick factor was just getting too high," she said with a grimace. "Who knew he was a psychotic stalker? I guess now I'll have to hold auditions for another partner."

"Don't think saving me means you get to keep dancing here," I said, dialing 911, "because I have a hard-and-fast policy against client-stealing, fiancé-poaching sneaks, even when they save me from certifiable whack-jobs."

Uniformed police showed up quickly and seemed inclined to arrest Solange for assaulting Mark Downey. I told them she had hit him to save me and suggested that Mark had killed Rafe. That got them on the radio to summon Detective Lissy, who arrived as the EMTs were carting Mark off to the hospital for some stitches and observation. He looked even more annoyed than usual, and kept a hand pressed to his side as if he had a stitch. He talked to Solange first and finally let her go.

"If I'd known it was going to be this much hassle, I'd just have let the nutcase have her," I heard her grumble as she descended the stairs barefoot, the police having confiscated her one shoe as evidence.

Detective Lissy approached me where I sat slumped against the hall wall, guarded by a policewoman assigned to make sure Solange and I didn't confer about our stories. "Miss Graysin," he said, looking down at me.

If he thought I was going to leap to my feet at his appearance, he had another think coming. I was too darned tired. I waited for him to continue.

"When I got to work today, I had one viable suspect for Rafe Acosta's murder. You. Now I have three. How do you explain that?"

"Just lucky?"

He burped and rubbed at his side. "That's not how I would characterize it. I'm not happy with this case. No, not happy at all. Fingerprint evidence appeared this morning, suggesting a certain Victoria Bazán was involved. Ms. Bazán, I'm subsequently informed, is uncontactable and untouchable for a variety of reasons I won't bother you with. Despite not being happy with how this evidence turned up, I'm on the verge of closing the case when you call to say you've been attacked by Acosta's real murderer. Miss Dubonnet supports your contention that Mark Downey attacked you and seemed to have a 'bizarre fixation' on you—one she was at a loss to explain since you're, and I quote, 'a passably pretty, third-rate dancer'—that might have included trying to get rid of your dance partners." He shook his head, bemused.

"He admitted he tried to poison Vitaly." At his puzzled look, I clarified. "Voloshin. My new dance partner. Mark spiked his juice with something. And he set the fire. He said it was so I'd realize how much I needed him, but I think that was about revenge because I told him we weren't going to be dance partners."

Rubbing a hand down his face, Lissy said, "Did he cop to Acosta's killing, too, while he was in confession mode? Or the gang killing near the airport two nights ago? Maybe the convenience store robbery on Prince? We've got plenty of open cases—he can have his pick."

The sarcasm in Lissy's voice didn't faze me. "No, just Vitaly and the fire. You'll have to solve the rest of those cases on your own. But he must have killed Rafe, don't you think?"

"Why not admit it, then, since he seemed to want you to know how far he'd go to win your affections?"

I gave him an incredulous look. "He's loony, not stupid. I'm betting murder carries a lot longer prison term than arson does."

Lissy sighed. "Okay, Miss Graysin. Come see us in the morning to sign your statement. Do me a favor and leave that Drake character at home. You're no longer a suspect. I think we'll hang this one on the Bazán woman, but I'll look into Downey's alibi for the night of Acosta's murder and follow up a little more before we close this."

He held down a hand and, after a surprised moment, I took it, letting him haul me to my feet. "Thanks."

He burped, nodded, and strode away, leaving me to stagger to the interior door, lock it carefully behind me, and stumble down the stairs. I was beyond exhausted, but I felt compelled to shower before falling into bed, needing to get the scent and feel of Mark Downey off of me. I began to shake under the stream from the shower head as I considered what might have happened if Solange hadn't been there. Tears joined the droplets of water streaming down my face as I tried to come to terms with the fact that I'd liked Mark Downey, that I'd spent a couple of hours a week with him for three years and never realized he had a screw loose. Maybe several screws. What did that say about my judgment?

Hair still damp, I tumbled into bed and fell asleep almost instantly, only to dream of Rafe facing a firing squad made up of the Bazáns, Solange, Mark, Sherry Indrebo and various other students, Maurice, and, most disturbingly, me.

Chapter 21

The next morning I awoke feeling unrested and grumpy. When I picked my jeans off the floor from where I'd dropped them last night, Sherry's thumb drive fell out of the pocket. Picking it up, I flipped it in one hand, tempted to just toss it in the trash. After all, it didn't have anything on it anymore. Instead, I decided to send Sherry an e-mail letting her know I'd found it so she could pick it up if she wanted to. She could take the thing to a computer guru and hope he could resuscitate her documents if the data on it was important to her. I shot her a quick e-mail from the laptop while my coffee dripped, not mentioning that I knew the drive was fried; she didn't need to know Tav and I had tried to peek at her documents.

After breakfast, I called a locksmith to get the locks changed and agreed to pay extra if he came today. Then I called Tav and told him about the scene with Mark Downey. "I'm ninety-eight percent sure Mark killed Rafe," I finished.

"Why would this Downey be at the studio that late?" Tav sounded thoughtful, not argumentative, and I could picture the line between his brows as he tried to puzzle his way through the details.

I shrugged, even though he couldn't see me. "Looking for me? Or maybe he planned it and hung around waiting for an opportunity to get Rafe alone."

"Then why not wait at his condo? And if he planned it, would he not bring his own weapon?"

His points were good ones, but I didn't want to acknowledge that because I wanted this whole thing over and done with, closed, finished. "I don't know," I said grumpily. "He could've had a knife with him but decided the gun would do the job better when Rafe pulled it out."

"That is probably what happened," Tav agreed after a short pause. "At any rate, Detective Lissy called earlier to say I was free to return to Argentina, so I have booked a flight for tomorrow afternoon. Before I leave, we have some things to discuss about the business. Does this evening work for you?"

"Sure," I said around the lump in my throat. I hung up and swallowed hard, not sure if I was choked up because Tav was leaving or because I was worried about what he planned to do with his share of Graysin Motion. He sounded like he'd made a decision and I wondered what I'd do if he told me he was accepting Solange's offer. On the whole, I thought I'd be better off with Uncle Nico as a—hopefully—silent partner. Or possibly I'd mistaken my life's vocation and I should look into flipping burgers for a living; surely it was less frustrating than running a dance studio. But I wasn't a uniform person—I couldn't imagine wearing the same thing day in and day out—so that left out fast-food worker, cop, firefighter, and postal employee. Danielle could get me started on the path to career success as a union organizer, I mused. Nope. I wasn't a beige person, either, so no government jobs or corporate wonk jobs. Let's face it: I was born to be a dancer.

Buoyed by that realization, I took the stairs two at a time to meet Vitaly for our practice session. The floor refinisher was hard at work coating the ballroom floor with polyurethane when Vitaly arrived and the Russian dancer wrinkled his face into a grimace of disgust.

"Is stinking to highest hell in here," he said, tossing his dance bag into the corner of the small studio.

"Heaven," I corrected automatically.

"*Nyet.* Heaven is not smelling like this. This is hell."

I had to admit there was something to his logic as I opened all the windows and found a couple of fans.

We danced for almost three hours, with only short breaks for water, snacks, and for me to give directions to the locksmith when he arrived. Handing him a check an hour later and accepting the shiny new keys from him, I felt a load of worry I didn't even know I'd been carrying drop from my shoulders. I returned to the small studio to finish rehearsing, feeling like a cushion of air between the floor and my feet gave me a new spring. I was able to forget the past few days' woes and lose myself in the music and the movement, concentrating on the timing of our quick-step locksteps and working on the synchronization of our side-by-side movements. When we segued into the waltz, I envisioned being ethereal, floating, pointing my toes so hard they almost cramped as I raised one leg up and held it high with the strength of my abs while Vitaly pivoted me in a circle. By the time we finished, I felt renewed.

"We will winning at Blackpool," Vitaly said confidently, bussing my cheek as he left on the locksmith's heels. "Is certain."

I returned his toothy smile, feeling confident myself. "We make a good pair," I said.

"*Da,*" he agreed. "You is fulfilling your potentiality with Vitaly. None of that romance to detracting from technique." He flipped his hands as if shooing romance away.

I hadn't thought about that. Had Rafe's and my relationship detracted from our dancing? I always thought that it gave us a bit of extra zing, especially in the smoldering Latin dances, but maybe we'd been a bit too careful of each other's feeling in practice, not insisting on perfection, not being ruthless enough in our critiques of each other's performance.

"You should being gay," Vitaly said, grinning widely and throwing back his head to laugh like a donkey braying.

"I'll consider it," I said, closing the door behind him.

In my office, I wrestled with entry forms and fees for the next dance competition we'd be taking students to, until the logistics of it all drove me batty. I was almost willing to accept even Solange as a partner if she'd be in charge of the business end and let me focus on the dancing and teaching. I e-mailed all the students to let them know classes would resume as normal next week and to offer a "fire sale" discount of ten percent off for the month to coax back some of the wiffle-wafflers. I couldn't afford to do it, but I also couldn't afford to lose any more students. I resigned myself to subsisting on homemade bean and cheese tortillas, canned tuna, and carrots for the next month. An incoming e-mail from Sherry Indrebo said "THANKS!" for finding her flash drive and let me know she'd be by later today to pick it up. Swell.

*   *   *

When a knock sounded on the outer door shortly after six o'clock, it was neither Tav nor Sherry Indrebo, as I expected. Instead, a man with battleship-gray hair, wearing a belted navy raincoat, stood with his back to the door, looking out across the neighborhood. At the rasp of the dead bolt, he turned and I recognized Sherry's husband, Ruben Indrebo. The light rain misted his glasses and blurred his slight smile.

I pulled the door open. "Come in," I said. "I hadn't realized it was raining."

"Just a sprinkle," he said, stepping in and running his left hand over his damp hair. His right hand held a cane and he leaned on it slightly.

"I guess you're here for the flash drive," I said, leading the way to the office. "I know Sherry's anxious to get it back."

"Indeed." Instead of following me into the office, Indrebo continued to the junction with the hall and looked around. "A beautiful old home. It seems quiet," he observed.

"We're not back to our full schedule until next week," I said, explaining about the floor. Since he seemed interested in a tour, I stepped across the hall and opened the door to the empty ballroom. Newly applied polyurethane shone slickly and the sharp odor rose in almost visible waves. I coughed.

"I heard about the fire," Indrebo said in his mild voice. "What a shame. Do they have any idea how it started?"

"Arson. The police arrested a guy." I didn't feel like going into the details; it made me uncomfortable to admit that a student I'd known well had done such a thing.

Let the Indrebos read about it in the paper when Mark Downey came to trial.

"Do you believe in ghosts?" Indrebo asked, surprising me with a focused stare. His eyes hovered between blue and slate and I felt some of the force I was sure had propelled him to business success.

"No, not really."

"I'd think you'd be nervous to dance in here, what with your partner being murdered here." He pointed with his cane to a spot eerily close to where Rafe had lain.

"I guess I'm not the nervous type," I said lightly, closing the door. "Look, I don't mean to seem rude, but I've got a dinner thing." At least, I hoped my meeting with Tav would turn into a dinner date. "Let me get that flash drive for you."

"Where did you find it anyway?" he asked. "In there?" He nodded toward the ballroom. "Or maybe you've had it all along."

I gave him a startled look. "No, of course not. The floor refinisher found it wedged under a baseboard in the—" I bit off the words, suddenly realizing that he knew too much. How did he know where I'd found Rafe? All the paper said was "at a dance studio in Old Town, Alexandria." And why would he think I'd found the flash drive in the ballroom? Unless— My heart rate seemed to double, my heart pounding against my ribs so hard I was afraid Indrebo would hear. I stopped just outside the office door. "You know," I said, trying to sound mildly frustrated, not scared witless, "I left it downstairs on my dresser. Wait here and I'll be right back with it."

"I don't think so." His voice didn't get louder, but

steel threaded through the words. A gun appeared in his hand, aimed at my stomach, and I gaped at him wordlessly. "You must think I'm a fool, Miss Graysin."

"No, no, I don't," I stuttered. Killer, yes. Fool, no.

A smile played at the corners of his mouth, like I amused him. "Your partner made the same mistake of underestimating me. When he tried to blackmail my wife, he took on me, too, little though he understood that at the time."

"Rafe tried to blackmail Sherry?"

"Don't play dumb," he said wearily. "I'm sure you were in on it with him."

"I wasn't! I didn't know that—"

"No matter. Step back."

I took a giant step backward, happy to have a couple more feet between me and the gun. Not that a few feet would make much difference if he shot me. I needed to get out of the confines of the hall to someplace where I could maneuver. I rubbed suddenly damp palms against my jeaned thighs. Surely I could outrun a man with a cane? Maybe, but I couldn't outrun a bullet.

I played for time, hoping Tav would walk in, preferably with a SWAT team in tow. "What's on that drive, anyway? I mean, the *Post* already broke the story, so what's the big deal?"

"As you well know, the *Post* only had one story," Indrebo said, "the one that Acosta sold them, trying to get my wife to pay more for the return of the flash drive. She'd have paid it, too, if I hadn't told her to leave it to me. It's not just her political future at stake," he said, "it's my business. And as I explained to her when she was reluctant to have me meet Acosta in her place, it's my business—my money—that keeps her in politics. It's a symbiotic relationship—I have financed her campaigns and she's finally on the right committees—do you have any idea how long it took to maneuver her onto the House Armed Services committee?—to nudge business my way or pass certain laws that make the business climate more . . . favorable." He laughed, a mellow, grandpa-ish sound that didn't even hint at his ruthlessness. "There's a vote on the next-gen army helo coming up next week and it's vital for my company that she be at the HCAS meeting to cast her vote and sway any of her compatriots who seem to be waffling."

"You build helicopters?" I tried to keep him talking.

"Avionics for helicopters," he corrected me. "Never mind. But we're talking about hundreds of millions. And now that reporter, that McDill, is sniffing around, trying to connect his story about Sherry planting a spy in the Democrats' campaign office with Acosta's death, and I'm told he got the lead from you." His face hardened and he glared at me. "We're wasting time. Just give me the drive."

"It's downstairs," I said. "On my dresser."

He studied me, assessing my truthfulness, then stepped aside and waved me past him with the gun. "You go first. And don't try anything stupid because I'll be right behind you with this gun aimed at your spine. I don't think you'd do much dancing with a backbone shot to splinters."

The very thought made my calves and feet tingle. I moved as slowly as possible toward the interior door that opened to the stairs. "Why'd you use my gun to shoot Rafe?" I asked, turning slightly to face him.

"That was serendipitous," Indrebo said. "I had this gun with me, of course, but Acosta pulled out his gun at the very start of our conversation. It seems he didn't trust me." He chuckled again.

Rafe was smarter than I was, I thought.

"He wasn't really prepared to use it, though. It's harder than most people think to stand face to face and fire a gun at another human being. Shooting someone is a huge mental leap for most people, but physically it's just one quick step, a slight tightening of the forefinger." His finger tensed on the trigger and I flinched.

Indrebo laughed, reading my fear. "I smacked my cane across his wrist"—he tapped my shoulder with the cane to demonstrate—"and he dropped it. I recovered it and the rest, as they say, is history. Unfortunately, the thumb drive went flying when I shot him, and I couldn't find it. Not enough light, not enough time."

He prodded my shoulder with the cane and I opened the door, gesturing for him to precede me.

"Oh, I don't think so," he said, smiling. "Ladies first." He pointed with the gun and I started down the stairs, deliberately not flicking the light switch on the wall. Darkness favored me, I figured, since I knew every inch of these stairs.

"And Sherry had no trouble with you killing Rafe and wrecking her competition career?"

"My wife doesn't know I killed him," he said, a touch of irritation in his voice.

"Sure she doesn't." I rolled my eyes.

"She's good at not seeing what she doesn't want to see," he said drily. "An invaluable skill for a politician. I told her he didn't show for our meeting, that the studio was locked tight. If I'd told her the truth, maybe she wouldn't have sent you on a wild-goose chase for the damn flash drive and we wouldn't be here now."

A cheery thought and an excellent argument for total truthfulness between marriage partners. We had reached the landing with its pretty oriel window and I looked out, hoping to see someone I could signal. A red Jaguar I thought belonged to the neighbor two doors down nosed past and I half lifted a hand—not that the driver would have seen me or recognized my distress—but Indrebo poked the gun hard between my shoulder blades and said, "Don't even think about it."

I took another reluctant step down. The front door was tantalizingly near the foot of the stairs. I thought about hurtling down the last stairs, lunging for the door, and escaping through it. That plan relied on Indrebo being partially immobilized by his limp (so he couldn't catch me while I opened the door) and a lousy shot (so he couldn't shoot me while ditto). I decided to take the risk; once he got the flash drive, he was going to shoot me—I knew too much—so I didn't have much to lose by forcing the issue now. I was tensing my muscles for the leap when the cane's rubber tip dug into the small of my back and nudged me forward so I stumbled down the last three steps, landing hard on my knees and hands. The hardwood floor sent jolts up my arms to my shoulders and the pain in my knees brought tears to my eyes. I scrunched my lids together, determined not to let Indrebo see me cry.

"Where's the drive?" Indrebo asked, staring dispassionately down at me from one step up.

I breathed heavily for a moment on all fours, assessing my condition. Slightly winded, achy, and undoubtedly bruised, but not truly injured. I made a show of examining my hands, gingerly rotating my wrists like they were sprained, and rolling sideways to take the pressure off my knees. I tried to roll my jeans up high enough to inspect them.

"Stop stalling," Indrebo said, "or your knees will have bigger problems than a few scrapes and splinters." He aimed the gun at my right knee.

I gave him a wounded look and pushed to my feet, staggering slightly in an effort to make him think I was more shaken up than I really was. "Dizzy," I muttered, hanging my head by my knees.

"Oh, come—"

Before he could finish the sentence, I exploded from the crouch with all the force of my athletic dancer's legs, ducking my head and twisting slightly so my shoulders slammed into him at knee height. Suddenly off balance on the stair, he teetered and a shot rang out. White dust drifting onto me told me he'd drilled the ceiling. Locking my arms around his knees, I yanked with all my strength and he fell—*smack*—on his tailbone, letting out a yelp and a curse. He tried to bring the gun level to fire it at me, but the force of the fall had flung his arm upward and his elbow cracked against the stair behind him.

Unsure if I could wrestle the gun away from him without getting shot in the process, I whirled, sprinted three steps across the foyer, and reached for the doorknob. Crouching, I jerked the door open. Indrebo fired again. The bullet struck my left arm, twisting me with its force. I cried out. The pain burned through my arm like someone had hammered a red-hot spike through it. Blood dripped, splotching the floor. I was shot! The shock of it threatened to freeze me, but I knew hesitation equaled death. Flinging the door wider, I stumbled through it, gripping my bleeding arm with my good hand.

Wham! I thudded into someone running toward the door. The impact knocked me back, but the man—Tav, I realized—caught my wounded arm and I shrieked with pain. Large raindrops splatted me.

"My God, Stacy, I heard—"

"Gun, gun, he's got a gun," I babbled.

Tav scooped me up into his arms, ignoring my yips of pain, and ran toward the street. His feet slapped on the wet walkway. A steady stream of cars filled with people—witnesses, saviors, I thought—hissed past. Without hesitation, Tav jumped in front of a white van slowing for the stoplight. The startled driver hit her brakes. Horns sounded. Craning my head to look over Tav's shoulder, I saw Ruben Indrebo in my doorway, rage mottling his face, the gun pointed at Tav's back.

"Duck," I screamed in his ear. He threw us forward across the van's hood and a metallic ping told me the bullet had struck a car. When I opened my eyes to look, Indrebo had disappeared.

"Call the police," Tav was yelling at the frightened driver, who already had a cell phone pressed to her ear.

"And an ambulance," I whispered, strangely drowsy.

Chapter 22

"Another suspect, Miss Graysin?" The first thing I heard as I drifted up from an anaesthetized fog was Detective Lissy's dry voice.

I mumbled something and Lissy leaned closer, offering me a glass of water. I sucked on the straw, grateful for the water sliding coldly down my throat. "Not suspect," I croaked. I cleared my throat. "Killer."

"I'm inclined to think you've got it right this time," Lissy said, setting the cup back on the metal table.

"He admitted it," I said. My arm throbbed dully and I looked at it, seeing a bulky bandage beneath the abbreviated sleeve of the hospital gown.

"A flesh wound," Lissy said, making it sound like I'd stubbed my toe. "The docs stitched it up with a little IV sedation and gave you some antibiotics. A little rest and it'll be good as new." I frowned at him, unhappy with the way he was downplaying my gunshot wound. I'd been shot; I wasn't going to have the bullet hole in my arm dismissed as "a flesh wound."

Seemingly unaware of my pique, he stroked his yellow tie flat with one hand and said, "In case you were worrying, Indrebo's in custody. We caught up with him trying to board a charter flight for Minnesota."

I hadn't gotten around to wondering about Indrebo, but I was glad to hear the cops had apprehended him.

"We're not sure how involved the congresswoman was," Lissy continued, "and neither of them is talking."

"No surprise there," I muttered. The pair had been involved in politics long enough to know when there was no way to put a positive spin on a story.

"What I don't understand is why Indrebo came after you," Lissy said, leaning forward. "Did you see him the night Acosta was shot?"

"Flash drive." I fumbled for the water and drank again before explaining about the flash drive. "But there's nothing on it anymore," I finished. "The fire must have wrecked it."

"We'll see about that," Lissy said, a gleam in his gray eyes. "Where is it?"

He bolted from the room, cell phone in hand, when I told him. Kevin McDill, the reporter, was the next person through the door. I blinked in surprise at the sight of him. The fluorescent lights turned his dark skin muddy, but his eyes snapped with vitality and the ubiquitous toothpick was lodged firmly in the corner of his mouth.

"I hear you caught a bullet and got Ruben Indrebo arrested," he said. He glanced at my bandaged arm. "Doesn't look too bad. Care to tell me about it?"

Not too bad? Why was everyone determined to write off the bullet hole in my arm as nothing more serious than a paper cut or a scraped knee? I pouted but gave him the highlights of my encounter with Indrebo.

"I've been working this story since you pointed me toward it," McDill said, scrawling notes across a steno pad. "I'll tell you now, if you can keep your lips buttoned, that it was a source on Congresswoman Indrebo's challenger's staff who gave me the original story. He said that his source hinted that there might be more incriminating documents. I don't suppose you stumbled across anything?" His dark eyes fixed on my face.

So Rafe had gone to Sherry's Democratic nemesis with data from the flash drive, just as I suspected. I sighed. "I haven't seen any documents," I said truthfully.

McDill flipped his notebook closed. "Oh, well. It was worth a shot. This story will be big enough with your attempted murder, Indrebo's arrest, and the congresswoman's resignation."

"Sherry resigned?"

"She had no choice," McDill said. "Dirty campaign tricks, influence peddling for her husband, hints of an affair with a younger man, financial improprieties. She could have ridden out the scandal from one, or maybe two, allegations, but all of them? No way. She can kiss her political career bye-bye." He kissed his bunched fingers and flung them open, a strangely Gallic gesture from such a practical-seeming man. Plucking the toothpick from his mouth, he pointed it at me. "I owe you one."

A crowd of people filed in after he left: Mom, Dad, Danielle, Maurice, and even Vitaly. They crowded around the bed, surrounding me with flowers and kisses and concern, properly horrified by the bullet hole in my arm and eager to nurse me back to health. The only one missing was Tav Acosta.

He still hadn't shown up or called by the time Danielle ushered me down to her car to drive me home. I couldn't believe the hospital wasn't keeping me overnight—hadn't they noticed I'd been shot?—but the doctor dismissed me with a bottle of antibiotics, some pads and gauze, and advice to take it easy for a few days and visit the ER if my temperature spiked. Danielle seemed to tune into my feelings.

"You know," she said, "they send total mastectomy patients home after only twenty-four hours nowadays. Can you imagine them slicing off your boobs and whisking you out the door in less than a day? It happened to my friend Renee's mother when she had breast cancer."

Okay, breast cancer trumped my bullet wound. I quit moaning, even to myself, and said a quick prayer of thanks that Indrebo hadn't killed or crippled me. I flexed my arm carefully and it hurt, but I thought maybe I'd still be able to compete at Blackpool.

I felt markedly better after a good night's sleep and was trying a few cautious squats and lunges—exercises that didn't involve my arm—waiting for my coffee to brew, when the doorbell rang. An involuntary stab of fear took my breath for half a second, but then I remembered that Ruben Indrebo was safely parked behind bars and strode to the door. A peep out the window showed me Tav Acosta's tall, handsome form.

Happiness fizzed through me and I pulled the door wide. "I thought you were flying back to Argentina today."

"You did not think I would leave without saying good-bye?" He looked down at me with a lazy smile.

"I didn't know." Why did I feel so flustered? Maybe it was an aftereffect of the drugs from yesterday. "Oh, thank you for saving my life yesterday."

"You had done most of the saving before I got here," he said. "May I come in?"

"Oh, yes." I stood back to let him enter, automatically heading to the kitchen and coffee.

"You are injured. I will get it," Tav said, competently pulling mugs from the cupboard and filling them. I sat and watched him, enjoying the sight of him working— sort of—in my kitchen. Rafe never— I stopped the thought before it fully formed. I was determined to quit comparing the two men.

Tav brought my coffee to the table and then propped himself against the counter. "So you have solved the case and identified my brother's murderer."

"Well, I maybe half solved it," I said. "The solving gets easier when someone points a gun at you and confesses."

A half smile slanted across Tav's face. "Do not sell yourself short. If you had not kept after it, the police would have pinned it on Victoria Bazán and Indrebo would be free to kill again." I buried my nose in my coffee cup, uncomfortable with his praise.

"So," he said in a brisker tone, "about the studio."

I raised my eyes anxiously to his. "Yes?" *Please don't say you're selling to Solange. Please, please, please.*

"I have a proposition for you. You must promise to be honest in your response."

"Oookay," I said doubtfully. My knuckles whitened on the mug's handle.

"I have made arrangements to expand my export business to this area; I have signed agreements with several outlets—stores—in D.C., Virginia, and Pennsylvania. I need to be here to oversee the business for a while, maybe as much as a year. Since I will be here anyway, I thought I would hold on to Rafe's share of the studio for now and run it with you."

"As partners?" Doubt and hope collided in me.

He nodded and stepped closer until he was standing

right in front of me. "I have a degree in accounting and I am a whiz with numbers and organization. I could not help noticing when I went through the paperwork that you were—"

"Hopeless with numbers." I laughed weakly. "But you don't dance."

"True. But I am a fast learner." He smiled and reached his hand out. "Know where I can find a good teacher?"

I put my hand in his, feeling a tingle that had nothing to do with my wound as his fingers closed over mine. I stood and we were a mere breath apart. "As a matter of fact, I do."

I raised our clasped hands to dance position and put my left hand carefully on his shoulder. My stitches protested, but I ignored them. His left arm automatically encircled my waist and I leaned into his strength and warmth and steadiness. He smiled down at me, gaze slipping to my lips, and my voice trembled a little as I said, "Lesson number one: the frame."

"Now?" he said, looking a little uneasy. "Here? There's no music."

"Oh, there's always music." I squeezed his hand and we began to dance.

Read on for a sneak peek at the next
Ballroom Dance Mystery,

Dead Man Waltzing

Coming in June 2012 from Obsidian.

"One two three, *one* two three," I counted, landing heavily on the downbeat for the six elderly couples waltzing around me in my ballroom as rush hour traffic honked outside in the Old Town Alexandria streets. "Waltzing" was a bit of an exaggeration since collisions and missteps marred what should have been the graceful flow of the dance. Four of the six couples, though, were beginners, friends from a retirement community who had recently signed up for lessons, and I had hopes they would improve. "Keep your frame up," I suggested, nudging one large man between the shoulder blades. He drew his shoulders back stiffly; all he needed was a blindfold to look like a prisoner facing a firing squad.

"Better," I sighed, thinking we could work on relaxing and getting into the feel of the waltz in another couple of weeks. This was only their second lesson.

A short, plump woman in her seventies stopped moving, causing her even older partner to stumble. Mildred Kensington had been taking lessons at Graysin Motion for months, but hadn't shown much improvement. Still, she arrived each week with a sunny, pink-lipsticked smile and lots of energy, frequently with a new friend or two in tow. I had a soft spot for the spunky old lady. "Can you show us how to turn again, Stacy?" she asked.

"Of course." I glanced toward the door, wondering for the third time where Maurice was. He was supposed to be coteaching this class with me and it was totally unlike him to forget a class. Closing in on seventy—although he looked ten years younger—Maurice Goldberg had worked as a cruise-ship dance host before I hired him away to teach at Graysin Motion, my ballroom dance studio in Old Town Alexandria, Virginia, just outside the nation's capital.

Selecting the least rhythmically challenged of the men, I led him through the steps several times before encouraging the group to try it again. "Weight on your *right* foot when you offer your partner your *left* hand," I reminded the men as I cued up the Strauss CD.

"Hoover would pick this up faster than I am," Mildred complained after another circuit of the room.

Hearing his name, the Great Dane lifted his head and pricked his ears forward. White with black splotches, he usually lay quietly in a pool of sunlight under a window when Mildred came to the studio. No one had ever complained about him and I liked having him around, so he'd become a studio mascot of sorts. I gave him a surreptitious pat as I passed by and he thumped his black tail on the floor—not, unfortunately, in tempo. "Stop that, Hoover," Mildred complained. "You're throwing me off the beat."

The class ended fifteen minutes later and the group lingered, poking fun at each other's dancing as good friends do. The words "elephant," "rhino," and "diplodocus" occurred frequently. The early June sun still rode high at six o'clock and laid a yellow sunbeam road on the solid wood floor where it streamed through the street-facing windows. Some of the boards showed blackened strips where a fire had charred them a couple months back. I'd asked my refinisher to save the boards, if at all possible, because they were original to the Federal-era town home my great-aunt Laurinda had left me. He'd had to replace some of the more heavily damaged planks, but many of them were the very boards James Madison might have trod upon when the house belonged to his cousin.

Urging the group to practice at home during the week, I shooed them out the door by my office. It led to an exterior staircase that allowed dance students to come up to my second floor dance studio without going through my living quarters on the first floor. A darn fine arrangement. Before Great-aunt Laurinda had left me the house and I'd opened my own studio, I'd lived in an apartment nearly an hour from where I taught and danced, and the hideous commute had left me alternately drained and homicidal.

I had barely closed the door behind the seniors when a brief knock sounded. Unusual ... most students and the instructors walked right in. I opened the door and stood dumbstruck at the sight of the man standing on the small square landing.

"Detective Lissy," I finally said. "To what do I owe the honor?"

The man pursed his stretchy, too-red lips and crossed the threshold. Comb furrows tracked through his thinning, dishwater-colored hair, and his head seemed slightly too big for his thin neck. He wore an immaculate suit and a bland tie. He straightened the knot and the gesture slammed me back two months to when he had wanted to arrest me for shooting Rafe Acosta, my dance partner, co-owner of Graysin Motion, and former fiancé. I shivered.

"Ms. Graysin." Lissy acknowledged me with a sour smile.

"I'm guessing you're not here for the Latin class?" I said.

"Astute of you." He stepped farther into the narrow hallway and I backed toward my office. "Actually, I'm looking for Mr. Maurice Goldberg and thought I might find him here."

"Maurice?" What in the world could the police want with Maurice? "I haven't seen him this evening. Have you tried his house?"

"Now, why didn't I think of that?" Lissy said with mock-dismay. He passed me and poked his head into the ballroom.

I followed, becoming a little annoyed. "I told you he wasn't here," I said. "Why do you need to find him?"

"It looks much better than the last time I saw it," Lissy said, ignoring my question. "I like the new drapes." He gestured to the ivory velvet drapes I'd hung to replace the curtains incinerated by the fire. "Elegant."

His critique of my decorating efforts didn't distract me. "Why do you want Maurice?"

"You don't mind if I look around?" Lissy started for the smaller room at the back of the house that we called the studio to distinguish it from the larger ballroom.

"Actually, I do," I said, stepping in front of him. "Unless you have a search warrant." Being a murder suspect had taught me a few things.

Lissy stopped, looking down his sharp nose at me. He

was only a few inches taller than my five-foot-six, but he still managed to look down on me. It was an attitude thing more than a physical thing. The way the light from the hallway sconces hit him, I could see every little freckle across his cheeks and earlobes. "You don't have anything to hide, do you, Ms. Graysin?"

I balled my hands on my hips. "Tell me why you want Maurice, or say good night."

"Perhaps you know Corinne Blakely?" he asked, watching me closely.

I nodded. Who in the ballroom world *didn't* know Corinne Blakely, the grande dame of American ballroom dancing, a former champion, teacher, judge, and competition organizer who was leading the push for ballroom dancing to be admitted as an Olympic sport.

"I thought so." He made it sound like I'd admitted something criminal.

"Good night, Detective," I said, leading him back toward the door.

His voice came from just behind me. "Perhaps you haven't heard that she's dead?"

I whirled to face him. "No!"

"Yes."

"How?" Corinne must have been in her seventies; maybe she'd had a heart attack. But that wouldn't explain Lissy's presence. I cringed inwardly, awaiting his answer.

"Murdered."